$\mathcal{A}$ CANDLELIGHT INTRIGUE

CANDLELIGHT INTRIGUES

DEMONWOOD

Anne Stuart

A CANDLELIGHT INTRIGUE

For Bill Maier, with thanks for all his help
and for Maria and Lynda Jean, who like it best.

Published by
Dell Publishing Co., Inc.
1 Dag Hammarskjold Plaza
New York, New York 10017

Dell ® TM 681510, Dell Publishing Co., Inc.

ISBN: 0-440-11774-7

Printed in the United States of America

First printing—September 1979

PART ONE

Chapter One

"Are you entirely sure you know what you're doing, Mary Gallager?" my brother Seamus demanded of me. "You know Father never had much good to say for that side of the family."

"Father never had much good to say about anyone," I retorted. "Listen, Seamus, they might offer me a job. That's more than I've come to expect from anyone, friend or relative. And if they offer it to me, I'll take it!"

"But think for a minute, girl," my brother Patrick broke in, his normally placid blue eyes troubled. "Father and Ma have only been dead a month—surely you needn't rush into anything without first giving it careful thought."

I tossed back my heavy mane of hair and snorted ungenteely. "I've had years of giving this careful thought. As long as Father and Ma were alive and needed me I was glad to stay with them. But now that they're gone I need to do something on my own."

"I've not heard many good things about Maeve Gallager Fitzgerald and her fancy husband," Seamus said dourly, shaking his shaggy black head. "You may find yourself hundreds of miles from home, wishing you'd listened to your brothers. After all, it's not as if we didn't have homes for you."

"I don't want to be a poor relation! I want to earn my living just like anybody else." I heard the rising frustration in my voice and forced myself to calm down. I smiled ruefully at Seamus, that great black bear of an Irishman, and said, "Surely you don't think

Peggy would welcome me with open arms into her home. Or Maureen either." I turned to Patrick. "I'm too strong-minded to fit into another woman's household, and if you don't know it they and I do."

"I don't like the idea," Seamus protested. "My little sister forced to earn her living like a common drudge. And from the likes of Connell Fitzgerald! It's just not seemly."

"Seamus, it's the great grand city of Boston in the year of our lord 1897. Times have changed—it's no longer a disgrace for a woman to get a job."

"You should have been born with red hair instead of that black mane," Patrick noted gloomily. "You are the stubbornest female . . ."

I went over the conversation once more in my mind as I sat in the library of Connell Fitzgerald's Beacon Hill mansion. Despite my brave show of defiance to my protective older brothers, I was feeling very frightened and meek indeed, an unusual state of mind for the likes of Mary Gallager. I had always had more than my share of pride and foolhardy bravado. But in the lean weeks that had followed my parents' death I had had to swallow my pride more than once, and it would do me nothing but good. Or so Father McShane always told me. I contemplated the toes of my shiny boots with studied nonchalance, and wondered what the famous Connell Fitzgerald would think of his wife's lowly third cousin as she presented herself for his inspection.

I was not in my best looks that day, more by design than accident. As he walked into the paneled room he would see a woman past the first blush of youth, though perhaps not looking her full twenty-three years. Her sturdy young body would be covered in mourning at least two years out of style, her thick tangle of blue-black curls were hidden beneath the unflattering bonnet she had clamped down upon her head with disgust several long hours ago. Her face was pinched and pale, the generous mouth drawn in a prim fine line, her usually laughing green eyes narrowed and severe. Connell Fitzgerald needed a teacher for his troubled young son, and I intended to get the job. If I had to appear as a stern, destitute female, or had to play upon my tenuous relationship I would do so. The new owners were moving into my parents' house next week, and I intended to be long gone before that happened. For if I had to move in with my brothers I was afraid I would never escape.

"Miss Gallager?" I looked up, startled, at the tall gloomy-looking man in the doorway. "Mr. Fitzgerald will be with you shortly. Could I get you anything? Some tea, perhaps, or sherry?"

Right then I could have done with a stiff belt of the good Irish whiskey my father had kept around for added moral fiber, but I could see that such a request might be looked at askance. So I smiled faintly and shook my head. And waited.

I was both glad and sorry I wasn't to see my cousin Maeve. Perhaps she would have felt the blood tie more strongly, perhaps she'd changed from the spoiled, willful girl I'd known in my youth. Maeve's family had always had more money than my hard-working parents, and their beautiful only daughter, seven years my senior, always made it quite clear to me at the infrequent times we met that the Patrick Gallagers were at best poor relations, at worst as bad an embarrassment to the Matthew Gallagers as any Shanty-boat Irish could be.

No, I doubted I'd have much luck with her. She'd prefer an elegant French nanny to her raw-boned third cousin, and I didn't know if I blamed her. Connell Fitzgerald might prove more amenable—at least, I certainly hoped so. After all, I had always gotten along better with men than with women; perhaps it was caused by being the only daughter with six sons. Women to me had always seemed a little sly and sneaking—you never really knew where you stood with them. No, I would do better with Connell Fitzgerald. I could speak to him frankly, man to man, and not have to worry about secret resentments and hidden motives.

"Miss Gallager?" I jumped nervously, but it was merely the gloomy secretary once more. "Would it be possible for you to come back tomorrow? Mr. Fitzgerald will be tied up for quite some time."

Ah, the curse of Mary Gallager! I was losing my temper, as I was wont to do. With great strength of mind I swallowed the hasty retort that rose to my lips. "I would rather wait, if you don't mind. It's a long trip into town and I'd as soon not have to make it again." Actually, I didn't know if I could afford to come again. I had borrowed the trolley fare from a grudging Seamus, but once it was spent I doubted he would advance me any more toward an object he disapproved of so strongly.

The gloomy man looked even gloomier, his sepulchral voice dropping a notch. "Very well. I can't say how long it will be, though. Mr. Fitzgerald is a very busy man."

My temper flared and broke. "Mr. Fitzgerald asked me to come here today!" I shot back. "I hardly think I'm asking too much of him to keep this appointment." All the half-remembered newspaper clippings and whispered rumors began sneaking back, and I recalled how proud and arrogant the wealthy Mr. Connell Fitzgerald was touted as being. Having experienced his high-handed ways before I'd even met the man, I found I was rapidly beginning to dislike my cousin-by-marriage intensely. I fell back to contemplating my boots, scowling.

"Certainly, miss," he said emotionlessly.

And in the end I had waited three hours and forty-five minutes when the door finally opened and Connell Fitzgerald strode in.

At that point I could almost have wished he had waited a bit longer. I was at low ebb, tired and nervous and angry. Angry at his careless assumption that I could wait, angry at the intolerable situation I found myself in. Nobly I swallowed my rage as I rose and turned to meet him.

My first reactions to him were a-jumble. I had seen his portrait in the papers so I had a general idea of what he looked like, but I was completely unprepared for the somewhat overwhelming effect of Connell Fitzgerald in the flesh.

He was a tall, strong-looking black Irishman—in general appearance and coloring he was very much like me. His jet black hair curled around a high forehead, his eyes were a deep piercing blue set in a smooth, tanned face. His nose was strong and slightly crooked, his mouth large and thin-lipped, his jaw firm and pugnacious. And on his face was the nastiest expression—combined contempt and boredom with the world in general and me in particular. I told myself that I didn't like him very much. If this was what millions of dollars did to one, then he could keep it.

Those scornful blue eyes swept over my slightly dowdy form, and I stiffened with unconscious pride. "You wanted to see me, Miss Gallager?" he said abruptly, and despite my instant dislike for him I couldn't help but notice the lovely timbre of his voice. It was low-pitched and musical, the kind of voice that could beguile a girl to do almost anything. Some girls, that is.

"There was really no need to see me personally," he continued with cool disdain. "Murphy has full instructions to take care of Maeve's financially embarrassed relatives with discreetness and generosity. I'm sure if you'll simply speak to him on your way out . . ."

This was clearly a dismissal. I stared at the man, dumbfounded, my mouth agape in fury and disbelief, my cheeks flaming. "Mr. Fitzgerald," I said with steely calm, "I came to see you about a position, not for a handout. I don't know which of Maeve's relatives you've been dealing with, but I'll have you know that Patrick Gallager's children wouldn't touch your filthy money if they were starving!" I started for the door

13

with as much dignity as I could muster, which, under the circumstances, was considerable.

"If you're interested in a job then you'd be touching my filthy money anyway," he said reasonably, a trace of amusement in his bleakly handsome face. "What position were you interested in?"

"I heard that your son needs a tutor," I muttered with little grace.

He looked down on my not inconsiderable height with a total lack of concern. "He does. But I'm afraid you wouldn't be suitable. You are my wife's cousin, are you not?" The tone in which he said the word "wife" spoke volumes. "I had in mind someone a little older. And not related. Part of Daniel's problems is his reliance on too many relatives."

I felt panic clutching at my middle. He was dismissing me without even a hearing. Desperately I said, "I'm only a third cousin, sir. I've seen Maeve a handful of times in my life—I don't see that that constitutes a relationship. A mere connection, perhaps."

He raised an eyebrow, seeing me for the first time. "Semantics, Miss Gallager," he dismissed my protest. "And you're still too young." But he signaled me to be seated as he strode behind his highly polished mahogany desk. For some reason I had caught his interest, and I felt the first vague stirrings of unease.

"I'm not too young. I'm twenty-three!" I said defiantly, perching gingerly on the edge of the horsehair sofa. "And I've had experience."

"Twenty-three," he scoffed. "Such a very great age, to be sure." The cold, scornful expression on his face had lightened somewhat, and his eyes held a spark of amusement in them, almost despite himself. "Tell me about your experience, then."

I proceeded to do so. "I was trained at the Simpson Institute for Teachers. I've taught Sunday school and tutored neighborhood children in their studies . . ." This sounded lame even to me.

"And have you done any professional teaching?"

"N . . . n . . . no."

"And have you had any experience with . . . shall we say, troubled children?"

"No," I confessed unwillingly. "But that doesn't mean I wouldn't be good at it. I've always had a way with children—I know I could do it if you'd only be giving me the chance." I could hear the Irish slipping into my speech as it did when I grew agitated, and I forced myself to calm down. "Mr. Fitzgerald, there's nothing I could do to make you give me the job of tutoring your son. I can only tell you that you'd be making a great mistake if you didn't." I sat back, a little breathless at my daring.

To my amazement his harsh features softened into a smile. A fairly cynical one, to be sure, but a smile nonetheless. And I was aware of the most alarming reaction within me.

"I'd be making a great mistake, would I?" he repeated softly. "Well, Miss Gallager, I've made many mistakes in my life. I suppose I should avoid making any more." There was a note of bitterness in his voice, the same note it had held when he spoke of his wife. He rose abruptly, as if he'd already wasted too much time on me. "Be here tomorrow at nine o'clock with some personal references and my sister will explain the duties."

I had risen when he had and I stared at him with sudden panic. "Are you offering me the job?"

"I thought you practically demanded it," he answered irritably. "Do you want it or do you not?"

Clearly the man was a bully. "I'll let you know tomorrow," I said grandly.

"Miss Gallager," Connell Fitzgerald demanded, "if you don't want the job then why did you come here today?"

I met his dark-blue gaze in the tanned, handsome face candidly. "Oh, I want the job, Mr. Fitzgerald. It's certain things about it that I'm not liking."

"And would you be so good as to tell me what those things are?"

"It's you that I'm not liking," I answered sweetly.

He stared at me in amazement for a moment, then let out a ripple of laughter. "Excellent, Miss Gallager. By all means continue to feel that way. I only hope your dislike of me won't prejudice you against my son. I have the feeling you might be just what he needs."

I rode the trolley home in a grumbly mood. The house in Cambridge seemed colder and emptier than ever as I let myself in the basement door and made my way through the autumn-damp rooms to the big cozy kitchen that was the heart of the house. I kept my mind a perfect blank until I had stirred up the fire in the stove, made myself a cup of strong, peaty tea and settled down with my mother's warm afghan around me. And I sat there, lost in thought, until the sound of someone knocking awoke me from my reverie.

It was Pauline, youngest and dearest of my bevy of sisters-in-law, her pregnant body ponderous, her pretty face alight with curiosity. She'd been my best friend since I was thirteen years old, and her marriage to my brother Luke hadn't diminished the relationship in the slightest.

"Did he offer you the job?" she demanded, helping herself to a cup of the still warm tea and pouring half the contents of the sugar bowl into it.

I settled back into the comfortable rocker. "That he did."

Pauline's sharp brown eyes watched me for a moment. "Then what's troubling you? I thought it was what you wanted above all things—a chance to get away from Cambridge and all your family."

"Not you, Pauline," I protested.

"Yes, even me. It's time you had a life of your own, not living through your sisters and brothers and nieces and nephews. And since you won't have Michael . . ."

"I thought you understood!" I cried, pained by her defection. "There's only going to be one man in my life and I'll know it when I see him." I wrapped the afghan tighter around me. "Michael Flynn is simply not the man."

"Ah ha," said Pauline, and I felt alarm rise in me anew.

"What do you mean by 'ah ha'?"

"Nothing, nothing at all. Just 'ah ha.'" She leaned her plump, pregnant body across the well-scrubbed kitchen table. "And you've met him, then?"

"Met whom?"

"The man you've been sitting around waiting for for twenty-three years. I must say it's about time—I thought the day would never come."

"I don't know what you're talking about," I denied it hotly. "The only man I met today was Connell Fitzgerald."

"Mary, I've been your closest friend for ten years. Haven't we always been honest with each other?"

"And did it never occur to you that I wasn't caring to be admitting it to myself, much less to you?" I answered roundly.

Pauline leaned forward and put a hand on mine. "Don't fret, lovey. It's not as bad as all that."

"It's not bad at all—the problem is really quite simple. Connell Fitzgerald is a handsome man. I noticed it. A perfectly normal thing, after all. It shouldn't stop me from taking the job." I was arguing more with myself than with her, rocking back and forth nervously.

"A perfectly normal thing, indeed. Except that you've never been really interested in handsome men. What with your six great big strapping brothers you've grown up more like a wild lad than a girl—a bigger tomboy I've never known. More than one young man has complained of your hard heart." She took a deep gulp of her tea and helped herself to the last of my sugar. "If the man's upset you this much then it's more than a natural appreciation of manly beauty. Maybe you shouldn't be taking the job."

"Maybe I shouldn't," I echoed unhappily. "But I've

17

got to get away from here!" I threw aside the afghan and began pacing the brick-floored kitchen. "Pauline, I'll tell you the truth, but you must swear never to tell a soul. I didn't even like him."

"And who says liking has anything to do with loving?"

"For God's sake, I'm not in love! I only just met the man."

"Hush, hush," she soothed me. "Tell me what happened and let me be the judge. You were sitting there in his house, feeling frightened and lonely and unhappy, and in walked . . ."

"Control yourself, Pauline," I said sternly. "He's an attractive man," I admitted against my will. "And a very unhappy, cynical one too. At first I thought he was the coldest, proudest, most disagreeable person I'd ever met."

"And then?" she prompted.

"And then he smiled." I felt myself flushing, remembering with alarm the intensity of my reaction to that smile. "I felt as if . . . as if my knees had melted."

She laughed then, a full-throated roar. I stared at her in mute rage while she continued to enjoy my unfortunate situation.

"I don't consider the situation to be all that amusing," I said stiffly.

"I'm sorry, dearie." She mopped her streaming eyes. "But I never thought the day would come when I'd hear you talking like a moon-struck weanling! I rejoice to hear it."

"The man is married to my cousin," I reminded her sourly. "And even if he weren't, he's a bit beyond the reaches of a Shanty Irish girl past her prime."

"Mind what you say, girl!" she protested. "I'm the same age as you are and I don't consider myself past my prime. Why, you're prettier than you've ever been, and so am I, if your damned brother would just leave me alone long enough to stay unpregnant for more than half a year at a time." She glared at her distended

18

stomach in disgust. "The situation is not that bad, Mary darlin'. Maybe you've just sort of . . . come awake. Like Sleeping Beauty, and now you'll be able to appreciate men in their natural role."

"And pray, what may that be?"

"As husband and lover and protector," she replied. "Not as a peer. For heaven's sake, Mary, you've more men friends than you could shake a stick at. Men have other uses, you know. As any number of them have been trying to tell you these last few years."

"I don't need a protector," I said stubbornly. "I'm entirely capable of taking care of myself."

"And you don't need a husband or a lover?"

"Not now," I said sadly. "I've got a horrid feeling that I'm doomed, Pauline. When the Gallagers mate, they mate for life. Haven't you heard of my great-aunt Moira, who hanged herself when her young husband was drowned? Or Aunt Mary, whom they named me after, who was jilted at the altar and never looked at another man?"

"And you'll be feeling the same desperate way after clapping eyes on Mr. Connell Fitzgerald? Faith, he must be some man!"

"Lord, I hope not," I said devoutly, my sense of humor returning. "Not that it would do me any good—he didn't like me one bit. I don't know that he really likes any women."

"You were ever one to jump to conclusions," she clucked. "What makes you up and decide that?"

"Just a feeling I had. The way he looked at me—with such dislike and contempt. And I'd never even met the man!"

"Well, that solves your problem, then. If the man doesn't even like you all you'll have to suffer is a few soulful longings for what will never be. It will do wonders for your emotional growth—you can have nice, tear-filled nights like you should have had when you were seventeen, and in a year you'll be ready to fall into a good man's arms and appreciate him. If the

19

man's as unpleasant as you say, I can't think why you'd want to have anything to do with him in the first place."

"You don't think I'm asking for trouble?" I questioned dubiously, longing to be convinced.

"Devil a bit," she replied cheerfully. "And besides, who says you'd even see that much of him? Isn't he always traveling around on business or off in Europe with his fancy wife? Pardon me, I should say Cousin Maeve. I doubt you'll see him above once a month. If it bothers you so much, why don't you talk with Father McShane first?"

"Because I know exactly what he'll say, and I know it's the truth. Adultery of the heart is just as great a sin as adultery of the body, and Father McShane thinks I have far too many sins of the heart already. He thinks I should marry Michael and raise a large family of Catholics."

"And so you should," she agreed stoutly. "And you'll be far more likely to do just that and be happy about it once you've got this . . . this wanderlust out of your system. You go and teach that young boy, and come back in a year and start raising a family of your own. Michael will wait."

"But I don't want him to wait," I lied. The thought of being able to fall back upon the strong shoulders of Michael Flynn comforted me in my moments of self-doubt.

"Well, whether he will or not isn't up to you, my girl. And I think it's the world's best thing for you to get away like this." She finished off her cold tea and made a face. "But don't you dare tell your brother I said so."

Chapter Two

Pauline, good, wise, ever-pregnant Pauline, was right as always. I didn't set eyes on Connell Fitzgerald the next day, or the day after that, or for the entire week I was being prepared for my demanding task. Instead, I spent all my time with his sister.

Lillian Fitzgerald was somewhere on the shady side of forty—a short brown woman with soft eyes and absolutely no pretensions to style or beauty. Her silky brown hair was piled untidily on top of her small head, her deep-set brown eyes peered near-sightedly at the world with a constant expression of both defiance and alarm, her tiny hands clasping and unclasping with genteel nervousness. When I was first ushered into her presence by the dour Mr. Murphy she had risen from the couch and rushed toward me in a whisper of brown silk, throwing her arms around me like a long-lost relative. As indeed, she made it clear from the start, she considered me to be.

"Just the thing for dear Daniel, Mary," she confided. "Someone young and female and blood-kin. I do think blood ties are so important, don't you? When Con told me he had persuaded you to come to us I nearly wept with happiness—we couldn't have dreamed of anyone more perfect for helping us out."

That was the term she always used, "helping us out." I think it offended her idea of family ties to realize that I would be a paid employee, and therefore one of the lower classes. The Fitzgeralds had a proud heritage, descended from Irish kings and only one step (and an ocean voyage) away from the landed gentry that were a far cry from the hard-working Gallagers. The beauty of their grandmother, the fabled Countess of Carradine, was legendary. It must have been galling when Connell threw himself away on a lovely nobody like Maeve. But then, perhaps he'd married for love. If so, he'd made a bad choice of it in my cousin.

My duties were soon made clear, even if they weren't couched in those terms. I would, in a week's time, be transported northward to the Fitzgeralds' country estate in the northeast area of Vermont, where awaited my young charge. There I would remain throughout the winter, readying him for the first school he had ever attended in his life.

"But he's ever so bright," Lillian assured me, blinking those kind brown eyes nervously. "I'm sure you won't have any trouble with him. And the house is fully staffed—anything you want you need only request." She hesitated. "It will be lonely, of course. Demonwood is comprised of several thousand acres of woodland in a rather desolate area of the country. We have some charming neighbors, but I don't expect you'll see them anymore often than you'll see Connell and me." She made a slight face, so slight I couldn't be sure whether I had imagined it. "And Maeve, of course. Even though Demonwood is our home, we don't seem to spend much time there. Connell is always busy, and Maeve is always traveling. And I . . . well, I suppose I'd best be frank." She leaned closer to me, and I caught the scent of violets emanating from her brown silk body. "Connell has decided that I was becoming too possessive about Daniel. That I should live a life of my own, in the city, with more people around me. Up until this year I've been his teacher, his confidante, his mother." There was anger in her soft, pouting mouth. "I'm sure you realize, my dear, that your cousin Maeve is no sort of mother at all. Her own pleasures and parties come first with her, and always have. Though how she can resist such a sweet, charming, sensitive child I will never understand. She's

a cold, heartless bitch, and I don't mind saying so."
She looked at me defiantly, as if daring me to defend
her.

"I've only seen her a few times in the last ten years,"
I said hurriedly. "I really don't run in the same crowds
as she does."

Lillian patted my hand. "Be glad that you don't, my
dear. It's a fast, wicked life that will only end in sorrow for her and anyone who gets too close. Like Connell," she said grimly. And then quickly changed the
subject.

The week passed in a whirl. My six brothers came
over every night, singly, in pairs, and on one momen-
tous occasion en masse, to plead, to threaten, to cajole
me into making my home with one of them. Their
wives came over, singly, in pairs, and en masse, with
an amazing variety of objects, from lace-trimmed un-
derdrawers to several little-worn and much-cherished
dresses that would do wonders for my sparse wardrobe. It felt rather like a trousseau for a blushing
bride—a thought that I quickly shied away from.

We had all come to the conclusion that I must give
up my half-hearted attempts at mourning, for financial
as well as spiritual reasons. We could scarcely afford an
entire wardrobe of funereal black. Besides, they all
knew as well as I did that Molly and Pat Gallager
wouldn't have wanted a year of sorrow and drab
clothes in their honor. So I accepted the bright-hued
garments with profound gratitude, sternly shutting out
thoughts of how Connell Fitzgerald would react to a
certain rose-colored dressing gown. My sisters-in-law
all loved me dearly and were all deeply grateful that
I had chosen an independent life of my own, rather
than joining one of their already crowded households.
They would have preferred to see me settled with Michael, but accepted my anticipated departure with un-
abated cheerfulness that would vanish whenever one
of my brothers appeared with fresh arguments about

23

the foolishness of my decision, and their suddenly somber and disapproving faces would send me into barely controlled giggles.

The night before my departure for the wilds of Vermont I was invited to dine on Beacon Hill. Connell would be out, as he had been everyday I had been there, but Lillian and I would contrive to entertain ourselves. We had become surprisingly close in the short time since I had met her, and the thought of leaving a new friend filled me with some regret. Her instructions on the care of young Daniel were foolish and overprotective in the extreme, but I could see through her fussing to the real love and devotion she had for him and promised I would do all that I could to provide the love he would be missing.

I dressed with care for that evening, in one of Pauline's dresses that she had declared never fit her properly. Indeed, as she was short and thin and I was tall and amply rounded, there was some truth to her observation. It had been made for an elegant lady who had bestowed it upon her maid, who happened to be Pauline's mother. None of the Gallagers, decent, hard-working folk though they may be, could afford such a fine dress of blue-watered silk. Even Maeve's staunchly middle-class parents were unable to outfit her in such luxury. It had taken a multimillionaire like Connell Fitzgerald to dress her in the style she obviously felt she deserved.

"It will be the perfect thing for you, Mary," Pauline had declared when I protested over the richness of the present. "Some evening when your Miss Lillian is visiting she might have a few people in, and some young man will lay his heart at the indigent cousin's feet, and you'll be set for life. And you can snap your fingers at Connell Fitzgerald."

"I wish you'd forget what I told you," I begged her, acutely uncomfortable by her harping on my momentary weakness. "I don't know what got into me—nerves, I suppose, at the thought of leaving everything that

24

I've known. I haven't even thought of the man in days."

Pauline smiled her knowing smile, her eyes merry. "That's as may be," she murmured. "But you'll have the dress anyway. I doubt I'll ever spend more than a few months without a baby in my belly, and someone should get some use out of the elegant thing before it's out of style. It'll make him regret what he's missing."

I looked at my reflection in the mirror, smoothing the lovely material over my rounded hips. Until this night I had never been more than superficially interested in pretty clothes. Now, despite my protestations to Pauline, my appearance was tremendously important.

The dress was extremely flattering, and not quite as indecent as most evening dresses tended to be. My black hair hung down in a tangle of loose curls around my neck, my green eyes shone with excitement, and my pale skin was faintly flushed. I looked more like a woman about to meet her lover than a teacher going to dine with a spinster cousin-by-marriage, and the truth of that observation made me blush even more. For I couldn't help but admit to myself that I hoped I would catch a glimpse of Connell Fitzgerald before he went out on whatever mysterious business he conducted at night. More importantly, that Connell Fitzgerald would catch a glimpse of me in my expensive and flattering clothes. The image Pauline had conjured up of that handsome and haughty man mooning after me in a lovestruck daze was immensely satisfying.

I had forgotten, of course, how very beautiful my cousin Maeve was. I had plenty of time to remember, for the ever-tactful Mr. Murphy ushered me into a salon that I had never seen before. An obviously masculine room, the only feminine note was the huge portrait of my cousin Maeve, dominating the room, her laughing, golden presence overwhelming and subduing the surroundings. I stared up at her painted likeness, and told myself it was the painter's art and that no woman could have hair so gold, eyes such a glorious shade of lavender-blue, skin so translucent. And knew that I lied to myself, and hated her all the more.

"Good evening." That lovely voice spoke from the door, and I whirled around in surprise, my silken skirts swirling around my ankles. I hadn't really expected to see him, so invisible had been his presence through the last week.

"Mr. Fitzgerald." I controlled my stammer, but just barely. He was dressed in evening clothes, and if anything he looked more elegant and disdainful than before. I tested my reactions, just a pinch, so to speak, and was relieved to find none of that treacherous melting. It had been a mirage, then, brought about by nervousness and rage.

"You look very lovely tonight," he said in a bored tone of voice that told me he couldn't care less. "I'm afraid Lillian is discommoded this evening. She suffers from the migraine, you know." Those chill blue eyes raked over me with indifferent curiosity, and I could feel myself flushing.

"No, I hadn't known. In that case I'll excuse myself." I started toward the door, expecting him to move aside with that insolent grace. The damned man did no such thing, just stood there staring down at me with the beginning traces of amusement.

"Where are you running off to, Mary? And why are you blushing in such a charming way? I have better things to do with my time than seduce innocent young relatives of my dear wife."

"I'm sure you do." My head snapped up defiantly. "And I have better things to do than bandy words with a rude, arrogant, railroad magnate." I made it sound like an aspersion on his parentage. "I'll be saying good night to you, Mr. Fitzgerald."

He still did not move, but that lazy smirk had vanished. "I was forgetting how much you dislike me,

Mary. Well, I'm afraid you'll have to swallow your distaste for the evening. I happen to be your employer, and there are certain things I had better make clear before you take that train tomorrow morning."

"You could have spoken with me any time this last week," I pointed out rudely.

"I didn't care to talk with you this week. I had other, more important things on my mind than an impudent colleen I was fool enough to hire." He was losing his temper, which was preferable to that condescending charm that emanated from him at odd moments.

Of course, I was losing my temper too, and a grand thing it is when it goes completely. "Certainly, Mr. Fitzgerald, sir, I understand," I said in a superficially meek tone of voice that was belied by my flashing eyes. "And what is it you'd be wanting me to do?"

His anger subsided as quickly as it had come, leaving in its place a bored, unhappy man. "In the first place, you might bring yourself to call me Connell. We *are* related, even though you prefer to look upon it as a mere connection." He smiled then, and my heart sank. It hadn't been an hallucination the other time—it was happening all over again. And it was his smile that did it; the lost, half-loving smile that he no doubt bestowed on serving maids, stockholders, cab drivers, and indigent cousins-by-marriage with equal indifference. Bravely I controlled myself and met that charming smile stonily.

"I merely want you to have dinner with me while I explain a bit about the situation at Demonwood. Is that asking so much? In the meantime you could be taking pity on a lonely man by agreeing to bear him company. You shouldn't let that pretty dress go to waste."

"You needn't try to charm me," I warned him darkly. "I'm a level-headed young woman and not easily moved. I've been around too many Irishmen all my life to be taken in by blarney."

He stared down at me for a long moment, conflicting

and unreadable emotions playing across his handsome face. "All right, I won't try to charm you. I'll be completely straightforward and honest with you, but I give you fair warning. I'll expect the same honesty from you. Inasmuch as you're capable of it—being a woman, you're not likely to do too well in that area. There's nothing I detest more than liars."

I watched him out of narrowed eyes, considering. Clearly, the man had known many liars in his life, most assuredly my dear Cousin Maeve, for one. As I was neither adept in the art of prevarication nor particularly fond of it I found the promise easy to make. "Fair enough," I agreed, and held out my hand to shake on it. He stared down at it for a minute, and amusement lightened his dark face. He grasped it, and the touch of his rough, long-fingered hand sent an unpleasant little shock through my body. Without a doubt, the less I saw of Connell Fitzgerald the safer my immortal soul would be.

Dinner was a sumptuous feast—there was enough food to feed my entire family, and they were all heavy eaters. Course followed upon course, and staunchly I plowed through each one, having a murderous time keeping my mind on a dozen different things, among them which fork to use, how much to eat, what that funny-looking thing with the pink sauce could possibly be, how much of the potent wine I could safely imbibe, and most of all, what in the world I could say to the man who was sitting across from me, watching me out of those cynical dark blue eyes while he ate barely a thing.

"And what has my sister told you about young Daniel?" he asked at one point, when I had given up thinking of entertaining and witless things to say.

I swallowed the rich, sickeningly sweet dessert that I had taken far too much of, and cursed myself for a glutton. "She told me that Daniel was a very delicate boy. He should be kept out of drafts, protected from the rough climate, and overstimulation isn't good for him. That he is very high-strung and sensitive, and should be given unstinting love and approval, not criticism." I rattled this off like the lesson it had been, almost word perfect. It wasn't until I finished that I realized how like a parody of Lillian's nervous voice I sounded, and I threw a quick glance at my employer's stern face, wondering whether I had offended him.

"And what did you think of that?" he asked me in even tones, his face impassive, his eyes on his glass of wine.

I felt I was being tested, and for the life of me I couldn't guess what the right answer was. The only thing for it was to tell him the truth, as I had promised to do. "I thought it was probably a bag of moonshine, sir. And what he needs is some fresh air and a good fight with the local bully." I held my breath, waiting for the explosion. None came.

His eyes met mine for a brief moment, then he went back to examining his wine glass. "I doubt there is a local bully, Mary." And he drained the pale liquid, his expression unreadable across the candle-lit, damask-covered table. The flickering, shimmering lights bounced off the highly polished silver, the Waterford crystal, the prisms flashing rainbows from the silver chandelier and the sconces, turning the formal dining room into a fairyland. But I was no fairy princess, and Connell Fitzgerald was no Prince Charming, for all he might look like one with his black curls tumbled rakishly across his high, tanned forehead, and those devilish blue eyes in a mockingly handsome face.

"I'll ask one more thing of you, Mary Gallager," he said softly. "Don't believe everything that's said of me, girl." There was a curiously endearing note in his lovely voice, and I could feel my treacherous heart pounding against the thin, blue silk of my dress. Before I had a chance to respond, he signaled the butler that we were finished.

Very politely he pulled my chair out for me, very politely he took my arm and led me to the hall. Murphy appeared from nowhere with my serviceable wool cloak over his arm, and with the grace of long practice, Connell took it from him and draped it around my shoulders. His hands seemed to linger for a moment longer than necessary, but that was probably wishful thinking on my part.

"How did you come here tonight?" he asked abruptly.

"By trolley, sir."

"Stop calling me sir." He turned to Murphy, and something about his movements made me realize his problem. He was slightly, politely drunk, and he was obviously one of those men that drink made evil-tempered, rather than mellow. "Escort Miss Gallager home, Murphy."

"Very good, sir," Murphy replied, all staunch correctness, and opened the wide front door for me. I stared at Connell's back for a moment, perplexed. Then, shrugging, I drew my cloak more closely around me and sailed out the door without a backward glance. If Connell Fitzgerald could be rude and enigmatic, why, then, so could I. What matter that I wouldn't see him again for long, long months—perhaps never? I had been more disturbed by his sudden gentleness at the table than his subsequent ill temper. If he stayed nasty I would have no trouble whatsoever fending off my sinful longings if and when he returned.

The house was dark when I finally arrived home that night. I could have wished I'd had a more loquacious companion—Murphy was his usual lugubrious self, and the only advantage his company afforded was the paying of fares and protection from amorous young men. As I had recieved a substantial advance on my salary from an embarrassed Lillian, and had long ago learned to deal with amorous young men quite effectively, I couldn't say much for Murphy's assistance, but beggars cannot be choosers.

With great correctness Murphy took the key from me and opened my door. "Could I offer you a cup of tea, Mr. Murphy?" I asked politely, hoping he wouldn't accept.

I should have known the very correct Mr. Murphy would refuse to enter a lady's house unchaperoned. "No, thank you, miss. I will be here at seven o'clock tomorrow morning to escort you to the train."

"All right," I replied, stifling my surprise. I had had no idea what arrangements had been made for my transportation, trusting in God and Mr. Fitzgerald. "I'll be ready then, Mr. Murphy."

"I trust you will, miss," he said gloomily. "In the meantime I think your young man wants your attention."

I jumped, startled, as Michael Flynn appeared from the dark corridor of my house. The situation was extremely compromising, what with him being in his shirtsleeves at close to midnight, red hair tousled around his handsome, bovine face, and I turned to make some sort of fumbled explanation to my disapproving companion. But he had vanished into the night, no doubt full of salacious tales to bear to his cynical master about the sluttish tendencies of the new tutor, and I turned to Michael with a sharp annoyance not untouched by fear at the thought of losing my position.

"And what are you doing here at this hour, Michael Flynn?" I demanded, shutting the door behind me. "And who let you into my house? One of my matchmaking brothers, no doubt. I'd be pleased if you'd find your coat and hat and take yourself off before I have to summon assistance."

"Ah, Mary," he said woefully, and my hard heart softened a bit. He was a handsome boy, with shoulders twice as broad as any man I knew, a kind handsome face, and a good, loving heart. That his heart was filled with love for me brought me as much pain as satisfaction, for, good man though Michael was, he simply woke none of the tender feelings in my breast. Indeed, when he looked at me with such a lovesick, hangdog expression on his simple face it made me irritable. Since I was six and he was eight I had been able to wind him around my little finger, and I didn't fancy ruling the roost for the rest of my life. Unfortunately Michael Flynn was the kind of man who'd enjoy just that sort of relationship, with a few cuffs to my head thrown in to make him feel he was a man after a night at the tavern.

"And what're you doing here?" I repeated.

"I came to say good-bye," he announced with great dignity, having visited that tavern already. "Seamus told me you were leaving tomorrow. You couldn't even tell me yourself, Mary!" he reproached me, and I noticed with weary annoyance that he was drunk too. I seemed to have more than my share of drunken men that night.

"Michael Flynn, you've been drinking," I said severely, if needlessly. "Come into the kitchen and I'll make you some nice strong coffee to take the edge off you. Your mother would die of shame if she knew you were wandering around in a state like that."

"I don't want anything, Mary. I just want you!" he wailed mournfully, shambling after me. "And you, you cold-hearted jezebel, you offer me coffee!" He sank into my rocker in disgust, the old chair creaking in protest against his sturdy weight, and proceeded to fall sound asleep.

I stared at him for a moment, filled with a sudden sense of loss. The chair and the man in it were closely identified with my whole life up to that point, and tomorrow morning I would leave them both behind; the chair sold along with the other furnishings to the nice young baker who was buying my parents' house, and Michael to whatever clever young lady might snap him up. I couldn't resist a sigh, wondering if I were as great a fool as I suspected I might be.

A snore emerged from his sleeping form. "Michael," I said sharply, to cover my momentary indecision. There was no response. I poked him in his ribs, always a highly effective action with the lad. He snored on. I tugged at his massive body, and only managed to pull him out of the chair and onto the floor.

"Michael!" I cried in disgust. "Wake up, curse your black Irish heart. You can't stay here!" He curled up on the rough brick floor like a little baby, deaf to my cries. As a desperate last resort I went to the pump and filled a bucket with icy water and proceeded to throw it on his head. And still he slept.

"Well, all I can say, Michael Flynn, is that you must have drunk a snootful, and it's a sorry man you'll be if any of my brothers catch wind that you spent the night here." And giving up in disgust, I went in search of some blankets to make the poor drunk comfortable before retiring to my little bedroom on the first floor, for the last time in my life.

Chapter Three

I was awakened early the next morning, before the first light, by the sound of voices below me in the kitchen. My first reaction was blind panic, which was swiftly replaced by anger and relief when I remembered my sodden suitor. Throwing a blanket around me, I made my way downstairs to the basement to see what visitors Michael Flynn was entertaining in my absence.

I expected to see Mr. Murphy standing there, as disapproving as a Calvinist minister. It came as a horrid shock to recognize Connell Fitzgerald there in my homey little kitchen, a saturnine expression on his face, while Michael, shirtless, barefoot, and amazingly cheerful for one with a hangover like he deserved to have, stirred the fire and casually outlined our wedding plans.

"As soon as we've made enough money, Cousin Connell, Mary and I are going to tie the knot." A nice blast of heat rose from the old cast-iron stove to meet the nice blast of heat rising from my temper. "So I wanted to make that clear to you and any boy-o who happens to be around. She's promised to me," he said, one large thumb thumping his hairy chest, "and I won't be having you forgetting that."

"My man Murphy has already apprised me of the situation," he answered smoothly, with far more courtesy than my loutish suitor deserved.

I'll just bet he did, I thought hopelessly. Aloud I said, "What are you doing here, Michael? And Mr. Fitzgerald. I wasn't expecting you this morning."

Michael jumped, and had the grace to look abashed; something that didn't escape Connell Fitzgerald's seemingly indolent attention. Only for a minute though. With foolhardy courage I couldn't help but admire, Michael sped across the room and drew me into his hairy embrace.

Now I'd been kissed before, and by Michael Flynn for that matter, but I had never been half-strangled by a passionate embrace designed to show a man's ownership of me. And not by a half-naked, hairy bear of a man with his breath reeking of stale whiskey. I struggled ineffectually, but I'm afraid it merely made the embrace appear more passionate. Wishing to God I had thought to put on nice, heavy shoes so that I could trample on his bare feet, I held still and waited until he finally drew back with an expression of glazed satisfaction, I leaned back and slapped him as hard as I could across his oafish face.

"How dare you?" I demanded, and proceeded, verbally, to march up one side of him and down the other, all the time aware of my cut lip and the distant, amused interest on Connell Fitzgerald's face. So much

34

for any fantasies I'd allowed myself last night, I thought grimly.

The problem with Michael Flynn, and the problem with most of the possible suitors I had met in my twenty-three years of life, is that they're none of them man enough for the likes of me. I need a strong hand and a worthy opponent in the battle of life, not a sweet, lovesick young law clerk.

"And you can leave now," I finished, thrusting his shirt, boots, and jacket against his unprotesting body. "And you can be sure it'll be a long time before I forgive you for this drunken display. You're just lucky Seamus and the others don't get wind of it."

"But, Mary," Michael protested, "this was Seamus's idea."

I stared at him, dumbfounded. Then I picked up his teacup full of freshly made tea and hurled it at his head. The coward left at a dead run.

I turned to the other occupant of the kitchen and smiled demurely. "I'll be with you in a few minutes, Mr. Fitzgerald. Help yourself to some tea."

"Thank you, Mary," he replied with a ripple of laughter in his lovely voice.

The trip to the train station was made in total silence. Connell Fitzgerald sat opposite me in his elegant plush-lined carriage, his cynical blue eyes staring moodily out of the window. And I sat primly in the corner of the luxurious vehicle, my eyes demurely downcast, except when I thought he wasn't looking. Every now and then I would sneak a glance at his distant, handsome profile, and wonder why in the world he had come to see me off on the north-bound train instead of his dour dogsbody, Murphy. He hadn't even objected to my one stop at the house in Clarence Street, for one last tumultuous farewell with my oversized family.

It had been all I could do to bid a polite farewell to Seamus with the memory of his perfidy still fresh in my mind. The sooner I was away from my matchmaking kin the better, I thought, my eyes drifting upward to meet the clear blue ones of my employer. Quickly I lowered my own, feeling a flush mounting my pale cheeks.

"Your family will miss you," he said suddenly, and I jumped nervously.

"I suppose so," I agreed. "But they should have enough family around to keep them busy while I'm gone."

"I would think so," he said drily, returning to his contemplation of the dirty city streets as the carriage made its slow but steady way through the early-morning traffic. But from then on, every time I tried to sneak a subtle little look at him, just to make sure his face was set in my memory, I found him watching me with a curiously quizzical expression that made my stomach contract in the most alarming fashion. And once more I was glad that I was going three hundred miles away from temptation.

Our arrival at the train station was a lesson to me in the advantages of being rich. Casually Connell Fitzgerald helped me out of the carriage, casually he nodded to a porter who dropped an irate lady's bag and rushed to do his bidding, casually he put one strong hand under my slightly trembling arm and guided me across the crowded platforms. I glanced at the large clock over our heads and jumped.

"We're late," I said nervously. "I'll miss the train."

The look he cast me was coolly amused. "The train won't leave without you," he stated with bored conviction, and indeed, I believed him. No train company would dare to antagonize Connell Fitzgerald of the far-flung Fitzgerald enterprises. And I was to find out later that he owned the railroad, or at least a goodly part of it.

"Just in time, sir." Murphy appeared from out of the milling crowd. "Miss Gallager's bags are in her room. I'll see her the rest of the way." The man seemed uncommonly eager to rid Connell of his burden, and it was with surprise that I watched him wave his secretary away.

"Meet me in the carriage, Murphy," he ordered abruptly, and pushed onward through the crowds of arrivals and departures, his hand still under my willing elbow, seeming to my romantic mind to burn through the thin cloth.

And finally I was handed over to another smartly dressed porter, along with a sizable sum of money, if I could judge by the affable expression on the man's face. "He'll take care of you," Connell said in a suddenly harsh voice. "I wish I could be as sure . . ."

I stared up at him, bewildered, and noted for the first time how very tall he was. I was a tall woman, yet he seemed to tower over me. "What do you mean?" I demanded, suddenly frightened. "What could possibly go wrong?"

Whatever he replied was lost in the sudden blast of the train whistle, and the sound of the conductor roaring, "All aboard." All around us couples were embracing, bidding each other a teary farewell.

"Take care of yourself, my darling," a young husband said into his wife's plumed hat beside us. A look of devilish amusement passed over Connell's usually impassive features, and a moment later I found myself swept into his strong arms.

"Good-bye, darling," he murmured, and his mouth came down on mine in a kiss that was both lighthearted and yet totally devastating to one in my already precarious state of emotions. And the next thing I knew I was placed gently but forcibly on the train while it moved slowly down the platform, and I stared out the open door at Connell's quickly receding figure with dazed eyes.

"This way, ma'am." The porter grinned, and with a great effort of will I pulled myself together, following his sturdy figure down the narrow hallways.

I had many long, long hours to remember that kiss. The train ride from Boston to the tiny Vermont town of Lyman's Gore took a full seven hours—seven hours to wonder what had prompted Connell to kiss me like that, seven hours to wonder how I was going to bear being so far away from the only life I had ever known. At least I wouldn't have to worry about my guilty passion. A flowery-scented note from Lillian had reassured me on that head. She and her brother were off to Europe in the next few days, he for a round of business meetings and no doubt to trace his errant wife, with Lillian as his unwilling companion. She doubted they'd see me before the spring. And it was with both relief and admitted regret that I watched the barren trees fly by my window and knew that it was the end of November and spring was far, far away.

I put *Pride and Prejudice* down on the seat beside me and stared out at the bleak landscape. It was admittedly comfortable in my luxurious private room, but I was getting a little uneasy, alone with my thoughts and the memory of Connell's quixotic farewell. So it was with relief that I greeted the tentative knocking on my door.

"Do you mind if I join you?" A voice broke through my reveries, and I looked up in surprise at my fellow passenger. Warm brown eyes smiled down at me, set in a face that was so handsome it might even be called effeminate. Wavy brown hair curled over his brow, his body was clothed in a suit of Irish tweed, and his smile revealed a row of even white teeth. He wasn't quite as tall as Connell Fitzgerald, and his build was slighter and more delicate. After a long, considering moment I smiled in return. I had read Miss Austen's masterpiece seven times in my short life, and I decided that Mr. Darcy could wait till later.

"Thank God, you smiled," he said ingratiatingly, seating himself opposite me and holding out a strong, well-manicured hand. "I'm not usually this forward, you know, but I couldn't resist. I knew you'd be traveling up today, Miss Gallager, and decided it was my duty to keep an eye on you. I'm Peter Riordan. I'm going to be your neighbor, you know."

"Are you?" I inquired somewhat coolly, not sure if I enjoyed brash young men.

My standoffishness didn't seem to daunt him. "It took me this long to talk the porter into telling me which car you were in. Con was ever a secretive devil when it comes to me. Mustn't trust me."

"Does he have reason not to?" I questioned with an attempt at frivolity, and was surprised to see the stricken look that passed over his open, expressive face. "Well, I'm glad you found out," I continued hastily. "I've been spending far too much time alone with my thoughts, Mr. Riordan. I'm afraid I'm homesick already."

"Peter," he corrected, smiling once more with a smile that would have captivated me totally only a week ago. Compared to Connell's smile, it was the difference between Irish whiskey and weak tea. "And don't you worry about that—we won't give you time to feel lonely. My mother and I own the land adjoining Connell's. Nothing so grand as Demonwood, mind you, but then, what is? We have just a few hundred acres and a comfortable house—but I won't bother describing it to you. You'll be seeing it soon enough." He glanced out the window at the tracings of snow on the ground. Snow that to my city-bred eyes was an amazement. "It looks like a mild winter this year. We're about due for one."

"Snow on the ground already and you call it mild?" I questioned in astonishment.

"We usually have at least a foot by this time, Mary, my girl. I may call you Mary, mayn't I?" He was very sure of himself, was this Peter Riordan. "Winters up here are a sight more difficult than in Boston—as you'll soon see. But you needn't worry about it. We're used to it. We don't let a little snow get in the way of our social life."

"Is there a social life?" I questioned idly. "I gathered from Lillian that things are pretty secluded."

"To the Fitzgeralds I suppose it might seem so. We manage to have a good time anyway." His brown eyes as they met mine were frankly admiring. "You're Maeve's cousin, aren't you?"

"Her third cousin," I corrected cheerfully. "Not quite in her class, I'm afraid."

"You've the look of her."

I gave him a skeptical glance. "No one's ever said *that* before, and I'll take leave to doubt it."

"But you do," he insisted, winning a small corner of my vain heart forever. "Not in your coloring, of course. But certain expressions you have . . . didn't Connell mention it to you?"

I remembered his initial, inexplicable look of dislike, and wondered whether I might not have hit upon the reason for it. "No, he never mentioned any family resemblance."

He tilted his head to one side and viewed me as he might a painting. "I suppose you're not the great beauty she is," he admitted truthfully if not tactfully, "but you've got a sweeter expression. And kinder eyes. Besides, I've always had a weakness for black hair and green eyes."

"How fortunate for me," I murmured in dulcet tones.

Peter laughed good-naturedly. "I can see why Connell hired you. He never could abide milk-and-sugar misses. But I can't understand why he'd want to leave the country just when you're going to Demonwood. The moment he described you to me I decided to head north. Too many winters in the city have taken their toll on me—it's time to rusticate for a season and redirect my energies."

I had stiffened uncontrollably at the start of his last speech. "I don't suppose it occurred to you, Mr. Riordan, that Mr. Fitzgerald hired me to tutor his son, and for no other purpose?"

He smiled at me, unabashed. "Oh, I'm perfectly willing to believe that's all you had in mind. After all, Con's married to one of the most beautiful women of the last decade, and your cousin to boot. Even if it is a marriage made in hell for both of them. I'm even

40

willing to believe that Con hired you with only the purest of intentions on his part. After all, you're not in the usual style of his amours. But I've known Con for almost twenty years, and I'm willing to bet you that he's at Demonwood by Christmas, with or without his wife and sister trailing behind him."

"And what is it you'd be willing to bet?" I demanded, for unfortunately gaming ran in all the Gallagers' blood. Even to my brother, Ronan, safely bestowed in the priesthood.

"A kiss," he replied promptly, a rakish grin on his face.

"And what am I to have if I win? I wouldn't count a kiss from you as any great prize."

"What about my hand and heart?"

"No, thank you. Something else."

He appeared to consider the matter. "All right, if you win, I'll have Connell treat you to a weekend back in Boston in the spring. How would that be? By that time you'll be dying to get away from that poisonous child."

"It sounds agreeable enough," I said slowly. "But why do you call Daniel 'poisonous'?"

"That, my dear lady, I'll leave for you to discover. In the meantime we have much more important things to discuss, such as the story of my life." And he proceeded to beguile the rest of my hitherto tedious and maudlin trip with amusing and highly unbelievable tales of his childhood and college years, his various short-lived professions, and other entertaining subjects, while I listened to them with half a mind only, still remembering my last sight of my cousin's husband, and wondering what would happen if and when we met again.

Chapter Four

I was glad of Peter Riordan's company in more ways than one. When we finally arrived at our destination it was fully dark, and that dark, combined with a brisk wind and the beginnings of a freezing rain made me wonder whether I had been a fool to take on this frightening job so far away from all I'd ever known and loved. As I stepped from the train, the rain whipped at my heavy blue serge skirts, tugged at my already disarranged hair, and added a note of gloom to my troubled spirits.

"This way, Mary." Peter put a firm hand beneath my elbow and guided me across the almost empty railway platform. And his touch left me sadly unmoved. "Good evening, Carpenter," he greeted a small, bundled-up figure waiting impatiently beside a carriage. "You see what I've brought you? A new teacher for darlin' Daniel."

"Good evening, Mr. Riordan. Good evening, Miss Gallager," the figure said grudgingly. "Welcome to Vermont."

"Oh, I've already welcomed her," Peter reassured him jovially. "And in return for bringing such a treat, how about a ride to my ancestral acres?"

"Certainly, sir," Mr. Carpenter answered correctly, if without enthusiasm. "Would you mind if I took Miss Gallager home first? The wife's been keeping dinner for her and you know how Mrs. Carpenter is when she's kept waiting."

"I do, indeed," Peter said lightly, helping me up into the carriage.

"How far is it to Demonwood?" I asked once we started moving. I had been up since daybreak and exhaustion was just beginning to set in. I devoutly hoped it wouldn't be long before my new, albeit temporary, home.

"Not too far, sweet Mary," he replied with sudden gentleness, and I wondered with a spasm of nervousness whether he was about to pounce. I squirmed back into the plush corner of the carriage. I had no doubts about my ability to defend my virtue, but I really didn't relish the thought of proving it right now. Besides, Peter had been charming and so friendly, and I had the uneasy feeling that I'd need a friend where I was going. "Another twenty minutes or so," he continued after a moment, and I relaxed against the velvet cushions. "And Stonewalls is only another half hour away from Demonwood—you won't be deserted, you know."

Could he read my mind? It was an eerie feeling. "I'm sure I'll be too busy to feel deserted."

"Perhaps," replied Peter, not sounding at all sure himself. He leaned forward across the carriage, and I could feel his breath warm on my face. "I'm going to say something to you, Mary, and I want you to remember it. If anything happens, anything goes wrong, you can always come to me. I'll see that you're safe, I promise you. And that's with no strings attached."

This was the second veiled warning of the day, and my overtired Irish temper began to smolder. "What could go wrong?" I demanded bravely. "Is there something I should know that you aren't telling me?"

The silence in the carriage seemed to stretch and grow, with only the sound of the wind sighing through the tall trees and the clip-clop of the horses' hooves penetrating the gloom. Then he laughed, a convincing, self-deprecating little laugh. Except that I wasn't convinced.

"Oh, you might find dear little Daniel more of a burden than you think. Or the remoteness of the place might drive you mad after all your years in the big city. Or you may very well love Vermont—there's no telling. I'm just saying that if you don't, if you have any problems, you know that you have a friend."

I was touched, skeptical, and still faintly alarmed. But Peter Riordan had the air of a man who knows when he's been indiscreet, and I knew from experience with my brothers that I would get no more out of him. So, with all the patience in the world, I leaned back and shut my eyes.

Before I realized it the carriage had drawn to a halt, and blazing lights illuminated our shadowy, dark faces. "We're here," Peter announced unnecessarily, his voice suddenly hushed, and I felt my stomach tighten. I, who had never before been nervous a day in my life, stared out the window through the lightly falling snow at the monstrous structure that was Demonwood.

"Elegant, isn't it?" Peter's voice was ironical as he handed me down.

"It is that," I breathed, momentarily cowed at the massive grandeur of the place. I had never seen such a glorious, hideous thing in all my life. Four stories high and made of stark, drab-colored wood, it looked very new, very expensive, and very cold. Even the light shining from the windows facing the drive and pouring from the open front door did little to alleviate the gloom of the place. I couldn't control a little shudder of apprehension.

"Are you cold?" my companion asked solicitously, hurrying me up the wide front stairs and into the mansion. I stopped short just inside the door so that I could fully appreciate the lofty, repelling atmosphere of the place.

The entry hall, (and, indeed, the entire house, as I was soon to discover) was large and cold and bare, with the marble floors and the lofty ceilings screaming aloud the very newness and the pretensions of the place. The walls were a particularly repulsive shade of brown, the curtains cold, shiny silk, and a blast of icy air seemed to swirl and eddy through the still, damp atmosphere. I had never seen a more unwelcoming entrance, and I turned to Peter in helpless dismay.

"It affects you that way, does it? This monstrosity is Maeve's pride and joy, so you'd best not criticize it when one of her spies is around."

"It's . . . it's very grand, isn't it?"

He laughed, and took one of my unresisting hands in his and clasped it warmly. "Very grand," he agreed, "and very new. Connell had it built for . . . before he met Maeve." I noticed the abrupt change in his wording but forebore to comment on it. "But it's pretty much Maeve's creation. Con leaves it to her and Lillian and the boy whenever he can. If you ever find you're desperately in need of more comfortable surroundings you'll know where to find me."

This was the second offer of shelter in a matter of minutes, and my sense of unease grew. "I'm sure I'll be fine," I lied, unclasping his hand with gentle firmness. Peter Riordan was a very handsome, sensitive young man, but at that point I wasn't interested in handsome young men. In the back of my mind hung the image of a tired, cynical man, and the feel of his mouth on mine lingered, flooding my chilled body with a guilty, telltale warmth.

"I won't say good-bye, Mary," he murmured, oblivious to the tortured workings of my brain. "I'll be over in the next few days to see how you're doing, and to give you a tour of the countryside. You ride, don't you?"

"Yes, but . . ."

"No buts, my girl. Connell would have no objections to your taking the air with me. You can't work all the time, and you'll find there's precious little around here to keep you occupied." He recaptured my limp hand, brought it to his lips, and kissed it lightly, his mouth soft against my work-worn hand. "You remember what I told you, Mary," he said softly, his voice pitched low. "Till then," he added in a louder voice, and left me.

I watched his departing figure out of tired eyes, feeling mildly bereft. It seemed a day for leave-takings, and I wondered how long it would take me to get accustomed to this new life. I had had more change in one day than in the rest of my twenty-three years. It was with great weariness and trepidation that I turned to face the woman approaching me across the highly polished floor.

"Miss Gallager?" Her face was pink and round and should have emanated goodwill, but her tiny little black eyes were as cold as the wind howling around this lonely mansion, and her small pink mouth was pursed in a prim, disapproving pout. Her uniform of black bombazine with its rows of fussy jet trim was molded to her sturdy, round little figure, and as she moved toward me on oddly mincing little feet her keys jangled at her ample waist, proclaiming beyond any doubt her status as housekeeper and chatelaine of Demonwood.

Before I could even open my mouth she continued, "I'm Mrs. Carpenter." Her steely glance raked over my travel-worn form, and I thought I detected a barely audible sniff of disdain. "Mr. Fitzgerald informed me that you would be coming, although I hadn't known that Mr. Riordan was such an old friend." Her expression said clearly that it wasn't for the likes of me to associate with the gentry.

Determinedly I stifled the wave of explanations that flew to my lips. I wasn't about to justify my actions to this disapproving old witch. I met her tiny black eyes with cool unconcern.

Her eyes wavered first. "I'll show you to your room," she continued after a moment, her thin-lipped mouth expressing her contempt. "I'm sure you'd like to freshen up before you have supper." And if I didn't wish to I was clearly even more of a slattern than I appeared to be.

"Yes, I'd like that," I responded politely. "Is Daniel still awake? I'd like to meet him tonight, if that's possible."

"Mr. Daniel," she corrected frostily, "is always in bed by six-thirty. Tomorrow will be soon enough. Come with me." Her stiff, upright form swept ahead of me, and wearily I followed, my bravado vanishing. I had had such high hopes for my new life. I had never expected that I would have to cope with a hostile chatelaine and a child stigmatized as a little hellion by his father's friend. I felt like throwing my carpet bag down and indulging in a strong fit of hysterics.

Instead, I trudged along behind Mrs. Carpenter, head held firmly up, eyes straight ahead, as we traversed stairs and halls and then more stairs and halls, each one as ornate and elegant as the previous one, the only difference between them the various shades of olive green, puce, and a particularly rancid salmon-colored one. It wasn't until we reached the very top floor when my guide stopped to let me get my breath. She wasn't even winded.

"I decided to put you up here," she informed me with sudden false cordiality. "Mr. Daniel has been worried recently about ghosts and the like. There have always been silly rumors about this floor, and I decided that a teacher would be certain to be full of common sense—just the right thing to calm his fears, don't you think? Set an example to us all."

And who's going to calm my fears. I wondered with a start of nervousness, staring at the tall, gloomy hallway. I prided myself on being a sensible young woman, but when it came to ghosts and banshees I was reduced to a quivering mass of terror. I gave Mrs. Carpenter my most endearing smile, determined to win an answering response. Her basilisk eyes met mine, then looked away. "I'm sure this will be lovely," I said gamely after a moment or two.

She responded with a genteel snort, opening the door at the back of the hallway. I was less than entranced.

The room was made up of half-windows; their cold panes staring in at me like so many eyes. A sharp breeze was blowing, rattling the panes, and the room

47

was colder than any room I'd been in during my not too opulent life. Surreptitiously I pulled my black wool cloak around me. The space was huge and sparsely furnished, dominated by a massive four-poster bed—one of those dynasty-founding affairs.. The two walls that weren't floor-to-ceiling windows were paneled with intricately carved wood, made up of cupids, satyrs, and nymphs in positions that were absolutely embarrassing upon close inspection. I turned to my silent companion.

"It was once a studio for Mrs. Fitzgerald," she offered. "She tired of it a few years ago and this has been empty storage space until now. When Miss Maeve redecorated her bedroom we moved the old Fitzgerald bed up here, and I believe the paneling came from an old castle in Ireland belonging to one of Mr. Fitzgerald's ancestors. Perhaps even the Countess of Carradine herself." Mrs. Carpenter's voice took on a hushed reverence at the mention of that august name. "It amused Miss Maeve to have it installed. I do hope it doesn't disturb you?" Her concern was as false as her sudden, smirking affability.

"Not in the slightest," I lied cheerfully. "It'll be a little better with a fire," I added, shivering slightly. Mrs. Carpenter watched me stolidly.

"We don't allow fires in the servants' bedrooms," she observed, and noted with complacency the flush that mounted to my face.

"Mrs. Carpenter," I said with deceptive gentleness after a long moment, "before I'm here another minute we'd best get a few things straight. Number one, I am not a servant. I am a teacher. Number two, I have no intention of spending the night in this room without a fire to warm it. Ghosts I can stand, pneumonia is another matter." I stopped, at a loss for a moment.

"Is that all, miss?" Mrs. Carpenter murmured, visibly unmoved.

"Yes, Mrs. Carpenter."

"Then someone will be up with your bags shortly. And someone will kindle you a fire. Though I doubt it

48

will do you much good. Nothing seems to warm this room." On that sepulchral note she left me to my jumbled thoughts.

She was right, of course. The blazing fire added an aura of warmth to the cold, bare room, but no actual heat penetrated more than a few feet into the barren interior. Besides the bed and the cavernous wardrobe that had swallowed up my meager clothing there was a small writing desk and a large, uncomfortable chair. It was there that I sat and ate the poor meal Mrs. Carpenter had seen fit to send me, and it was there I sat, composing a bright, cheerful, lying letter to my brothers about the elegant house and the warmth of my reception. Finally my usually fertile imagination failed me, and I put the ebulliant missive aside and crawled wearily up into the soft, overwhelming bed, shivering against the chill of the rough, linen sheets. As I lay there in the cold, dark room I wondered unhappily how I would bear spending the next seven or eight months in this cold, unfriendly place without anyone to keep me company, not a friendly face in the state, as far as I could tell. Of course, Peter Riordan would be around as often as I let him; I knew enough about men to recognize that right off. But I was only fooling myself. It wasn't a friendly face or Peter Riordan that I wanted. I reached up and touched my mouth with suddenly trembling fingers, and on that thought I finally fell asleep.

Chapter Five

I had many strange dreams that night. At first I was alone on a train, traveling farther and farther into a snowy oblivion. There were no conductors, no train-men, no porters. I struggled with the windows on the coach, thinking I could escape that way, but they were firmly fastened. I ran down the aisle and tried the doors, but they were locked. And staring at me malevo-lently through the glass partition was Mrs. Carpenter, grim amusement written on her stern New England face. As I was beating on the door, begging her to let me out, two hands reached for my shoulders and turned me around to face the dark, tormented gaze of Connell Fitzgerald. And I watched him, mesmerized by those eyes, waiting for him to kiss me again; trapped by an inertia I was both powerless and loath to break, until I realized that I was awake, and stand-ing by my bed was a small, pale little boy with Con-nell Fitzgerald's dark eyes glowing into mine.

"Good morning, Daniel," I said softly after a mo-ment. Light was streaming through the many windows of the room. "I must have overslept. How nice of you to come wake me up."

I sat up sleepily and he jumped back, as if he was afraid I might bite him. "Mrs. Carpenter sent me up. She told me I had to come." His voice was low-pitched and sullen, and those brilliant eyes in his pale, thin face darted nervously around the room. He was defi-nitely not a beautiful child—his mother's spectacular looks had passed him by entirely, and the only resem-blance to his handsome father were those dark, de-spairing eyes. His ears stuck out from his closely cropped brown head, his transparent skin was dusted with tiny freckles, and his clothes were of a neatness and propriety seldom seen on a child his age. The wary expression on his anxious face touched me to the quick, and I wanted to reach out and comfort him, protect him from whatever demons had been torment-ing him. And demons, human or otherwise, had cer-tainly been at work on his fragile well-being. Of course I did no such thing.

"I didn't want to come," he continued more boldly,

his eyes flashing like blue fire. "I don't like it up here. Why are you sleeping here?"

I felt an irrational twinge of relief. It was the room that frightened him, not me. "Mrs. Carpenter put me here. I suppose we're both dependent on what Mrs. Carpenter thinks is right. What don't you like about the room?"

He stared at me as if I were simple-minded, a look of contempt that brought his father back to me with unpleasant force. "It's haunted, of course. You should know that. Mrs. Carpenter said you were no doubt a superstitious fool like all the other Irish and it wouldn't take long for you to get the wind up. *Are* you frightened?"

"Devil a bit," I replied cheerfully. "It's a little drafty for the likes of me but apart from that I'll get used to it in time. And I imagine there's a lovely view from up here."

"I suppose there is," Daniel acknowledged grudgingly. He moved away from the bed toward a wall of windows and looked downward, and I noticed again with increased surprise that I had never seen a cleaner child. I swung my feet out of bed and with enormous willpower prevented myself from swinging them right back in. It was desperately cold in the room, and it wasn't yet December. Bravely I left the bed and padded barefoot across the chill wood floors to the windows beside Daniel.

It was a revelation. All my fears, my doubts, my rages vanished as I viewed the landscape. A stark green and brown and white wilderness lay around me, lightly dusted with snow, tall majestic mountains on every side and not another house in sight. The bright blue dazzle of a lake shone with reflected sunlight, the clouds scudded along in the brilliant blue sky, and there was nothing I wanted more than to run outside and dance. If this was the land of Connell Fitzgerald's Demonwood I could be very happy here.

"It's beautiful, isn't it?" Daniel inquired in a small, proud voice.

"That it is, me lad," I replied devoutly. "Now if I could just get warm . . ."

He turned his sober face to me. "If you like I'll build up your fire. It should take some of the chill off the room. Or perhaps you'd prefer to dress quickly and come down for breakfast. The dining room's quite warm." He looked at me askance. "But I forgot. It probably takes you an hour at least to dress. It takes my Aunt Lillian that long, and my mother even longer."

"Well, I'm not one of your frail, hothouse flowers," I answered firmly. "I can dress faster than anyone I know. If you'll be so good as to leave the room, young Daniel, I'll be ready in five minutes flat."

"Shouldn't you call me Master Daniel?" he asked, jealous of his dignity.

"Well, now," I considered it, "I might, but then you would have to call me Miss Mary, and that gets a mite formal. How about Cousin Mary and Cousin Daniel?"

"Are you my cousin?" he asked incredulously, obscurely pleased by the thought.

"Third cousin once removed, or is it first cousin three times removed? Something like that. So maybe we'd better just call each other Mary and Daniel and have it go at that."

"All right," he agreed solemnly. "Mrs. Carpenter didn't explain that you were family," he added accusingly.

"Well, I'm not completely sure that she knows," I pointed out. "Now be off with you before I freeze to death—I'm just a poor city girl, not used to your rough climate."

Seeing the house in the daylight did little to change my initial impression. For some reason the very newness of the place created an aura of blank, impassive malevolence, an aura I couldn't shake off. Each floor looked the same as the next one, except for the main floor. Here an attempt at individuality had been made—there were some lovely rare pieces of furniture among the new and expensive stuff, the gaudy gilt trim had been applied with an even more lavish hand, and some of the family portraits on the walls had added a note of disapproving humor. Young Daniel led me through the house, oblivious to his surroundings, and I hoped I would soon have the same oblivion. I devoured a huge, well-cooked breakfast that was at variance with the unpalatable stuff Mrs. Carpenter had sent up the night before, and sat beneath that lady's beady little eyes, determined not to let her unpleasant face spoil my appetite. I leaned back in my elegant, uncomfortable chair, replete for once.

"Shall we start lessons?" Daniel asked in his solemn little voice.

"Oh, not today," I protested with deliberate indolence. "I think we should get to know each other a little better first. Why don't we go for a walk—it's stopped snowing."

"Aunt Lillian thinks the winter air is bad for me," he murmured. "And I'm behind in my studies."

"Cold air is bracing," I replied firmly. "And we can go for a nature walk and discuss the various trees and plant life we can find. You get bundled up and I'll meet you by the front door in ten minutes."

"But I don't want to go outside."

"Why ever not?" I questioned, willing to discuss the matter reasonably. "When my brothers were your age there was no keeping them inside on a day like this. All six of them would pile out the door before my sainted mother could say a word."

"You have six brothers?" he breathed, fascinated in spite of himself.

"That I do. And every one of them a hell-raiser. I think, Daniel, me lad, that it's about time for you to raise a little hell yourself."

"I wish I had even *one* brother," he said wistfully.

"Well, you might someday."

"No, I won't. Not ever. My mother said it nearly killed her to have me, and she'd never go through that torment again."

I stared at his plain, unhappy little face, so unlike the flamboyant beauty of his mother or the cynical attractiveness of Connell. "Well," I said after a moment, "she may change her mind. And then again, she may have no say in the matter. I think we'll spend some time on biology later on."

"I heard her tell Aunt Lillian that even if there were accidents she could see to it that there'd be no more little monsters to interfere with her life."

I was shocked to the depths of my Catholic soul. I had heard of birth control methods, and even, to an extent not shared by Father McShane, approved of them. Poor Pauline and her perennially protruding belly would be enough to change the mind of any woman. My dear cousin Maeve, however, was obviously referring to abortion, and although I could sympathize with some poor woman's needs, it still festered in my mind as little more than murder. And that her son should hear her . . .

"Well," I said again, "then I guess you might not have any brothers and sisters. But you already have tons of cousins."

"I do?" He brightened visibly.

"In Boston. If you learn very fast, and do just as you're told, perhaps I can persuade your father to let you come to Boston with me for a week and you could get to know them. There are twins just about your age."

He nodded avidly, looking more alive than he had all morning. "I'll go get my coat," he said hurriedly, and sped from the room.

"I wouldn't raise his hopes like that if I were you," Mrs. Carpenter's cold voice came from the far doorway. I jumped, startled, and wondered how long she'd been standing there.

"Why not?" I rose. "I think it's an excellent idea—the boy doesn't have enough outside influences."

"Miss Lillian thinks he has far too many," she replied slyly, pursing her narrow lips. "He's a delicate boy—too much excitement isn't good for him. I doubt he'll ever be well enough to go jauntering over the country with you."

"Then how do you expect he'll be able to go to school next year?"

A cold smile flitted across her deceptively cheery face. "Why, I don't expect him to be able to go away to school at all. Nor does anyone who knows him. You're a last-ditch effort, and it will do no good. Even his father has come to realize that Daniel is much too scared of his own shadow to be able to live a normal life."

"There's nothing wrong with the boy!" I said hotly. "Nothing that a little fresh air and sunshine and companionship won't cure."

"Do you really think so?" she asked scornfully, and I wondered what lay behind her antipathy. "We'll see, miss. We'll see."

We went for quite a hike that day, Daniel and I, partly to prove to myself he was as sturdy as any other little boy, partly to give us a chance to get to know each other without the shadow of Mrs. Carpenter's disapproval hanging over us. From the moment we walked out the massive oaken door I wanted to get as far away from that cold, unfriendly place as my legs could carry me. And Daniel, for all his initial objections, had the energy of any nine-year-old, and I soon found myself trailing behind him in a grim effort to match his sturdy little legs.

There was only a thin crusting of snow beneath our feet, and my stout brogues made their way through it with little difficulty. I started out our hike with a vague effort at pointing trees out to him, but when I referred to an aspen as an oak and a beech as a maple, Daniel kindly relieved me of the responsibility for identifying them.

"It's hard to tell them apart when they have no leaves," I excused myself.

"That's all right, Cousin Mary," he said grandly, obviously delighted to have been proven more knowledgeable than his teacher. "After you've been here a while you'll know the difference with your eyes closed." We had come to the edge of the pine forest, and Daniel suddenly shied away nervously, like a skittish mare.

"Let's go back, shall we?"

"But why?" I peered through the dark trees. "It looks like fairly easy going once we're in there."

"I don't like the woods," the boy said nervously. "That's how our house got its name, you know. Demonwood, like the forest around it. This leads up to the cliff . . ." he stopped suddenly, afraid he'd said too much.

"The cliff?"

"I want to go now!" he shouted, and pulling the hand that had rested so trustingly in mine, he turned and ran from me back to the house, ignoring my calls.

Chapter Six

I toiled my way back to the house very slowly, preoccupied with all the new ideas and emotions that had assaulted me in the last twenty-four hours. So caught up was I in pondering Daniel's strange, terrified behavior that I didn't hear the horse until it was almost upon me.

"Good morning to you, Mary Gallager," Peter greeted me from astride a tall, rangy gray mare. "And how are you enjoying your new job? I saw your little student take off like a bat out of hell a few minutes ago."

"Something frightened him," I confessed unwillingly. "I haven't the vaguest idea what. I suggested we walk in the woods a bit . . ."

"That explains it right there. Of course the little coward would run. Not that I can really blame him."

"Why is he a little coward? What is there about the woods?"

"Ah, you haven't heard of the ghosts of Demonwood? The forests around here are haunted, my girl. There are parts of these woods that have never seen the sun, never been trod on by human feet."

I looked back at the dark brooding pine forests that had seemed so welcoming from my attic windows and shivered. "What of it?" I demanded with false courage. "I'm sure the same can be said of most forests in North America. What's special about this one?"

Peter smiled down at me, his brown eyes warm and confiding. "I'd love to take you through there and show you just what haunts Demonwood. Are you game?"

Among my many faults, superstition could be accounted a major one. I hesitated, wishing I could decline Peter's kind offer. But I knew I would never be able to help Daniel conquer his fears if I didn't conquer my own, so meeting that limpid gaze firmly, I acquiesced with only a slight quaver in my voice.

As our horses picked their way delicately along the path I could see he was right about the lack of sunlight in the woods. Astride an exceedingly beautiful, high-strung mare with the fanciful name of Moon Maiden, I followed Peter's broad back through the forest, the only sound the creaking of the pines and the faint whoosh of their branches as they reached desperately toward the sunlight. I peered nervously through the tree trunks, searching for some sign of life in this still, dead place, but I was rewarded with nothing more than a few rabbit tracks in the thin layer of snow.

We were climbing steadily upward, the horses plodding dully along. Several times I started to speak, to ask Peter exactly where we were going, and several times I subsided into silence. I wondered where Daniel had run to—there had been no sign of him when we arrived at the stables seeking a mount for me. Robinson, the sullen, attractive groom, had merely cast a bored glance at me when I'd questioned him, his spaniel's eyes running over my rounded body in a manner that made me feel decidedly uncomfortable. Perhaps Daniel was hiding somewhere in the sterile newness of the house, perhaps he had run in the opposite direction—down the road toward town. Perhaps . . .

"We're here," Peter spoke suddenly, and I drew to a halt beside him, my eyes staring across the magnificent panorama that even bested the view from my room. The range of mountains was snow-capped and overpowering in the distance, and the few ribbons of clouds in the bright blue sky were a perfect contrast.

"It's lovely," I breathed, entranced. "What's so terrifying about this place?"

Peter snorted. "I should have known you'd feel that way—romantic young lady that you are. Look down."

I did, and my sudden start must have communicated itself to Moon Maiden, for the skittish creature reared back, and it was only with a great deal of strength that I kept the horse under control, preventing both of us from tumbling down that narrow, treacherous cliff.

"It's rather steep, isn't it?" I said after a moment. "I still don't see what there is to frighten people."

"It's called Perry's Ledge," Peter said in a hushed, oddly exhilarated note. "It was from this very spot that Connell's first wife Kathleen jumped—or was pushed."

There was a long silence. "I didn't know he'd been married before," was all I said after a moment.

"Aren't you shocked?" my companion demanded, a nervous twitch marring his pale, handsome face. "You look as if I just told you this was a picnic spot. Can't you feel the aura of death and disaster about the place?"

"Now who's sounding like a romantic young lady?" I demanded in a cheerful voice, doing a magnificent job of hiding the very real distress I had felt upon hearing Peter's macabre news.

"It might interest you further to know that there was a great deal of talk at the time. Talk that Connell threw her down from here in a black rage. And he gets black rages, believe me."

"Why on earth was he supposed to have done that?" I questioned mildly.

"For the same reason husbands have been killing wives since the institution of marriage was invented. He thought that she was unfaithful to him."

"Then why hasn't he murdered Maeve yet? I somehow get the impression that she hasn't been the soul of fidelity."

"Because he never loved Maeve—he never expected anything of her but an heir. An obligation she fulfilled. That's what made Kathleen's death doubly sad . . ." he let it trail, knowing my curiosity would get the better of me.

"Why?"

"The main problem between Kathleen and Connell was her apparent barrenness. Perhaps she wouldn't have died if he'd known she was finally pregnant."

I couldn't keep the expression of sick dismay from my face any longer. "Are you trying to make me believe," I asked coldly after a long pause, "that Connell is a ruthless murderer? A man who killed his wife and unborn child? I thought you two were friends."

"We are. And I'm not trying to convince you of anything. I simply thought you should be warned."

"Why?" The question hung in the chill autumn air.

"Because I care about you, Mary Gallager, even though I scarcely know you. Connell's women haven't been known for their luck. And I wouldn't want anything to happen to you."

As we rode back slowly from that place of death, we talked exclusively of the weather, the view, and the likelihood of snow. By unspoken mutual consent we didn't speak of the murderous history of Demonwood, or the dark suspicions that still hung over the place. But somehow, beneath our light banter, ran the vision of Connell Fitzgerald and his dark, haunted eyes, and I wondered if I had made a very grave mistake in coming here.

"Then you'll come for tea on Thursday?" Peter demanded as he helped me from the mare. "And you can even bring the little monster—my mother, God help her, has a fondness for the brat."

"If you're sure it's all right," I temporized.

"My mother insists on it. Ever since I arrived home last night I praised you—your wit, your beauty, your . . ."

"You, Mr. Riordan, are full of it!" I interrupted indignantly, my cheeks flaming. I had the feeling he was mocking me, and my anger stirred into flame. "Good day to you, sir!" And I stalked from the stable with Robinson's boldly curious eyes on me.

"And good day to you, fair Mary. Dream of me tonight!"

But I didn't dream of Peter Riordan that night. I dreamt dark, horrifying dreams of Connell Fitzgerald throwing my lovely cousin Maeve down that treacherous gore and then turning to me, his dark handsome face desolate as he reached his strong, merciless hands to throw me down after her.

I awoke in a cold sweat, my covers scattered at my feet, the room like ice with the silvery, shivery moon shining in from all the windows. Wrapping the discarded quilts around me, I padded barefoot across the icy floor to poke some life into the dying embers of the fire. A faint warmth emanated from it, and I tossed the few sticks of wood Mrs. Carpenter had graciously allowed me onto the glowing coals. If the weather continued as it had, and indeed it would assuredly get much worse, I would have to move my bed closer to the fire. The small heat put out by the fireplace at its roaring best barely penetrated the cavernous interiors of my bedchamber, and I had no intention of freezing to death in a millionaire's home.

When my fingers had lost some of their numbness I trudged back to my disordered bed. Climbing up into its massive softness, I was about to drift back into a deep sleep when a curious noise brought me back fully into consciousness. It seemed to come from within the very walls, and it sounded quite horribly like . . . like chains clanking.

Now in the daylight I'm as full of common sense as the next person, but alone at night, with the full moon staring down at me and the wind whistling through the haunted forests that surround this cold, empty house, I was perfectly willing to believe in ghosts, witches, and all the hounds of hell. I huddled deeper into the heavy blankets, trying to shut out the hideous noise, and yet listening for it with an awful fascination. Perhaps this is what Daniel heard at night in the room beneath me, this added to his terror of life in general. Quivering with fright, I didn't blame him one bit. All it needed was a few ghastly moans to make the eeriness complete.

As if on cue, a low, hoarse groan issued from directly behind my bed, and I barely contained a shriek. I lay there, waiting for the next sepulchral sound, every muscle tense, every nerve screaming. But no sound came. No more groans, no more clanking chains. Whatever tormented soul haunted Demonwood, it had finally sought its rest. I would have a great deal harder time seeking mine.

When I awoke next morning the room was ablaze with bright winter sunlight, and for a moment I couldn't believe the eerie events of the night before had actually happened. I was an intelligent, modern young woman—surely I knew better than to believe in such things. Of course, if this had been Ireland it would be a different matter. I had grown up with tales of dark and mysterious doings in that dark and mysterious land, where leprechauns and faeries were only to be expected, as were their darker cousins, the banshees. But such creatures belonged in an old land wracked with superstition, not in this shining new country. Or so I argued with myself, so successfully that I almost believed it.

Young Daniel made no mention of any nocturnal occurrences last night, and I remained silent. The child was nervous enough without my adding to his dark fancies. Indeed, I had been prone to nightmares the last few days. Perhaps it had just been another nightmare, a bit more real than the others, no doubt, but a nightmare nonetheless. Daniel and I both needed bracing up, and that, along with ciphering, grammar, geography, spelling, Latin, and French, would be my main goal.

Lessons that day went better than I would have expected. Mrs. Carpenter had assigned us to a large, airy room on the second floor that overlooked the long drive, and by dragging the scarred table near the fire and wearing several layers of clothing, we managed tolerably well. It was beyond my comprehension why anyone would build a house with such lofty, icy rooms in a climate like this. A proper Vermont house would have low ceilings, small windows, and nice rag rugs on the floor. The Aubusson carpets did not fit the environment, although they provided the only spot of soft, subdued color in the dank, garish house.

Daniel was a fast learner, once his interest was caught, and I assumed he must have inherited his quick brain from his father. Certainly Maeve had never shown any aptitude for book learning. My rusty Latin was put to the test quite thoroughly, and I realized I would have to do extra work as well as Daniel if I expected to keep far ahead of him.

After lunch, I had enough sense not to suggest we take another nature walk. I had no desire to repeat yesterday's fiasco, and Daniel needed an hour or so to himself. The time would come when he wished for my company, I hoped, and I could wait patiently enough until then.

I took a brief stroll around the house, my feet scuffling through the thin layer of snow, my hands tucked warmly inside my fur muff. The chilly air was bracing against my skin, giving me a ruddy glow I knew would be very attractive and I laughed at my own vanity. What did it matter how pretty I looked with only a handful of hostile or indifferent servants and an unhappy nine-year-old boy to appreciate it? Even Peter, attractive and attentive as he was, aroused no strong emotions in my breast. It might be his flippant, flirtatious manner, too easy to be believed, or it may have been the memory of a pair of brooding dark blue eyes that kept me from viewing him as a possible suitor. Considering how eligible a party he was, I was being nine times a fool not to make more of an effort in that direction. But I had always been a fool.

The grounds surrounding Demonwood were not much more appealing than the formal house. Granted that it was the worst time of year to see them, with just a thin, icy covering of snow on the ground and the cold brown earth peeking through in patches, granted the leafless trees and ornamental shrubs looked menacing this time of year. It still seemed all too calculated. I think I preferred the dark, brooding, untamed woods with their hint of menace to the lifeless formal display around me.

"Lovely grounds, ain't they, miss?" Robinson appeared out of nowhere, a leer on his handsome face. I think he knew very well my reaction to the stilted, formal gardens.

"Lovely," I agreed unenthusiastically. "Do you do all this work by yourself, Mr. Robinson?"

"By no means!" He appeared affronted. "In the spring and summer we have three men working here, and we could do with a fourth if Carpenter had his way about it. Takes a lot of work to keep gardens like these in order."

"I'm sure it does," I replied encouragingly. Despite his repulsively familiar manner, he at least seemed to have slipped his surly disdain, and I wished I could make further inroads. Everyone around this place was so damned unfriendly, and I had been longing quite desperately for my bevy of brothers and sisters-in-law and their exuberant offspring.

"Not that you'd be interested," he continued slyly. "But I know something you might find fascinating. You strike me as a very curious young lady."

Not knowing how to reply to what I suspected was a veiled insult, I merely watched him, waiting for him to continue.

"Yes, you seem like a very curious one. Though it's not too safe to be curious, miss. As you'll very likely find out before too long." He wiped his nose on his sleeve and stared at me out of his damp, lustful eyes. "Like that boy. Young Daniel. He's already found out more than he ever wanted to know. He's already learned that if you poke around in places where you don't belong you might uncover things best left hidden."

"I'm sure that's true," I said coldly. "However, an inquiring mind is a good thing if used in moderation."

Robinson laughed then, a low, insinuating chuckle, and it was all I could do not to turn and run from his leering presence. "Well, miss, I'll tell you. If you take a horse and follow that path through the woods to your left, you'll find. . ."

"I know exactly what I'll find," I broke in. "I'll find Perry's Ledge where a tragedy occurred a number of years ago. A tragedy that's much better forgotten and not hinted at by everyone."

Robinson did not appear to be affronted by this, merely nodding his head knowingly. "Master Peter must have taken you there. Young Daniel wouldn't, I know that for a fact. But you see, miss, people can't forget about it. Because she can't rest, and neither can her murderer. The memory hangs over this place, and people say sometimes at night you can hear her wailing and moaning."

I could feel the skin prickle along the back of my neck, and tears of sheer panic start in my eyes. "You're lying," I said hoarsely, all my primitive beliefs coming to the surface. "You're just trying to frighten me. Why should this house be haunted by her? Wasn't it built after she died?"

"She died barely a month after it was finished. Her that had designed every board, every room, every window, and never got to live in it for more than a few weeks. Is it a wonder that she haunts the cursed place?"

With great effort I pulled myself together. "Have you been spreading tales like this to Daniel? If you have, it's no wonder the poor boy's frightened half out of his wits. You should be ashamed of yourself, for spreading such a pack of lies!" My voice grew bold and forceful and my temper rose, but the groom wasn't fooled for a minute.

"But you believe me, miss," he stated flatly. "You don't think it's a pack of lies, nor does anyone else. Murder was done here, murder most foul, and someone's gotten away with it for far too long."

"I've heard quite enough, thank you." I was in a towering white-hot rage by this time. "You'll have to find more fertile ground for your lies and slanders—I won't listen to them. Good day to you."

"So that's the way it is," the young man said maddeningly as I turned to leave.

Reluctantly I turned back, the very curiosity he had discovered in me coming to the fore. "What do you mean by that?"

"Nothing, miss. I just wondered why a pretty young lady like yourself would be here minding another woman's children instead of having her own. I should have known there'd be a reason behind it."

"What do you mean?" I repeated.

"Why not a thing, Miss Gallager. Mr. Connell is a very handsome man." And with that he turned and left me, before I could voice one of the half-dozen protests that sprang to my lips. I watched his exaggeratedly broad-shouldered, swaggering figure amble off with impotent rage, my fingers clenched inside the warm muff.

"I don't like him," Daniel spoke from behind me, and I jumped, startled.

"How long have you been standing there, young man?" I demanded crossly. "Don't you know you shouldn't eavesdrop?"

Those dark blue eyes in that pinched cold-looking face stared at me blankly. "I wasn't eavesdropping. Robinson knew I was there the whole time."

"I'm sorry, Daniel, I shouldn't have snapped at you. But that man makes me so mad!" I growled.

His brow cleared. "I'm glad you don't like him either. He likes to frighten me at night. He comes up to my room and tells me stories that make me have awful dreams. And then he laughs at me and calls me a sissy."

"Daniel, he's a mean, nasty man, and you mustn't pay any attention to him. If he bothers you again, tell me, and I'll . . . I'll stop him." How, I couldn't imagine, but Daniel seemed satisfied with my promise. I hoped I wouldn't have to break it.

Chapter Seven

Thursday dawned bright and clear, and a little warmer than usual. My feet when they touched the bare floor beside my mammoth bed didn't scream in protest, and the early morning sunlight had warmed the cavernous room to a comparatively tropic extent.

Against my will I was looking forward to our outing this afternoon. I hadn't seen or heard from Peter in three days and despite my summary dismissal of him as possible husband material I had missed him, missed his warm, flattering brown eyes and his soft, lying tongue. There was something sneakingly, surreptitiously threatening about Demonwood, with its servants ranging from dimwitted (like Molly whom I scarcely saw and the harmless and surly Mr. Carpenter) to malevolent, like Adelaide Carpenter and the surly Robinson, the latter perhaps the most frightening of the lot. I wondered how Connell could have hired such a motley crew, and decided we would have to find more ways of escape, Daniel and I, if he was ever to turn into a normal little boy. My questions about neighboring children had drawn blank stares from Molly, the maid of all work and cold denials from the disapproving Mrs. Carpenter. Perhaps Peter's mother would be more forthcoming.

I dressed with extra care after lunch, choosing my sister-in-law Barbara's pink-striped suit with the ruffled overskirt as just the right sort of teatime wear. My thick curling black hair I dressed with severity—by the time we arrived at Stonewalls it would be in its usual disarray. There seemed no way I could control the riotously waving locks, and I had long ago given up trying. I only hoped I wouldn't look too blowsy for the older woman. My pale, fine-boned face with its saucy green eyes and overgenerous mouth was flushed with excitement, and I took the steps down to the main floor two at a time.

The difference between Demonwood and Stonewalls was the difference between night and day, between happiness and despair, between guilt and security. Or so it seemed to me that day. It was a smaller house in comparison to the Fitzgerald grandeur, but with an easygoing elegance that seemed even more costly than the ostentatious wealth of our house. We were met at the front door by Peter, dressed in a coat of Irish tweed that my brothers would have given an arm for, and his welcoming smile was all I could have asked for. He even included Daniel in the warmth of his greeting, but my silent charge was unmoved. Perhaps he knew full well Peter's distaste for him, and returned the feeling in full. I really couldn't tell.

"Oh, lovely lady, I have counted the days until you came," Peter said, bringing my rough, hard-working hand to his lips and kissing it with as much elegance as if it had been the hand of a countess. "And you grow more dazzling everyday—surely Vermont air must agree with you. I can't wait to have my mother meet you."

"I don't believe a word you say, Peter Riordan. The words come a little too easily," I said suspiciously, tossing my head back, not unmoved by the pressure of his warm, firm lips.

He laughed merrily. "You distrust my gift of gab, as they call it? No, I've always had a way with words, but you, dear lady, raise me to new and glorious heights."

"Why are you talking so funny?" Daniel inquired coldly.

Peter cast a look of acute dislike toward the boy. "I'm flirting, young Daniel. But with more seriousness than I've ever had in my long, misspent life."

"You talk the same way to my mother," he observed with a deliberate lack of tact. "Were you flirting with her?"

Peter's face turned a mottled red, and the look he bent at my charge was almost murderous. Before he could say any of the harsh things that were springing to his lips I interrupted smoothly. "Isn't this a charming house! So much cozier and nicer than Demonwood, I think. Has your family always lived here?"

Both gentlemen cast me a look of melting gratitude, and Daniel moved from the shelter of my skirt now that the crisis was temporarily past.

"Since the middle of the century," Peter replied proudly, leading us down the warm, paneled hallway to the back of the house. "My mother would love to tell you the history of the place—just give her half a chance." He opened the door into a cozy little drawing room. "Mother, they're here."

As we moved ahead of him into the room I heard Daniel give a little squeal of pain, and I suspected that Peter had succumbed to temptation and given the child a good pinch. Not that Daniel hadn't deserved it, but I wondered why Peter should dislike him so. And vice versa. Unless it were the embarrassing truth that Daniel had blurted out, either consciously or unconsciously. Peter Riordan was obviously the type to flirt with almost any woman, be she young or old, ugly or attractive, married or single. And I didn't for one moment believe he was serious about any one of them, including my humble self.

"My dear, I'm so glad to meet you at last," a soft voice murmured from the depths of a chintz-covered sofa. "Peter's told me so much about you."

She was exactly as I had imagined her. Frail, old in that lovely way a few select women can manage to grow old, her white hair piled high upon a still aristocratic head, her face with just a faint tracing of crepey wrinkles. But the blue eyes were just as sparkling and lively as they must have been in her youth, and the faint flush on her cheeks suggested a youthful confusion and shyness. In her prime she must have been the equal of my cousin Maeve and more.

"Come sit down beside me, Miss Gallager, and tell me all about yourself." She patted the sofa beside her frail, delicate form and gingerly I did as I was bid. I am a fair bit above average height and definitely on the strapping side, and Mrs. Riordan's diminutive stature made me feel like a hulking farm girl fresh from County Cork.

"Tell me," she continued, "how do you like Demonwood?"

"It's . . . it's very grand, isn't it?" I said with what I hoped was noncommittal praise.

Her faded blue eyes met mine, not for one moment fooled by my attempt at tact. "It's a monstrosity, you mean. We all think so. Everyone, that is, except Maeve and her familiar."

"Her familiar?" I echoed, bewildered.

"The pleasant Mrs. Carpenter," the old lady clarified. "That woman makes my skin crawl."

"Which one?"

"Both of them," she replied flatly. "I warned Connell Fitzgerald when he married that woman that no good would come of it. I suppose I shouldn't say such a thing—after all, she is your cousin." She leaned over and poured a cup of weak tea into a fine bone china cup. "But one of the privileges of old age is speaking one's mind, and I've been indulging in it frequently of late, haven't I, Peter?"

"You have indeed, Mother," said her son fondly. "I've learned better than to try and shut you up when you've got an opinion to express. I hope you're not shocked, Mary?"

"Not in the slightest," I replied firmly. "I . . ." I was about to confess my own dislike of my wayward cousin, when I belatedly became aware of Daniel's solemn little face watching us as he nibbled on a tea cake, his protruding ears moving with each bite. "I scarcely know her," I amended hastily. "This is a lovely house . . . have you lived here long?"

She cast me a speaking glance from those wise blue eyes, as if to say she was not fooled by my change of subject. But she launched into the tale of the Riordan's tenure in northern Vermont willingly enough, how they had traveled up here with their family friends the Fitzgeralds in the middle part of the century and bought country retreats that bordered on each other. As the years passed the Riordans had lost a bit of their money and sold their land, while Connell's father and then Connell himself had expanded the Fitzgerald holdings of rich timberland. The controversial subject of Maeve Gallager Fitzgerald was temporarily forgotten.

An agreeable hour passed, and the shadows began to lengthen outside the small-paned windows. With great reluctance I cast about in my mind for proper words to signal our departure, when I saw Mrs. Riordan give her son a meaningful nod.

"Well, Daniel, me lad," Peter said with false heartiness, "why don't you come with me and I'll show you our brand new foal? Misty had a baby just a few days ago."

"I don't like horses," he replied mutinously, which we all knew was a lie.

"And Mrs. Barton would love to see you. She's been saving some special treats out in the kitchen just for you to take home with you," coaxed Peter with unconvincing warmth.

"I'm not hungry."

"Daniel, dear," the old lady broke in with her soft, plaintive voice, "would you be an angel and go with Peter? I want to talk with Miss Gallager for a bit . . . about personal matters."

The poor boy was torn between his dislike of Peter and his obvious adoration of the man's mother. A variety of emotions played across his pale face, but affection for the old woman won out. "All right," he replied grudgingly. "But I'm doing this for you, not him."

"Daniel!" I said in a warning voice.

"Excuse me, if I was rude," he muttered, then glared up at his companion. "Let's go," he added in a tone of deep resignation.

"It's a great shame those two dislike each other so much," she sighed as the door closed behind them.

"Yes, indeed," I agreed. "I wonder why?"

Those sharp blue eyes met mine with uncomfortable acuity. "I think you might have a good idea, my dear. Daniel hates Maeve and anyone connected with her. He's quite naughty as far as my poor wayward Peter's concerned, and I'm afraid my son reacts with infantile spite. But it wasn't about Daniel that I wanted to talk with you, Miss Gallager. We have something a little more private to discuss. Which is why I asked Peter to take care of the boy for a while—so that we might

71

talk, woman-to-woman, without interruption from those clumsy men."

"I'm flattered that you wanted to be talking to me," I replied frankly, "but I can't think what about."

"Can't you? Well, I'll come straight to the point. My son is very attracted to you."

"But we scarcely met!"

"Don't you think there's such a thing as love at first sight? Ah, I can see by your blush that you do. I wonder if I dare to hope that blush was for Peter?" There was just the most delicate trace of inquiry in her soft voice. Numbly I shook my head. "No? Well, that's a pity, but I don't despair. I will be frank with you, Mary. I may call you Mary, mayn't I?"

"Of course," I murmured, embarrassed by the situation, by the old lady's charming inquisitiveness, by life in general.

"Well, as I said, I will be frank. My son has involved himself most unfortunately with a . . . a married woman. This sordid affair has been continuing on and off for over a year now. He's tried to break off with the creature, but the sad truth of the matter is that he's simply bewitched by her. And now, suddenly, for the first time in ages he's shown interest in another woman. You, my dear."

"That's . . . that's very flattering," I fumbled.

"It's more than flattering, it's a miracle!" she breathed. "But he needs encouragement—he mustn't fall back in that harlot's clutches!"

Things were moving too fast for me. "I'm sure he'll grow out of it, Mrs. Riordan," I said soothingly. "He must have been getting over it already when he came up here—otherwise, why would he choose to bury himself in northern Vermont, away from his . . . his mistress."

"You don't really understand yet, do you? For the past year and a half Peter has been carrying on an affair with his best friend's wife!"

"Maeve?" Although I'd somehow half-expected it, the words still came as a shock to me. How any woman

72

could prefer Peter's bland and superficial charm to the fire and ice of Connell Fitzgerald's magnetic presence eluded me completely.

"Maeve Gallager Fitzgerald," she verified with sour satisfaction. "I've been hoping and praying that she would let him go before Connell found out—that she'd tire of him before we had another . . . another tragedy."

An ominous chill settled over my body. "What do you mean by that?" I had to ask.

Those wise blue eyes, no longer as kind as they had first seemed, met mine. "One wife of Connell's has met with a cruel, violent end at the hands of a murderer. They say once you've killed, the second one is far easier."

"No," I breathed in horror. The very idea repelled me. For obvious reasons—reasons I did not care to examine too closely, even by myself, the idea of Connell as a cold-blooded murderer was completely unacceptable to me.

"We have to prevent such a thing from happening again," Mrs. Riordan was saying, oblivious to the torments I was going through. "And you're the only one who can help."

"I . . . I can't marry your son to save him from another woman!" I cried desperately.

"I'm not expecting you to. I just want you to encourage him a bit. Flatter him, accept his attentions. After a while he should appreciate the difference between a sweet young thing like yourself and the jaded tastes of that . . . that courtesan. And if, after a few months, you find that you return Peter's affection, then, so much the better. From the moment you walked into the room I decided I wanted you for my daughter-in-law, despite your background." She dismissed my working-class Irish heritage with a small shrug.

All my rebellious nature rose up at this cavalier disposition of my future. Beneath Mrs. Riordan's soft and gentle appearance obviously lurked a will of iron. "And if I don't come to care for him? Not in that way?" I argued.

"Well, then, his heart might be broken, just a bit," she shrugged her shoulders in a delicate French gesture. "But that, to my mind, is better than being disgraced. Or murdered." Her voice was cold and flat, and I wished I could shut out that soft, nagging tone with its nasal, well-bred accent, so far removed from Con's softly lilting voice, shut out the horrid ideas that were seeping into my mind against my will. "Mary, will you help me?"

"I . . . I don't know. I can't promise."

She watched me measuringly for a moment, then nodded, satisfied. "I don't need your promise, Mary Gallager. You've a good, generous heart. You'll see your duty, and you'll do it. You wouldn't condemn my son to the bitter and sordid life he's been leading of late."

"All finished gossiping, Mother?" Peter poked his handsome golden head through the door. "Young Daniel's out in the carriage already—he's had enough of my company for the day."

"We're through, darling," his mother beamed, untouched by her knowledge of his weaknesses. "You may escort Mary back to Demonwood if you wish. We'll hold supper for you."

"Thank you for a lovely tea." I rose and took her hand. She grasped mine firmly, as if shaking on a bargain, and it was all I could do not to snatch my hand back.

"Come again, Mary. Come soon, and come often." She pulled me down with surprising force and pressed her dried wrinkled lips against my cheek.

"I've never seen Mother so taken with anyone," Peter breathed in my ear as he bundled me into the carriage. "What magic did you use to charm her?"

"Nothing," I replied glumly.

"Is something wrong? You were looking rather

shaken when I came to fetch you. I hope she didn't disturb you in any way?"

I pulled myself together. "No, not at all. Your mother's a lovely woman, Peter. I'm so glad you took me to meet her." This was not entirely truthful but I was nothing if not tactful.

He leaned back against the velvet cushions, a smug expression on his boyish face. "I thought you'd like her. She's a marvel, isn't she?"

"She is that," I agreed wryly, thinking back to the promise she had all but wrung from me. A promise I had refused to give, but was already, instinctively fulfilling. But how could any woman resist such a handsome cavalier? Only a foolish girl half in love with a shadow.

"Do you have to come home with us?" Daniel demanded in a petulant voice from his seat in the corner of the carriage.

"Daniel, I won't have you being rude," I warned him in a deceptively mild tone of voice.

"Sorry," he muttered gracelessly, his luminous blue eyes flashing his dislike. "But I still don't see why he has to come home with us. We see enough of him when my parents are home."

"Daniel, Mr. Riordan is a friend of your father's. And a friend of mine, for that matter," I said sternly.

"Yes, ma'am."

"Little monster," Peter muttered tactfully. "Will you go riding with me tomorrow? Without your charming chaperone?"

"My chaperone, as you call him, happens to be the reason I'm here."

"But you don't have to stay with him twenty-four hours a day, do you? What about three-thirty?"

"Not tomorrow. We've taken too much time off from our studies already." Score one for me against the autocratic old lady.

"Then what about Saturday? Surely you aren't expected to work on the weekends too? Connell wouldn't be such a slave driver."

"Perhaps. We'll have to see how much we accomplish tomorrow." The moment the words were out of my mouth I realized what a mistake they had been. From the gleam in Daniel's eyes I knew that if he had anything to say about it we wouldn't accomplish a thing until Peter Riordan was out of reach. "On second thought," I said abruptly, and the boy's face fell, "I believe I will ride with you on Saturday. The outing should do me good."

"Bless you, lovely lady. I knew you couldn't be so cruel to a poor, heartsick young man," Peter declaimed. "You won't regret your generosity."

"I will if you don't stop all these blandishments," I said sternly. "You've a bit too much of the Irish in you at times, my boy. And Daniel will accompany us. You two should learn to get along."

Chapter Eight

I sat curled up on top of my bed that night, my room unusually warm. There was a deceptive softening in the air outside, and for once my cavernous quarters no longer resembled an ice house. I hunched cross-legged over my writing tablet, struggling with a letter to my family in Cambridge. Not that I usually had trouble with words. Both on paper and vocally I had never been reticent, nor terribly selective, for that matter. If I gave Seamus and Patrick and the others even an inkling of the undercurrents that beset this strange household I would be out of here by the scruff of my neck in the time it took for the letter to be delivered and read. And I didn't want to leave Demonwood, haunted and unappealing as it was.

For one thing, I had grown fond of young Daniel. He was so alone, so shut away from everyone and everything. I wanted to bring him out in the open, to set his child's heart free. But that would take time and care and a firm hand. Lillian had failed by giving in to his fears and demands. I would help him face his terrors, both of the night and the day, and present him to his . . . to his parents a whole, normal young boy.

Ah, curse you, Mary Margaret Gallager, you were going to say "present him to his father," I admonished myself sternly. It's his father's eyes you want to see filled with gratitude—you don't give a tinker's damn what Maeve thinks of you. She's never liked you before and it's doubtful she'll start now. It's Connell's admiration you want, you wicked, sinful girl.

Wearily I thought back to Father McShane's warnings. I had always been willful, too eager to look before I leapt, too foolhardy to really consider all sides of the situation before making a decision. And it usually was the wrong one. Yet I never learned. I knew at the time I shouldn't have come to this house. But I had closed my ears to my conscience, shut my mind to the warnings of my soul and come here.

I stretched out across the bed and shrugged. What's done is done, I told myself sternly. Regrets won't do you a bit of good, me girl. Deliciously I wiggled my toes. If I had my choice of one thing in this world, one outrageous thing that I could change, it would be that I could go barefoot whenever I pleased.

I hated shoes, always had, always would. They made me feel I was being smothered. I stared down at my toes admiringly, and wiggled them again. Such a delicious, free feeling. Some day I would run through grass barefoot, and feel the tiny strands tickle my feet. After a lifetime of city living such an event had never come close to fruition, but if I stayed on at Demonwood I would have more than enough chances. Or if I stayed at Stonewalls.

The thought had crossed my mind once or twice, I

must admit. Michael Flynn was charming and dull and no doubt very worthy, and I would be near my family. Whether or not that was a good thing would have to be proven. Peter Riordan was rich and handsome and very entertaining—I could do far worse than marry him. I had his mother's blessing before I had known him a week. Perhaps it was fated. I wiggled my toes again.

Pauline had given me a few clinical details about marital duties. The mechanics of it I understood all too well, and the idea seemed faintly distasteful to me. The thought of Peter's strong, healthy body possessing mine filled me with a feeling akin to dismay.

The room was growing steadily colder, and, tiring of my ruminations and struggles with my missive, I tossed the paper to one side, blew out the lamp, and crawled beneath the warm, heavy covers of my bed.

Now, of course, my thoughts continued, quite against my will, if it was Connell Fitzgerald's body covering mine . . .

It was almost with relief that I was distracted from that wholly disturbing thought by the first groan. And I was no longer warm and toasty in the great big bed —my skin had turned to ice.

But worse was to come. The chains began clanking again, a musical accompaniment to the moans and groans of the poor creature in torment. And then a new sound pierced my consciousness. A horrid, muffled sound. Like someone dragging something across the bare floor. Something like a body.

Being a good girl I immediately took refuge in prayer. I had finished three hail marys and two Lord's prayers (chanted in a loud, impassioned monotone) when the noise finally ceased. The clanking, shuffling creature moved away into the night, leaving its poor victim scared witless, too frightened to even relight the lamp beside her bed as a safeguard against further night terrors.

* * *

"You look tired, Mary," Daniel observed over breakfast. We were in the austere formal dining room as usual, seated half a mile away from each other across the shining oak table with the too-ornate legs. Snow was falling lightly outside the windows, covering the gardens with a flattering blanket of white.

"I didn't sleep well," I replied thoughtlessly. Immediately he pounced.

"Did something keep you awake last night?" he demanded. "Did you hear anything, anything out of the ordinary?"

"Why do you ask?"

His deep blue eyes grew large and solemn. "It's haunted up there. Robinson says so. You can hear the ghost of Kathleen Fitzgerald wandering around, weeping."

"Nonsense," I said stoutly, conveniently forgetting my state of abysmal panic the night before. "There's no such thing as ghosts." I took a gulp of hot, steaming coffee sweetened with maple syrup. "The little folk, maybe, but no ghosts."

"You'll learn," the child said darkly, barely nibbling at the delicious sweet roll. Mrs. Carpenter, despite her sour temperament, was an inspired cook when she cared to be.

The door to the kitchen swung open just then, and Mrs. Carpenter herself, every square inch of her form radiating contempt and disapproval for us lowly creatures, edged her way into the room on her tiny, mincing feet. She cast her usual scathing glance at poor Daniel, and what little appetite he had vanished altogether. He quickly excused himself and slipped from the table, leaving me to face the woman alone.

"I've heard from Mrs. Fitzgerald," she announced in her prim little voice. "It appears I was mistaken in putting you in the old studio. I hadn't realized you were a connection of the mistress." Her tone said "poor relation" in suitable disparaging accents. "She insists you have one of the better bedrooms on the third floor."

Immediately all my suspicions were aroused, and I met her cold gray eyes with a limpid gaze. "I wouldn't think of moving, Mrs. Carpenter! I love my room—so far above everything and with such a heavenly view. I couldn't put you to the bother of moving me after all this time. The attic will be just fine for the likes of me."

"Mrs. Fitzgerald wishes you to move downstairs."

I could be equally stubborn. "But I don't wish to move," I replied sweetly. "Don't worry yourself about such a little matter, Mrs. Carpenter. When Cousin Maeve returns we can discuss it. I'm sure she'll understand my feelings."

The housekeeper opened her mouth to protest, then shut it again with a tiny snap. "As you wish, miss," she replied after a moment, and left the room abruptly. Leaving me to sit there and wonder what in the world had prompted me to hold onto my haunted room.

I had more cause to wonder that night, when I finally retired to my aerie. Moving up the dark, shadowed stairs, my candle barely making a dent in the inky blackness, I cursed myself for being nine times a fool. Finally I fought the temptation to stare back over my shoulder into the deserted (I hoped) stairwells. With fumbling fingers I locked the door behind me, with fumbling fingers lit the lamp beside my bed. If the ghost of Kathleen Fitzgerald wanted to harm anyone she would go after her usurper at the very least, or more likely her murderer. She'd have no cause to harm a poor Irish lass who was only trying to earn her living.

I undressed quickly in the chill room, stopping long enough to toss a few logs on the fire before climbing into bed. This time I wasn't such a fool as to extinguish the lamp. I lay back in the soft bed, waiting for my body warmth to penetrate the covers, and stared at the eerie shadows overhead.

I must have drifted off to sleep, for the next thing

I knew the fire was almost out and the wick had burnt down low in my bedside lamp. And Kathleen Fitzgerald moaned and clanked and shuddered behind the walls.

If there is one thing I hate, it is to be awakened from a sound sleep. My rage upon such occasions had cowed even my brothers. Without thinking I reached out for the nearest thing at hand, which happened to be a copy of *Northanger Abbey,* and sent it hurtling against the wall. At the same time I yelled fiercely, "Curse you, Kathleen, shut up!"

There was a stunned silence, and suddenly I was wide awake and rather horrified by my actions. But no avenging spirit flew through the wall to smother me in my bed or mesmerize me into walking out the windows. After a full minute or two I heard a tentative clank from behind my bed, and a quiet groan issued forth. I reached out and pounded firmly on the paneling with my fist, quite pleased with my daring. "Go away, Kathleen," I said sternly. "I'm trying to sleep." And the shade of Kathleen, whoever or whatever it was, shuffled off into the woodwork, leaving me to enjoy the first good night's sleep I'd had since she'd decided to haunt me.

November blew into December, and the snow deepened around the unfriendly mansion, piled into drifts alongside the road and gradually filled up the woods around Demonwood. And as the days grew shorter and colder, my life settled into a comfortable pattern. Lessons with Daniel in the morning, rides with Peter in the afternoon while my charge either studied or played outside. And of course, once a week we would all drive over to Stonewalls for tea and the gentle conversation of Peter's mother.

She never alluded to our conversation of my first visit, and she never sought another tête-à-tête. Instead she smiled benignly upon me, content that I was fulfilling her request. I think it never occurred to her that I might fail to adore her charming, weak-willed son.

That I might have someone else, someone forbidden, in mind.

The Riordans were the only people we saw outside of the staff at Demonwood. Oh, to be sure we went to Mass every Sunday, Daniel and I, with a grudging Carpenter to drive us. But we weren't encouraged to mingle with the other worshipers. Indeed, I doubt if it would have done much good—most of them spoke only French. Even Father LeJeune's command of English was limited. The one time I tried to make confession he got hopelessly lost between my sins of the body and my sins of the mind, so that I ended up doing penance for having committed adultery when all I'd done was . . . was imagine. But I suppose one could never be too penitent, and my guilt was so great that I dutifully said all the rosaries he requested, and a few more for good measure.

The lack of social intercourse was perhaps the only drawback in my new rural life. I missed having females of my age and background around to gossip and dream with. I missed having males to berate and tease, like my brothers. But Daniel was beginning to open up to me, it seemed, and I couldn't have found a more charming and attentive beau than Peter. But all the time I had the feeling I was waiting, waiting . . .

It was going to be a lonely Christmas without the loud, buoyant crowd of Gallagers to celebrate the season. I had planned the time as best I could—Peter would spend Christmas Eve with us (much to Daniel's dismay) and we in turn would spend the next day with the Riordans and their assorted relations. It would be pleasant, but it wouldn't be the same as family, as I think Daniel knew. He never mentioned his parents or his beloved Aunt Lillian, but I was sure he missed them. I had no idea whether this would be his first Christmas without them, and I was tactful enough not to inquire. But I was determined not to show my loneliness—this had to be a happy season for him.

For the most part gifts were no problem. I had put the long evening hours to good use, and made a shirt for each of my brothers and crocheted new shawls for my five sisters-in-law. Three of them were pregnant and the other two likely to be soon, so I decided against anything close fitting. Another shawl would do for Mrs. Riordan, and Peter would have to settle for embroidered handkerchiefs. I had no intention of encouraging him with anything more personal.

Daniel was my hardest subject, and it took me days until I hit upon the perfect present. I sent Peter into Lyman's Gore to purchase a small set of snowshoes—no longer would he have an excuse not to go out in the rapidly deepening snow. I tempered the present with a package of sweets I knew were his special delight, and began to look forward to Christmas with a little more equanimity and a little less trepidation.

"We still have a bet, you know," I reminded Peter as we made our way through the silent, drifting snow up toward Perry's Ledge. Despite its gloomy history we had made it one of our regular destinations, preferring it for its seclusion and rather frightening beauty. The path through the woods was oddly free from drifts. And I deliberately shut my mind to the thought of poor Kathleen with her newly pregnant body tumbling down that cliff.

"What bet?" he demanded, flashing his winsome smile. "I don't remember making any bet with you."

"The first day we met," I prodded him. "On the train. You bet me that Maeve and Connell would return home by Christmas."

"Oh, *that* bet! But I believe I said that Connell would return home, not necessarily Connell and Maeve. If I know Con he'll ditch that parcel of women as soon as he can." He smirked at me. "And I remember your forfeit. You should have reminded me sooner and I would have done something about it."

"What would you have done?"

"Written Connell, begging him to return by Christmas," he replied shamelessly. "I couldn't imagine a better present from you than a kiss, even at the price of having my worst rival present."

"And I can't imagine a better present from you than a trip back to Cambridge with Daniel," said I blithely.

"I don't remember Daniel being part of the bargain."

"I didn't know Daniel at the time. All you have to do is persuade Maeve . . . and Mr. Fitzgerald to let me go. I'll take care of the rest."

"I'm sure you will. Have you heard from any of the travelers? They still might be planning to return for Christmas."

Smiling, I shook my head. "They don't plan to return till April at the earliest. I received a long, newsy letter from Lillian yesterday."

"Ah, yes, dear Lillian. And how is she surviving without her precious child?"

"She's fine." I ignored the sarcasm in his voice as I kneed Moon Maiden onward. "She loves Florence and might very well stay on when Connell and Maeve leave for Paris."

"I find that hard to believe," he observed cynically. "Since she was fourteen years old and their mother died, Lillian has clung like a leech to Connell and then to Daniel. Con had the good sense to separate her from the boy before too much harm could be done, but I don't expect she'd willingly leave *his* side. For all her soft bland exterior Lillian has all the determination of an Irishwoman when there's something she wants."

"She says she has several very interesting beaux, including one rather dashing British colonel," I defended her. "Besides, what has she ever done to make you dislike her so?"

His face took on a grim, bleak look before he ducked it against a sudden gust of wind. "Let's just say she . . . interfered with my plans once too often. We've never been close; not since she caught me skipping lessons one day with Father LeJeune and tattled to my father. I've never forgotten the hiding I got that day, and I've never forgotten who I had to thank for it. Mealy-mouthed bitch."

I cleared my throat ominously. "I happen to like Lillian. And she happens to like me. So I'd prefer it if you wouldn't malign her to my face."

There was genuine surprise in his warm brown eyes. "*She* liked you? I must say I'm amazed. She usually goes after Con's women with claws unsheathed. Kathleen had a hell of a time with her. Fortunately poor Maeve is able to hold her own."

"I am not Con's woman!" I repeated with great resignation. "I wish I could convince you of that."

"Well, darling Mary," he smiled, "if you're not he's an even bigger fool than I thought him."

I leaned down and patted Moon Maiden's silky, smooth neck, partly to hide the flood of color that washed over my face. "Why do you think him a fool?" I found myself asking.

Peter sighed. "Because after Kathleen died he decided that all women were whores, and then he married poor little Maeve and proceeded to make her just what he expected her to be."

I had known Maeve and her reputation far longer than my companion had, but tactfully I refrained from mentioning it. "So you're saying that Maeve is a whore?" I asked limpidly.

"Damn it, no!" He whirled around, startling his horse. "She was fool enough to fall in love with Connell, and he's turned her into a cold, broken-hearted woman."

There's something touching about a man in love, and I kept my wicked tongue still. Even though I felt a twinge of annoyance that all that devotion wasn't directed at me, I realized I was being a dog in the manger. I didn't want Peter Riordan's hand and heart —at least I didn't think I did.

"Let's go back," I said gently, breaking into his obviously unhappy thoughts. For once I felt years older than my companion, even though I was at least ten years his junior. I put my hand on his tightly clenched fist, and he grasped it like a drowning man.

"Sometime, Mary," he said hoarsely, "sometime I'll have to tell you things that will make you hate me. Things that will make you turn away in disgust . . ."

"Hush, now, darlin'," I soothed him. "You don't have to be telling me a thing. We're friends. Friends accept each other with their faults and their virtues, and there's no need for confessions and explanations."

"But I want to tell you!" he insisted. "I need to make you understand . . ."

"Well, then, to be sure," I agreed. "Anything you want to tell me, anytime, I'll be glad to hear. But let's come away now—it's a cold, morbid place here. I can't think why we ride here so often." I stared down the ravine and shivered.

"You're right," he agreed with more life. "Let's get away from here and never come back." And he started off through the dark, threatening woods at a fast trot, leaving me to struggle behind him with mingled concern and irritation.

Chapter Nine

It snowed and snowed the entire week before Christmas, and Daniel and I were housebound and wild with anticipation and frustration. Even my charge greeted the advent of Peter's presence on Christmas Eve with enthusiasm, and we set forth for Mass in surprisingly high spirits. The sun had finally appeared that morning, leaving a world covered with three feet of freshly fallen snow. The half moon was shining brightly down from the sky, lending a silvery glint to the fields and woods as we sped along to the tiny church, and for the first time in many months, since my parents had died and I had first laid eyes on Connell Fitzgerald, I felt at peace with the world.

The church was jammed with people, and Peter greeted Father LeJeune like the old friend he was, bearing with good humor his remarks on Peter's lack of piety and fidelity to the mother church.

"But just think, Father, of all these sins I'll be busy atoning for. Isn't penitence a delight in the Lord's eye? Think of all the delight I'm bringing Him, then."

"You're a blasphemous young man," Father LeJeune admonished him cheerfully. "Come and see us more often. You never can tell, you might even enjoy it."

Peter smiled, but the smile was a little stiff. "I'll come back, Father. When I feel I've the right to come back."

The rotund little cleric immediately caught the seriousness of Peter's tone, and answered with equal solemnity. "You've always the right. Maybe now more than ever, my son."

But on the ride back through the deep, clean snow he seemed to throw off his pensive mood, and the Christmas carols he led with his melodious tenor were the buoyant, joyful ones, full of peace and goodwill. And Daniel and I, soprano and alto respectively, joined in with fervor and some not altogether unsuccessful attempts at harmony, so that we arrived back at Demonwood an hour later winded and hoarse and laughing.

But even the warmth of the holiday season failed to lighten the cold dark of the house. The servants had been given the night off, of course, but awaiting us was a cold collation of sliced turkey, ham, and beef, cheeses, fruits, breads, and desserts—enough for an army. But by that time the three of us were so hungry we felt we could easily devour the entire spread, and we set to with a will.

Carpenter had cut us a small pine tree and set it up in the book-lined library, the only room lacking the oppressive elegance that permeated the house. A warm, crackling fire was blazing merrily in the hearth, and while Daniel and I began the pleasant chore of trimming the tree with our homemade ornaments and the elegant crystal decorations that Maeve had sent, Peter busied himself with making a hot rum punch.

The tree-trimming was a lengthy and argumentative process—the placing of each piece involved much discussion and experimentation. When the tree was finally completed to our satisfaction and the myriad of tiny candles lit, we curled up in front of the fire and proceeded to distribute our small tokens to each other. To my surprise Daniel had even managed an offering for his old enemy. We all made much of each other's choices, and the feeling as the three of us gathered around the fire in the warm, cozy room was peaceful and friendly and relaxed.

"I guess I lost my bet," Peter remarked lazily as he admired my handkerchiefs. "Who would have thought Connell would be such a fool?"

"Hush," I hissed sternly, gesturing to Daniel's recumbent form.

"The boy's been asleep for the last half hour," he answered. "I may not care for the lad but I'm not totally devoid of tact." He took a deep drink from his hot punch, and a potent concoction it was. "But still, I must say it surprises me that Connell hasn't found some excuse to return to Vermont. He never could stand much of Maeve at one time."

"Peter," I said with the beginnings of anger in my voice, "I wish you wouldn't be wrecking Christmas with your nasty insinuations. I've only met Mr. Fitzgerald three times in my life, and the man made it very apparent that he didn't even like me." Except for that kiss, my treacherous mind remembered, and could feel my cheeks burning in the glow of the fire.

"Did he now?" Peter sat up straighter, looking much impressed. "Then this is more serious than I thought. Connell usually charms all women with complete impartiality. If he didn't charm you there must be even more behind it all than I thought."

"Damn it!" I cried, losing my temper. "Why do you insist that the man has any interest in me? I'm not so irresistible, you know."

"That's where you're wrong, darlin' Mary. I find you completely irresistible, with your black hair streaming down your lovely white shoulders and those witch's eyes. And I know Con well enough to be sure he would agree." He leaned back and sighed. "It's just as well that he's not coming back early. When it came to both of us wanting the same woman I never stood a chance. Until now, maybe."

A particularly nasty thought entered my mind, and once there, I couldn't dislodge it. "You aren't," I asked with ominous stillness, "by any chance courting me to get even with Connell, are you?"

He looked profoundly shocked, and I regretted my evil suspicions. "If you think that, my girl, then you haven't looked in a mirror recently. You're the purest, loveliest thing that's set foot in this house for many a month . . ."

"I have no doubts I'm the purest," I replied wryly, smoothing my green velvet skirts around me. "But the loveliest I'll take leave to doubt. Maeve is my cousin, you know. I've seen her all my life."

"But you're more beautiful," Peter insisted, presumably having been blinded by his lethal punch and the sweetness of the night. "You've a softer look to you, a warmer, gentler expression . . ." He rose on his knees and leaned toward me, a determined expression on his face. "Oh, Mary . . ."

"I hope I'm not interrupting anything," a light, high voice lilted from the doorway. We both jumped, startled out of our firelit reverie, to see my cousin Maeve herself standing in the door, a breathtaking vision of loveliness in pale blue velvet trimmed with ermine, her pretty face smiling with what seemed to be innocent pleasure. I knew that look well. She'd had the exact same expression on her face when last I'd seen her, and I had the uncanny feeling we'd called her up like an evil faerie at the christening feast. At that time she'd been watching the hired boy get the tanning of his life from her slightly drunken father, and all for a misdemeanor she herself had committed, and then blandished the poor simpleton into taking the blame for. An unpleasant chill ran down my spine at the sight of that lovely, smiling face.

And then her husband appeared behind her, a head taller and much broader, his face and expression in the shadows. "I won," Peter whispered in a voice filled with both triumph and despair, and leaned over in front of them and kissed me full on the lips.

There was nothing I could do, short of struggling, and I was determined not to present such an undignified picture. The situation couldn't have been more compromising, and I cursed a fate that always presented me to Connell Fitzgerald in another man's arms. Torn between tears and laughter, I wished more than anything I was a thousand miles away from this god-forsaken house with those haughty, handsome people staring down at me.

When Peter finally released me I rose from my seat on the floor with great dignity, brushed off my skirts, and advanced to greet my cousin.

She spoke first, those lovely lavender-blue eyes traveling up and down my ample figure with just the right amount of amusement and disdain. "Well, my cousin Mary. How charming it is that you could come and help us with poor little Daniel. I declare it's been years since I last saw you. You were twelve and a dreadfully dirty, unattractive little tomboy—so uncivilized. I must have been fourteen at the time." She had been twenty, but if she wished to take six years off her age I had no objections. I was too caught up in the cheerful malevolence that was emanating from her affable, beautifully smiling face. In previous years we had always been on polite, if distant terms. The waves of angry emotion billowing forth were nothing short of frightening.

"It's good to see you, Maeve," I murmured politely after a long moment. "We . . . we hadn't been expecting you."

"Apparently not," she noted with a chill smile. She turned back and addressed her companion carelessly over one delicate shoulder. "Darling, didn't you send word that we were due home for Christmas? My poor little cousin has been caught in the most awkward situation. One might almost say compromising. Trust you, Peter, darling. You never could keep your hands off the ladies." She moved into the room, her bell-like skirts swaying gracefully as she walked. Those lovely eyes took in the sleeping form of her only son, and her pretty nose wrinkled in distaste. "Shouldn't Daniel be in bed at this hour?" she questioned plaintively of the room in general. "I know I'm not the world's best mother, or so Lillian is always telling me, but I should think it would be way past his bedtime."

My already beet-red face flushed even darker. Once more I felt like a gawky, overgrown schoolgirl, and inwardly I cursed Maeve for always having the power to make me feel that way. "I decided to let him stay up later than usual tonight. Since it's Christmas Eve."

"But don't you think he's stayed up late enough?" she inquired sweetly. "Do take him up to bed, Mary dear. There's a pet." And she turned her pretty back to me and smiled up at Peter, who was staring at her, his face a queer mixture of dislike and helpless infatuation.

With great determination I swallowed the wave of anger that welled up in me at her dismissal. I controlled my desire to curtsy mockingly and went to Daniel's sleeping form.

He was light and small-boned for his age, and I picked him up without any great difficulty. He murmured something unintelligible and nuzzled against my shoulder, and I held him closer to me. Turning to the door, I met for the first time in many months the dark blue gaze of Connell Fitzgerald.

"Good evening, Mary," he said after a moment in

his gentle, measured tones. I thought I could read anger and disapproval and disdain in that quiet, charming voice, and a feeling of desolation settled over me. "I'm sorry we interrupted anything."

I met his scornful gaze bravely. "You interrupted nothing," I replied with great calm. "Good night." And I started past him into the hallway.

"When you've finished putting the boy to bed," he said in that same voice, "come back to the library. I'm sure it's far too early on Christmas Eve to go to bed."

To my tired ears there was a faintly menacing note in that, and I longed to refuse outright. But he wasn't the sort of man one refused lightly. I allowed my wicked eyes to stray toward his mouth—that mouth that had touched mine so tantalizingly last time we met. I swallowed, then nodded.

It only took me a few short minutes to undress the sleeping child and tuck him under his heavy covers. Stirring up the fire in his small, neat room on the second floor, I left him with a light kiss on his momentarily untroubled brow.

My feet and heart were curiously light as I made my way back through the deserted hallways to the library. And I knew very well why I felt like dancing, despite the nervous pounding beneath the low-cut bodice of my green velvet evening dress.

I stopped in front of the full-length, candlelit pier glass at the top of the stairs as I caught sight of my reflection. The woman in the mirror was both familiar and yet different, and I wondered why. My hair was its usual unruly tangle of blue-black curls, my eyes green and shining with excitement, my cheeks flushed in my normally rather pale face. My elegant dress showed off my healthy figure to advantage, and yet I knew full well that next to Maeve's delicacy I would look like an overrobust milkmaid. Certainly Peter's attention had vanished the moment she walked into the room.

"It won't do you any good," an unpleasant voice

hissed at my right elbow, and I jumped a foot in the air.

"Good evening, Mrs. Carpenter," I greeted her with a shaken calm. "I thought you and Mr. Carpenter had gone to visit relatives."

"You think I'd be gone when my lady was coming home?" she demanded, her tiny black eyes in her disconcertingly merry little face watching me with cold contempt.

"You knew they were returning tonight?" I questioned. "Why on earth didn't you tell us?"

She smirked, a cold, thin-lipped smirk that was at such odds with her rosy-cheeked visage. "You didn't ask, did you, miss?" She started to glide away when her words came back to me.

"What did you mean—it won't do me any good?" I questioned her retreating form.

She turned back for a moment, the balefulness of her expression unleashed. "Just what I said, miss. He'll forget all about you—he won't even look at you with her around. No matter how much you primp in front of the mirror. He won't be able to take his eyes off her."

"Who won't?"

She looked disconcerted for a moment. Quickly she recovered herself. "Mr. Peter," she snapped. "Or any other man, for that matter."

I felt an odd sense of relief that she had mistaken my interest. I put on my saddest frown over my too expressive face. "It's true," I agreed woefully, and started down the stairs. "Merry Christmas, Mrs. Carpenter."

There was no answer.

Considering how volatile were the relationships among the three people in the room, I was surprised at the ambience of peace emanating from the trio. As I approached the door I had time to notice both how alike and yet how different they were, with their attractive faces and their aura of wealth and security and breeding. Only Con stood out with that reckless, bitter look in his deep, unfathomable eyes, his cold disdain for his companions brutally obvious. For a moment I had the odd fancy that he belonged more in a band of raiding Celts, not trammeled in here among the rich and the righteous.

And Maeve, for all her middle-class upbringing and her slightly drunken father, seemed far more at home in her setting than her cynical husband. She was sitting next to Peter on the horsehair loveseat and laughing into his hopelessly bedazzled eyes while Connell looked on, a familiar expression of bored impatience on his dark face. I hesitated for a moment in the doorway, wondering whether or not I should quietly slip back upstairs to my room, when he turned around, some sixth sense informing him of my presence.

He rose with leisurely grace and gestured me into the room. Peter made a futile move, trying to rise, but one of Maeve's slim, possessive hands was on his tweed jacket, holding him firmly by her side while she flirted with him under her husband's nose.

My choice of seats was distinctly limited. I could either drop into Maeve's or Peter's laps or curl up next to Connell on the matching loveseat. At that point my nerves were at such a pitch that I didn't even want to look at the man, much less cuddle with him, so with studied nonchalance I seated myself cross-legged on the faded and beautiful Oriental carpet in front of the merrily blazing fire, and accepted the glass of dark amber liquid Connell silently handed me.

"Con, darling, we must do something about these furnishings," Maeve pouted prettily, letting poor Peter come up for air. The look he shot me was filled with desperation. "The rest of the house is so elegant, this room is positively shabby in comparison."

"This is my study," he answered with cold civility. "I didn't invite you in here, and if you don't like it you may leave."

I started guiltily. "I'm afraid it's all my fault—I was

the one who asked Carpenter to put the tree in here. I didn't realize it was your study, or I would never have suggested it. It was the only really comfortable room in the house . . ." I let it trail off as I realized the tactlessness of my remark, and was rewarded with Maeve's brief glance of amused dislike. A moment later it was gone, and if I hadn't known Maeve from childhood I would have doubted its existence in the first place.

She laughed, her light, brittle laugh. "Well, I'm sure you can tell what sort of household little Mary was brought up in. Shanty Irish with no pretensions to taste or refinement," she dismissed her family. "The poor little thing can't recognize an elegant house when she sees one." She laughed again, and the sound grated on my nerves.

Before the retort that was on the tip of my tongue could spill over, however, Connell broke in smoothly, "And how are you liking Demonwood, Mary?" His voice was flat and uninterested, but it served to change the subject.

"She loves it, don't you, Mary?" Peter broke in eagerly, edging away from Maeve's possessive grasp. "It's as if . . . as if she belongs here."

"Really?" Maeve questioned with spurious sweetness. "Now isn't that remarkable? While I have never felt more than slightly comfortable way out here in the wilds. I suppose you must be a farm girl at heart, Mary."

I was becoming more and more unhappy, sitting in that room with those three preoccupied people and their hidden tensions. Maeve seemed caught up in making spiteful remarks about my manners, looks, and tastes; Peter kept throwing beseeching glances in my direction; and Connell Fitzgerald just sat there, a remote, angry look on his strong-featured face. For all he cared I could have been a thousand miles away.

I took a deep sip of the drink he'd handed me and felt the warm glow of good Irish whiskey spread through me. The fire was warm at my back, the room smelled of whiskey and evergreens, and I wished more than anything that they would all go away and leave me to curl up peacefully near the hearth.

"Where's Lillian?" I questioned suddenly, belatedly noticing her absence. I couldn't contain a feeling of strong disappointment—my only ally in the house and she had chosen to stay in Europe. I had been looking forward to her warm heart and sympathetic ear.

Maeve wrinkled her pretty nose in distaste. "She was persuaded to remain behind. I think by her retired colonel. If luck is with us we may never have to put up with her again except for short intervals. She and that prosy old bore certainly deserve each other."

"I may remind you that you are speaking of my sister," Con said with quiet menace.

She pouted prettily. "Well, you can't expect me to be a hypocrite and pretend that I like her. It's a well-known fact that she detests and disapproves of me. It will be so pleasant to have my house to myself for once, without her pious, preaching ways."

Her husband stared at her stonily for a moment, and I wondered how he could be immune to such enchanting loveliness. I drained the glass of whiskey and rose on slightly unsteady feet. Although my father had maintained that the ability to drink hard liquor was a necessary part of a young girl's education, I was quite unused to such a large amount after Peter's lethal punch. I longed to escape from the suddenly stuffy, tension-filled atmosphere of the room—if I stayed there any longer I would either cry or fall asleep.

"Retiring so soon, little Mary?" Maeve teased, and my temper flared. My junoesque stature had always been rather a sore point with me, and her constant harping on it had the same effect as waving a red flag before a bull. I always felt like a strapping giant around her delicate beauty—there was no need for her to remind me.

"Yes," I snapped, starting for the door. Connell was there before me, his tall frame towering over me, making me feel deliciously fragile after Maeve's carping remarks.

Without a word to his wife and guest he took my unwilling arm and accompanied me out into the hallway. I heard Peter's protest as I blindly followed him. "Which room are you in?" he demanded abruptly, and I felt a quiver of alarm not unmixed with delight.

"Up in the attic," I replied. "In the old studio. Why?"

A suddenly amused expression crossed his face. "I thought I already assured you that I have no designs on your . . . your virtue, cousin. Everything that goes on in this house happens to be my concern."

"All right," I accepted it. I tried to free my arm, but his grip tightened painfully.

"Before I forget, Mary, I wanted to warn you."

"Warn me about what?" I demanded.

"About encouraging Peter's attentions. His affections are lightly and easily given. If I were you I wouldn't expect anything from him."

"And what the hell business is it of yours?" I raised my voice, my temper breaking.

His eyes closed in exasperation, and I noticed in the flickering lamplight that he had absurdly long lashes for a man. "You happen to be in my care—as your employer and . . . connection I happen to be responsible for you." I could tell he was mocking me, and I longed to lash out at him. "I wouldn't want to have to return you to your brothers in, shall we say, damaged condition?"

"My brothers have nothing to do with this!"

A twisted smile lit his face. "I think they'd disagree with you on that. I had a visitation from all six of them the night you left, and very definite they were about the care and treatment of Mary Gallager. And I don't think your violent fiancé would take kindly to your having an affair with another man."

"Mr. Fitzgerald," I replied with dangerous calm, all my Christmas spirit vanishing, "I think it's become necessary for me to set you straight on a few things. First of all, I have no fiancé, and never had one. It's perfectly true that Michael Flynn spent the night in my house that night, but he spent the night on the kitchen floor, stone drunk!"

I couldn't tell whether he believed me or not. "It's none of my concern anyway."

"Exactly my point. Nor is my choice of companions while I'm here your concern."

"I agree," he said stiffly. "I merely thought for your own well-being that I ought to warn you. Apparently you don't care what sort of trouble you get yourself into. I don't know why I expected any better of you."

I felt a small, clutching feeling inside at his words. I opened my mouth to speak, but he continued on in his cold, angry voice. "But one thing I will not have. I won't allow any sort of indiscretions in this house— my son has been exposed to too much of women's infidelity as it is. You'll have to conduct your no-doubt numerous love affairs at some other place and time."

"Oh, will I now?" I demanded, livid. "Well, if you say so, sir. I suppose I'll have to send around letters to the three score or so men who are simply dying to seduce me, and tell them they'll have to wait. Or would you like to pass inspection on them all? Of course, that's only the men in Vermont—it doesn't include three or four hundred from Cambridge who've enjoyed my favors in the past." I stopped for breath, glaring.

To my surprise a smile cracked Connell's stern visage. A smile, and then a reluctant laugh. "All right, Mary. Send the first twenty or so to me and if they pass muster I'll let you use your own judgment on the next hundred."

"What's so amusing?" Maeve questioned archly from the study door. "I don't think I've heard you laugh in over a year, Con, darling. My little cousin must be good for you." She smiled up at me benevolently, her pearly white teeth shining in the lamplight. "Do watch out for him, Mary dear," she warned sweetly. "My husband has a habit of breaking hearts."

"I think," I said with great calm, "that you all should know that I am entirely capable of taking care of my own heart and morals without instructions, advice, and warnings from the three of you!" Peter had appeared in the doorway and was watching us with a dazed expression. At that moment the clock struck midnight. "And I wish you all a very happy day on the birth of our Saviour." With great dignity I turned on one heel and left them, those three handsome and unhappy people, alone in the hallway.

Chapter Ten

If I had hoped to sleep late the next morning I was disappointed. The night had been a fitful one, full of tossings and turnings, and I hadn't drifted off until the first streaks of dawn were spreading across the mountainous horizon. The dreams that followed were filled with hints of danger and torment, and the memory of Connell Fitzgerald's mouth on mine had returned full force, not to be banished by common sense and guilt. My unhappy thrashings must have woken me up in the icy stillness of early morning, and I was about to pull the covers over my head when I realized I was not alone.

"I was wondering how long it would take you to wake up," came Maeve's soft voice from across the room. "You do sleep soundly, my dear."

I sat bolt upright in bed, pulling my covers around me. "What are you doing here?" I demanded ungraciously.

She was seated by the fire, a fire she had just managed to poke into life, clad (or almost clad) in a filmy, black lace negligee that could only have come from Paris. It exhibited her slender curves and silky skin in a manner that could only be called provocative, and I wondered that her husband had let her escape from his bed. Her hair hung down her back in a tawny wave, and her lavender-blue eyes glowed in the dark.

"How can you stand this room?" she questioned lazily, ignoring my query. "I would think you'd turn to ice by the morning."

"I find it bracing."

Her pretty pink lips curved into a pout. "I'm sure you do. Nevertheless, I think it would be better if you moved to one of the rooms on the second floor. Heaven knows there are enough of them. I can't imagine what Mrs. Carpenter was thinking of—to put you up here."

"I gathered it was Lillian's idea." I rose from the haven of the bed and stalked over to the fire, trailing quilts and blankets behind me. "And I intend to stay in this room—I like it. But you didn't come creeping up here to talk about my sleeping arrangements, did you, Maeve?"

Her light, silvery laugh filled the room. "Poor little Mary," she mocked. "I always could put you in a rage, couldn't I? You really are no challenge at all, you know."

Silently I counted to ten, drawing a deep breath. When I had finished I was a bit more in control of myself. "What is it you want, Maeve?"

"Why, to warn you to stay away from my husband, of course," she replied sweetly. "I've seen the way you look at him, the way you primp in front of mirrors when you know he's going to be around. Oh, yes," she recognized the look of annoyance on my face. "Mrs. Carpenter told me about that. She thought you were interested in Peter Riordan, but I knew better. It's my husband you want, isn't it?" There was no change in her lazy, curious tone.

"No, it's not," I said flatly. "Your husband is a mar-

100

ried man and I'm a woman with strong morals. And even if he weren't married I wouldn't be interested." God, what a liar I was becoming. "I don't see what it matters to you, Maeve. I've gathered from our family that you haven't been the image of a faithful wife."

She smiled at me, a sweet beguiling smile devoid of feeling. "The Gallagers do love to gossip, don't they? Con and I have a very civilized arrangement. He goes his way, I go mine. As long as we keep our various *affaires de coeur* relatively discreet, things go along quite smoothly. But I won't, Mary Gallager, have him trifling with my raw-boned cousin. If it weren't so insulting it would be amusing."

I chose my words carefully, masking the heady combination of hope, disgust, and fear that swept over me. "I can't imagine," I said slowly, "why you think your husband is enamored of me. For heaven's sake, Maeve, he's done no more than be polite. If he were looking for a . . . a mistress I'm sure he'd find someone a lot prettier and more of his station.

"Maeve," I said gently, "haven't you looked in a mirror recently? How could any man look twice at me with you around?"

"You'd like me to believe that, wouldn't you?" She rose, and her nightdress trailed on the floor around her. "I don't mind his meaningless flirtations, his short-term mistresses. He's always picked women of the world. Until you, Cousin. I've never been very fond of you. And I certainly don't care to be shamed in the eyes of my neighbors that my husband preferred a clumsy creature like you. If I find there's any basis for my suspicions I'll see that you leave, either by choice or by force." There was a note of steel behind her fragile voice, and I didn't doubt her for one moment.

The door to my room sprang open, and there stood Daniel, his dark blue eyes shining with excitement. "Merry Christmas, Mary," he burbled. "I've been awake for hours. You . . ." his voice trailed off as he spied his mother, and a look of dismay crept over his

101

expressive face, the blank unhappy look shuttering down.

"Well?" she said coolly. "Don't you have anything to say to me, Daniel? Or has my cousin tried to steal you away from me too?"

"Maeve!" I said in a warning undertone. At the same time her only child moved reluctantly forward and planted a chaste kiss on her proffered cheek.

"Hello, Mama. We weren't expecting you back so soon."

"Apparently not. Go back to your room, Daniel. We'll all have Christmas breakfast in another hour, and then you may see all the presents I brought back for you. You'd like that, wouldn't you?"

His lack of enthusiasm should have been evident even to the most disinterested of observers. His mother, however, had more important things on her mind, and at Daniel's nod she turned her back on him, dismissing him from her suspicious thoughts. "Remember what I said, Mary." And, taking one of her son's thin wrists in her hand, she swept from my attic bedroom.

I took a long time in my dressing that morning, preoccupied with my conscience and, I must confess, my vanity. Despite the absurdity of Maeve's accusations, one nasty, worrying little core of truth nagged at me as I dressed in a warm dress of forest green wool, wrestled with me as I tried to tame my wild black curls, subdued me as I pinched my pale cheeks to put a bit of color into them. I did lust after her husband, most shamefully, and for that I should announce at breakfast that I must return to Cambridge. My green eyes stared at me solemnly from the mirror, and I knew that I wouldn't do it. Just another week, I temporized. To let Daniel get used to his parents' return.

"My, my, don't you look lovely?" Maeve greeted me innocently from her seat at the head of the table, for all the world as if we never had a confrontation in the early hours of the morning. My usual seat, I noticed

102

with an unreasonable pang. "And who are you dressing up for, may I ask?"

I met her spiteful gaze calmly, seating myself as far away from her as possible. "It's Christmas, Maeve. And we're expecting visitors." She shrugged nonchalantly. "If you mean Peter you needn't have bothered. I told him we'd be otherwise engaged today. Though of course you'd know better than I would about Mr. Riordan's plans. Con, darling," she addressed her husband in plaintive tones as he appeared in the dining room door. "You're late. You missed my little cousin's lovely entrance. I'm sure it was planned for your approval—you know what an effect you have on women." She smiled up at him with deceptive sweetness, and I could feel a rush of color flood my face. I pulled my gaze away from Con's distant expression and concentrated on my cup of coffee.

"Maeve, couldn't you spare us? Just for this one day, couldn't you control your sick fancies long enough for us to enjoy Christmas?" His lovely voice was very tired, and I could feel my treacherous heart rush out to him. Deliberately I pulled it back. "Where's Daniel?"

"Here, Papa." My charge appeared from the kitchen, and never in my life had I seen such a change in anyone. I had expected him to receive his father with the same reserve with which he had greeted his mother. I was totally unprepared to see him launch himself across the room into his father's waiting arms.

Maeve and I were forgotten or ignored in the eager conversation that followed. Every country, every village they had visited in Europe was subjected to a myriad of questions that showed a heretofore undemonstrated interest in geography. The details of life at Demonwood underwent the same exhaustive treatment, all the while Maeve picked at her food, a disconsolate droop to her pink mouth.

When she could stand it no longer, she rose, deliberately knocking over her half-finished cup of coffee. "Why don't we finish this fascinating conversation in

103

the library?" she said brightly. "I would think a normal boy might be interested in the presents we brought home for him, at great expense and trouble."

Reluctantly he drew his attention away from his father. "Of course, Mama. It's just that it's been so long since I saw Papa. . . ."

"It's been five months longer since you last saw me," she snapped, her smile vanishing. "Come along." She started toward the door, then turned to me, as if suddenly remembering a victim. "Oh, Mary, you needn't rush your meal. We won't be needing you this morning. This will just be a family time, with the three of us." An expression of triumph curled her lips as I sat there, embarrassed and unhappy. I could feel Connell's eyes on me, an unreadable expression in them, and hurriedly I lowered my own gaze to my plate.

"Maeve," I heard him begin in his cold, angry voice, but her lilting tones broke through.

"It's Christmas, darling. I thought you wanted us to have a pleasant time today."

I stole a glance upward, to see the look of cold dislike he shot at her. "You're incapable of it, my dear."

"But for your precious Daniel's sake I must try, mustn't I?" she inquired sweetly.

I could feel the violence in the room, the barely restrained fury within the tall, lean man staring down at his faithless wife, and I wondered what she had done to merit such raw, fresh hatred. If, as Maeve insisted, things had been as civilly distant for so many long years, then I couldn't imagine how the dislike emanating from Connell could have been kept at such a fever pitch. Unless something new had come to disturb the already troubled waters of the Fitzgerald household.

My appetite vanished, I threw down my damask napkin and stood up. "Have a pleasant morning."

Con turned to me, an almost longing expression in his dark face. "We would be honored to have you join us this morning, wouldn't we?"

"No," snapped Maeve. "We'll . . ."

104

At the same time I spoke. "I'd prefer to be alone, thank you. If no one objects I thought I might go for a ride."

"The snow's too deep," he said, and I was aware of that strange intensity suddenly being directed at me. It was a mesmerizing feeling, and I steeled myself against it. Maeve seemed to know all too well how her husband affected me; it would never do for the man himself to recognize it.

"I'll manage," I responded coolly. "I'll see you all later." He watched me from those dark, hypnotic eyes for a moment, then shrugged, dismissing me. They left, and I stared after them with a feeling curiously akin to bereavement.

There was a biting wind whipping around the house, through the stunted bushes that were Carpenter's idea of formal landscaping. I pulled my cape closer around me as I scuffed through the freshly fallen snow.

Moon Maiden, my favorite mount, greeted me with a friendly whirrup as I entered the stable. Robinson looked up from his seat by the stall, a sullen look on his smugly handsome face.

I barely controlled a start of unpleasant surprise. I had assumed the stables would be deserted—assumed he'd have the holiday off with the rest of the servants. But for some reason, like Mrs. Carpenter, he'd chosen to stay and welcome the returning travelers. "What do *you* want?" he demanded in a sulky tone of voice, not bothering to rise.

The barely restrained insolence was even worse than his usual leering innuendos, and I controlled my anger with a noble effort. "Could you possibly saddle Moon Maiden for me?" I requested in my sweetest voice. "I thought I might go for a ride this morning."

"Well, you can think again. You ain't going nowhere, at least not on Moon Maiden, you ain't. She's the Madame's horse, and she'd skin me alive if I let anyone else ride her."

"Then why did you allow me to ride her before?" I asked, disappointment stinging me.

"Madame weren't here," he said faintly, and spat in the straw behind him. "Now if you were wanting I should saddle Lucifer for you. . . ."

"I'm not a good enough rider for a brute like Lucifer, and well you know it."

He rose, and swaggered across the brick floor to stand uncomfortably close to me, emanating an odor of sweat, horses, and some sickly sweet cologne, a Christmas present from a female admirer, no doubt. "I think you could handle anything or anybody you put your mind to, Miss Gallager." He smirked a loose-lipped smirk and leaned closer. "If I didn't have other irons in the fire I might be interested in taking you on. There's something underneath that prim and proper exterior. And Perley Robinson's the boy to bring it out. You'd be a right nice handful." He eyed my unfortunately lush curves with an appreciative eye.

"Oh, really?" I questioned icily, my rage bubbling to the surface. "Well, then, I suppose it's just too bad for me that you're . . . preoccupied." I turned on my heel to leave, but one grubby hand reached out and grabbed my arm, pulling my unwilling body closer until it rested against him.

"You oughtn't to be so high-and-mighty," he muttered roughly. He turned his head and spat again, then turned back to me. "There's others around here who ain't so particular." I squirmed helplessly against his grasp, disgusted and outraged. "Yessir, when it comes to certain things the mistress ain't so particular, and you don't have to be neither. I could . . ." I shut my ears to the coarse, nasty, vivid things he was suggesting, trying to shut my mind off too. I ceased struggling—it was only increasing his sense of power over me. ". . . and you'd like that, wouldn't you? I never met a woman who didn't."

"Perley!" Carpenter appeared at the door, looking like a small, gnarled, avenging angel. "Haven't you got

106

anything but bones in that pretty head of yours? Let her go, for God's sake!"

Reluctantly his grip loosened, and with an upsurge of energy I yanked myself free. "What business is it of yours?" he said sullenly.

"If anyone up at the house got wind of the fact that you've been interfering with the teacher you'd be in more trouble than you could shake a stick at. The Madame would have you turned off without notice, boy. She likes to keep her men to herself."

The thought of Maeve and this loathsome young stallion sickened me even more, and I turned and ran out of the stable. But not before I could hear the rest of Carpenter's warning.

"It doesn't matter to me what you do with the girl. But there's such a thing as time and place, my boy. Mr. Fitzgerald would just about break your neck if you touched her. Take my word for it."

I sped through the snow, paying no heed to what direction I was headed. Branches whipped at my face, pulling my hair free from the useless pins. I stumbled and fell once more, then rose and ran again, into the dark glowering confines of the woods, of Demonwood with its ancient maples, its young and threatening pines, anywhere away from that house of pain and sorrow, of evil desires that controlled all of us. Until by their own volition my feet began to slow, and I was moving through those woods at a slow, steady pace, trying to control the frightened, angry pounding of my heart.

It was a direction we had never wandered in, Peter or Daniel or I. The path I was following was wide and well-packed, only the most recent layer of snow was untouched. My curiosity aroused, I was no longer nervous of the haunted wood. Indeed, with the sun shining down through the trees, silvering the snow around me, I felt more at peace than I had in quite a while. There was no aura of violent death around here.

The path widened, turned a corner and joined with a narrow, well-kept road. My feet were wet and chilled through my moroccan leather boots, my cape and dress were snow-covered. If I were wise I would turn back, control my curiosity.

But the curiosity of a Gallager is a powerful thing, one that I couldn't resist on such a fine Christmas day. It would be my Christmas present to myself, a fine bit of indulgence after a thoroughly unpleasant, hateful morning. I would satisfy myself as to what lay at the end of this road, and if it turned out to be something horrid then it was no one's fault but my own.

I don't know what I expected. Not the sight that met my eyes some half a mile onward. Nothing exotic, threatening, or even terribly exciting. Just a rambling old farmhouse nestled among the trees.

No smoke came from the chimneys, curtains were pulled across all the windows, and snow lay heavy on the ground around it. But the place was as neat and trim as love and money could make it, the roof had been freshly shoveled, and a cleared pathway led straight to the front door.

Not being blessed with an active conscience that morning, I made my way up the front porch and peered in the window. A small chink in the curtains allowed me to see into a large, welcoming living room. The furniture consisted of looming shapes covered with holland covers, with a sad and deserted look to them. I moved to the door, hoping against hope that the caretaker of this place (and it was obviously well-tended) had forgotten to lock up.

The door opened without the slightest difficulty, and I hesitated on the porch for a moment. It was too easy—if I had any sense I would turn right around and head back to Demonwood.

At that moment a sharp wind blew, chilling me to my very bones. Without further hesitation I stepped inside the shelter of the house and shut the door behind me.

Chapter Eleven

My first order of business, after I had ascertained that the house was truly deserted, was to start a huge, roaring fire in the living room fireplace. Kindling and nice, dry maple was stacked beside it, with sulphur matches hung in a tin box on the freshly painted wall nearby. Once a goodly blaze had begun crackling, I took off my snow-covered shoes and began to explore the neat, enticing little house.

Faith, it was a lovely house indeed! Everything that Demonwood should have been, but missed by a yard. The floors were silky polished hardwood, the walls hung with delicately patterned paper, not the gaudy pinks and golds or the lugubrious browns of the Fitzgeralds' house. The furniture was old, beautifully crafted and infinitely useful. No delicate French settees for this house, thank you. Rag rugs covered the floor at various intervals, and the multipaned windows looked out over the countryside from their comfortable nest.

There were books all over the house—I couldn't remember if I had ever seen so many books. Books in the library, books in the living room, books in each bedroom, and even books in the kitchen. And then I realized that was part of the problem with Demonwood. Except for Connell's study (and my room, of course) there wasn't a single book in the entire house.

I wandered around the slowly warming room, staring at the leather and gold bindings, taking down an interesting volume now and then, whenever one happened to catch my eye. Whoever lived in this place had loved learning, and I found myself wishing that the owners were still around. They could have provided me with friendship when the Fitzgeralds began their hateful scenes.

I should have known, of course. And indeed, it was with a curious sense of destiny that I pulled down the worn copy of Keats and read the name written boldly on the flyleaf. Connell Patrick Carradine Fitzgerald.

And whose house would it be, I asked myself sternly, located a hand's reach from the stately halls of Demonwood. Where do you think the Fitzgeralds lived before they built that hideously new mausoleum? I went back up the twisted stairs to the front bedroom and looked once more on the paintings of the two children, so alike and yet so different. The boy looked very much like a livelier version of my quiet Daniel. Connell as a boy had had dark curls, the same glowing blue eyes as his son and a look of laughing devilment about him. Something had wiped that laughter from him, and I wondered if it had been Maeve or Kathleen. Or both.

Lillian sat beside him in the portrait, her soft brown eyes turned toward her younger brother with worshipful adoration, a plain little dab of a thing even then. And then I chided myself for my uncharitable thoughts. Lillian was my friend—it wasn't for me to judge her appearance.

I stayed in the deserted farmhouse until the fire died down, curled up in one of the covered chairs with the Keats for company. Very carefully I scattered the remaining coals on the hearth, straightened the dust covers and redrew the curtains. I hoped no one would realize anyone had been inside. I intended to come back here whenever I got the chance, and I had the strong feeling that they would try to stop me. But I wasn't going to give up the first haven of peace I'd known since I arrived in Lyman's Gore.

It was already dusk when I started back through the woods, and a full, silvery moon was rising over the dark and threatening trees. As I made my way at a leisurely pace my eyes wandered, and I noticed a deer standing in the clearing, her eyes shining in the twilight. I had always thought of deer as magic creatures, and her calm, passionless gaze seemed to speak to me, offering sympathy and reassurance. After a moment she turned and moved slowly away, trusting that I wouldn't harm her.

It was a good ending for not a bad sort of day, all told, and I returned to the house feeling curiously serene.

When I came down to breakfast the next morning Con was gone, leaving a sullen Daniel behind, his shining blue eyes dull with hurt and disappointment and what I almost thought I recognized as fear. But that was impossible, I told myself sternly. What could Daniel have to fear from his mother and me?

Maeve promptly took Connell's departure as a sign that she no longer need have anything to do with either her son or me. As far as I could see her days followed a slothful pattern. She would rise about eleven, eat a leisurely breakfast, and then be off visiting or riding with the ever-faithful Robinson. The latter's expression of smugness increased daily, and so disgusted was I with the blatant situation that I forbade Daniel the use of the stables. Not that my charge cared one way or the other—he was content to trot along behind me when I went for long angry walks through the ever-deepening snow.

In the first few days after Maeve's return Peter would accompany us, much to Daniel's dismay and my own pleasure. But as the days passed we saw less and less of his charming and gentle smiles, and only I knew or even guessed the torment he was going through over Maeve. For my lovely cousin was holding nothing back in her campaign to win her onetime lover back to her side. She would make a special effort to rise early on the mornings when she knew he was coming, and she would appear sleepy-eyed and flushed, her lavender eyes shining with sweet, innocent admiration, all her attentions riveted to Peter's suddenly stammering conversation. The full force of Maeve's feminine wiles was an awesome thing, and I didn't hold out much hope for Peter's powers of resistance. He was forever one to take the easiest course open to him.

I knew I could save him if I really wanted to, by as simple an act as lifting a finger, and yet I hesitated. With him loomed a full, peaceful life with an adoring husband and far more money than I would ever need, and yet still I was haunted by the specter of Connell Fitzgerald and his sad, mocking eyes. So poor Peter fought his battle silently and alone, until one morning we saw him riding across the fields with a laughing, wind-blown Maeve at his side, and I knew he was lost again.

As the new year began the air turned even colder, and the heavy snows, more a threat than an actuality so far, began in earnest. By mid-month another two feet had piled up around us, making my irregular visits to the old farmhouse lengthier and more difficult. But not even a howling blizzard could have kept me from going. Demonwood was surely not the most peaceful place in the world, with Maeve flaunting her various illicit relationships with mocking assurance and Daniel alternately frightened and defiant, all the time shutting me out, refusing to confide in me. And each time I came face to face with Peter in the rambling hallways of Demonwood the bemused expression on his face and the look of mild, guilty surprise wounded me in a way I knew was irrational but still painful.

Of course I had constant letters from my family. Scarcely a week went by without hearing from brothers and sisters-in-law, and I was sorely tempted to pour out my doubts and fears to them. Instead I wrote them bright and witty little letters, assuring them that I loved my job and that Maeve was charming. Which was not exactly a lie. Maeve *was* being charming, but not toward me. Father McShane had even told me it was reasoning like this that got me into trouble. And I knew he was right.

I was on my way home late one afternoon from the farmhouse when I noticed a difference about the huge new house as it stood like an eyesore amid the freshly fallen snow. The windows were blazing with light, and there was a vitality that seemed to flow out to me that told me Con must have returned. I quickened my pace along the snow-packed pathway.

"And where are you running to?" Maeve's mocking voice broke through my excited thoughts, and I turned to her in surprise, her dark-clothed figure framed against the twilit sky.

"Maeve!" A small, nervous laugh escaped me. "I didn't see you standing there. Are you on your way back to the house? I'll walk with you," I offered, having no desire for her company but determined still to keep up a friendly outward appearance.

"No, I'm not going back to the house," she snapped with sudden waspishness. "My beloved husband has appeared from out of the blue with an absolute horde of business friends, and I refuse to stay and play hostess to the bunch of them. Pompous old bores! It was bad enough being dragged all over Europe to serve as his hostess—at least his European associates were men of breeding and culture. I draw the line at his American merchant friends," she sniffed, and I couldn't help but wonder at her swift rise to snobbery. "I'll be back when they've gone, and you can tell my husband that during your next cozy little tête-à-tête. At least I know you'll be properly chaperoned." She started off through the woods.

"But where are you going?" I asked helplessly. "Does Connell know . . ."

She turned back to me, her lavender eyes blazing. "I, my dear, am going to spend the next few days with my maiden aunt in New Hampshire. Tell Con that, if you wish."

"You know as well as I that you have no maiden aunt in New Hampshire," I said sternly.

"Tell him any damned thing you please, Mary. Use your imagination." And without a backward glance she was off into the rapidly deepening twilight. My one consolation was that she headed in the opposite direction of Stonewalls.

I moved back to the house slowly, my heart thumping loudly beneath my tightly corseted chest. As I drew off my wrap in the back hall it was with a curious sense of fatality that I watched Mrs. Carpenter approach me, her deceptively jolly face wreathed in a smile, her prim little mouth curving upward in an expression of extreme malice.

"You're wanted in the library, miss," she announced. "Mr. Fitzgerald wants you to pour for his gentlemen friends."

"I . . . I . . ." I hesitated, some instinctive part of me knowing I was heading for trouble. "Where's Daniel?"

"In the library, miss, waiting for his tea. I told Mr. Fitzgerald I'd bring it as soon as you returned."

"But where is Mrs. Fitzgerald?" I questioned innocently, wondering what tale she had told them.

"You know as well as I she's gone, miss. No telling when she'll return."

"Does Mr. Fitzgerald know this?"

"I believe I heard Mrs. Fitzgerald mention it to him when they were upstairs," the old snoop admitted, her beady little eyes boring up into mine. "Tea will be ready in five minutes, Miss Gallager."

There was nothing I could do but head toward the library, taking only a moment to stop before a mirror and smooth down my crumpled dress of deep blue wool and try to untangle my unruly black curls. My green eyes shone back at me, and I knew the reason why.

My first impression of the library was that it seemed filled with about twenty loud, large men, all talking and laughing and smoking cigarettes and pipes and cigars, the blue smoke rising to the high ceiling and casting a haze over the room. I coughed reproachfully as I entered, and there was a mad dash to the fireplace as each gentleman doused his infernal smoking apparatus. All but Con, who stood off to one side, pulling gently on a pipe, an amused look in those fathomless blue eyes as he made the most casual of introductions. So casual that he omitted identifying me to the various middle-aged and elderly gentlemen who had accompanied him to his secluded house in the Vermont woods.

Smiling graciously to cover my nervousness, I seated myself on the horsehair loveseat and proceeded to pour out the strong China tea into the delicate, wafer-thin teacups that had come from Ireland with Con's grandmother, the legendary Countess of Carradine, or so Daniel had proudly informed me. My young charge passed the cups for me, his eyes unclouded for the first time in weeks, his body straight and strong in the gathering twilight. The look he flashed me was impish, and I wished with all my heart that his wretched mother would disappear off the face of the earth, leaving him with his father and Aunt Lillian. And, to be honest, with me.

One of the older gentlemen took the seat beside me, the springs protesting against his noble bulk, and proceeded to engage me in exquisitely and meaningless conversation. I gave all the required responses, my eyes focusing on Con's strong back halfway across the room, when suddenly my attention was riveted back to my companion.

"I must say, Mrs. Fitzgerald, that you're as lovely a creature as you've been reputed to be. I'm only sorry we've never met before—though of course I can understand your reluctance to accompany Con on his business trips. These semiannual meetings can be a great bore to an outsider, I'm sure, but I thought you should know what a treat it is for us that you consented to have us gruff businessmen invade your lovely home."

"Yes, indeed, Mrs. Fitzgerald," another, younger

man piped up loudly in the sudden stillness as everyone watched and listened with polite attention. "It's an honor indeed to be here, especially after Con told us so much about you. And he didn't exaggerate, no sirree bob, not one bit."

I stared up at them in dumbfounded horror, my eyes traveling in mute desperation from one affable, welcoming face to another, all of them equally gullible and friendly, with the sole exception of Con, who was watching my predicament out of narrowed eyes, making no effort to come to my assistance.

"But . . . but I'm not . . ." I stammered, and then Daniel flew to my side, a devilish grin on his pixie face.

Flinging his thin arms around my neck in a veritable stranglehold, he looked at me ingenuously, and said with great seriousness, "Isn't it lovely to have Father here with all his friends, Mummy? It's so much nicer than having him go away and leave us all the time. Mummy and I have been soooo lonely," he announced plaintively, and I could have murdered the little monster.

And then Con moved away from the wall, a wicked glint in his eyes. "We're all delighted to be here, young Daniel, your father especially." He lay one strong brown hand on my neck with the lightest, most casual of possessive gestures, and it was all I could do to control the little shiver that ran through me. "And we're so glad you decided you were up to acting as hostess, Mary dear." He smiled down at me, and in spite of myself I smiled back, knowing it was wrong but powerless to stop.

And in the background as we all trooped upstairs to change for dinner, I overheard one of Con's friends say to the other, "But I thought Con's wife's name was Maeve."

"Mary, Maeve, what's the difference?" his companion replied. "You know Con's always been devilishly secretive about her. After meeting her I can't say I blame him. A woman with a face like that should be kept away from marauding gentlemen like you and

116

me. All she'd have to do is snap her fingers and I'd be at her feet."

With great restraint I kept myself from turning around to identify the speaker. I had always been passably pretty, if a trifle on the robust side, but never before had I elicited such a response. And I knew the reason for my sudden irresistible beauty before I asked myself . . . it was Con, and my wicked reaction to him, that brightened my eyes and curved my lips into a soft smile when no one was looking. And it was for Con that I dressed and primped and laughed and half-danced down the hallways that lovely evening.

It passed in a flurry, far too quickly for my peace of mind. For the first time since I had been in this great, cold, gaudy house, I felt at home, and I received the mild flirtatiousness and accolades of Con's friends with cheerful grace. I was used to being surrounded by six brothers, and the sight of a long table filled with elderly and no doubt very rich and powerful men fazed me not one bit. I treated them all with impartial friendliness, all the time aware of Con's still, amused gaze from the opposite end of the table, a curious smile playing around his expressive mouth.

When I rose from the table to leave the men to their port and cigars, they all rose en masse to accompany me, and we trailed into the music room (Maeve had a room for every possible use) like a mother hen and her chicks. There we drank Irish whiskey and Irish coffee and I played the piano and sang all the old ballads and we were all very gay. And throughout it all I could feel Con watching me, those dark, unreadable eyes staring through me, and it was all I could do to remember the words of the songs.

Daniel kissed me with as much filial devotion as he had ever shown his beloved father, his eyes twinkling with more mischief than they had held during the three months I had known him. "Good night, Mummy dear," he murmured sweetly, planting a large, wet kiss on my proferred cheek.

As he moved to go upstairs, I couldn't resist giving him a small, loving hug. It was a dangerous fantasy I had been flung into by the Fitzgerald men, and, though I knew better, I couldn't resist enjoying it for the short time it lasted. But it was with a sharp twinge of recognition that I met Connell's suddenly longing eyes above Daniel's smooth brown head.

From then on I could no longer avoid the full implications of my masquerade. I smiled blankly at the outrageous compliments and subtle flirting of Con's friends, and as soon as I could manage it I rose.

"I'll be wishing you all a good evening, gentlemen," I murmured. "It's been a long day for me."

"Well, Mrs. Fitzgerald, it's been a long day for the rest of us too, and we'll be leaving first thing in the morning. Once you've retired I doubt we'll have much reason to stay up, will we?" the urbane gentleman on my left inquired of his companions. "We'll accompany you upstairs."

Silently I cursed him with all the profanities available to my limited experience. There was no way on God's earth that I could go up to my attic room with the twenty of them following behind me. As we mounted the elegant curving staircase my eyes met Con's imploringly. His response was a quiet smile.

One by one the gentlemen kissed my proffered hand, one by one they bid me good night outside Maeve's bedroom door, until Con and I were left alone there, a curious string of tension between us, while his guests wandered back to their rooms.

"What will Maeve say when she hears about this?" I whispered.

His cool blue eyes were unreadable in the candlelit hall. "She won't necessarily find out," he replied. "But I wonder why you went along with it."

My eyes flew open in outrage. There had been just the trace of an accusation in his lovely voice. "What did you expect me to do?" I gasped. "Tell all your friends that you were a liar? Especially with Daniel part and parcel of the whole scheme?"

118

He didn't reply, an enigmatic smile flitting over his dark face. One strong, gentle hand reached up and touched my tumbled hair. "You look very pretty tonight, Mary," he said softly. And then without another word he turned on his heel and left me, practically running downstairs.

I opened Maeve's door and went in. It would be the better part of valor to wait there an hour or two until I was sure all of Con's friends were asleep before sneaking up to my attic bedroom. Thank heavens they were all leaving tomorrow for another meeting up in Maine —I didn't think I could cope with another night like this, so close to everything I dreamed of, so dangerously close to my forbidden desires. Shutting the door behind me, I moved across the deserted room toward the oil lamp, my only source of light the dull gleam that came through Con's connecting door. The door that I suspected was kept firmly closed and perhaps even locked when Maeve was in residence, and was now welcoming me.

A wave of longing swept over me, primeval and so intense I could have wept. To hell with the guests, I thought suddenly, knowing that a moment's hesitation and I would be lost. I ran from the room, up the stairs and into my chilly, cavernous bedroom. There was only so much temptation I could resist.

Chapter Twelve

I played the coward the next morning, staying strictly cloistered in my attic bedroom until I saw carriage after carriage pull out along Demonwood's long, snow-packed drive. The last carriage held Connell, and before climbing in his tanned face squinted upward against the fitful sunshine, and I knew his gaze was on my windows. I only wished I could read the thoughts behind that unreadable face—whether the longing I had surprised on it last night had been a figment of my imagination, whether he felt regret or relief that I wasn't in Maeve's room that night, whether he was right now planning a polite letter saying that my services were no longer needed and I could return to Cambridge. But after a few moments he merely nodded, as if confirming something in his own mind, and climbed into the carriage. I watched them till they were out of sight.

There was no sign of Maeve that day or the next. Both Daniel and I were ill at ease, knowing instinctively a storm of some sort was due, dreading its coming but hating the long wait as well.

I was sitting up in bed well after ten o'clock the next night with my quilt tucked around me comfortably when my door opened and Maeve stood there, her thin, lithe body draped in a flowing cerise nightrobe, her golden hair a curtain down her back, a cheerfully malevolent expression in her violet eyes. I had seen that look before, and I could feel my stomach contract in dread. I pulled the quilt closer around me, shielding my opulent figure from her prying, scornful eyes.

The cords in her slender, swanlike neck stood out, and for the first time I noticed flaws in her perfect skin. In a few years she could easily look like a plucked chicken. Such observations cheered me, and I sat upright with a little more confidence. Even great beauties had defects—perhaps my strong, lush body had hitherto unforeseen merits.

"What can I do for you, Maeve?" I asked bravely, expecting an excoriating tirade on my manners and morals. Indeed, I had felt so guilty over my shameless masquerade that screaming tirades would have made me feel better.

Instead she smiled blandly, almost sweetly, and all

my suspicions were raised. "I merely wanted to tell you I've returned, Mary dear. And request your help in a small matter. After all, we are cousins. We practically grew up together—we're much of an age," she preened herself.

"You're seven years older than I am, Maeve," I said brutally, not lulled by her gentle beginning. "You just turned thirty."

"You little bitch," she hissed, her false affability vanishing. "Don't you dare mention that to anyone or I'll . . . I'll . . ."

"You'll what?" I called her bluff.

She smiled again, her pink lips curling into a smug little grimace. "That's exactly what I was going to talk with you about, Mary dear. It's not that I so much need your help . . . I demand it. And a few other things besides."

I huddled deeper into the quilt, suddenly very unhappy. "Such as?"

She leaned forward from her perch on the arm of the chair opposite me. "You think I wouldn't hear about your little party while I was gone? You must be an even bigger fool than I thought you were." She smoothed her skirts over her slender thighs. "I've warned you before. You are to leave my husband strictly alone, Mary Gallager. I know you stare up at him with those innocent green eyes, all sweetness and light. You're very wise to know that appeals to him. But I won't have it, do you hear? I won't have him trifling with my plain little virgin cousin while he ignores me!" There was a bewildered expression on her face, as though she couldn't comprehend how any man could resist her fabled beauty. All her life it had brought her everything she wanted . . . the idea of it failing her now was more than she could comprehend.

"Maeve, your husband doesn't even like me," I said vainly, and she laughed, a high, lilting laugh that set my teeth on edge.

"If you believe that then you're an even bigger fool than I thought you were. He's bewitched by you and your sweet little ways. But I won't have it, do you understand? I won't have you trying to take my place, queening it over his boring friends."

"Of course not, Maeve," I said soothingly.

A sly look came over the chiseled features. "Have you been bothered by nocturnal occurrences since you've been in this room, Mary darlin'?"

I was suddenly alert. "What do you mean?"

"Why, the ghost of poor stupid Kathleen, of course. Clanking her chains and moaning and sobbing behind the walls."

"How did you know?" I breathed.

"You silly, stupid fool!" she said dispassionately. "One would think you were just off the boat, to be taken in with all that idiocy. I had Mrs. Carpenter arrange that for you. I wanted you to leave Demonwood. You're a lot tougher than you look, though. You stayed."

"Indeed I did. Why should it be so important that I leave here?" I demanded.

She rose then, and glided across the polished floor to the ornate paneling beside my massive bed. With a deft movement of her beringed hand, the panel swung out into the room, leaving a gaping hole in its place.

"A secret passageway," Maeve said triumphantly. "It leads to an unused portion of the attics—the ceilings are too low to store much. At the end is a back stairway I had put in while Con was on one of his interminable business trips. It leads down to the stables and is really quite useful. I couldn't afford to give up such a convenient exit."

"Really?" I questioned coldly. "I suppose there's no need for me to ask why."

"No need at all. I either visit Robinson or take Moon Maiden and ride over to Stonewalls. We have beautiful nights this time of year." She smiled innocently.

"Peter told me he was finished with you," I protested weakly.

"And you believed him? You're even more gullible than I thought. Such innocence!" she mocked, leaning forward, and I caught a trace of her spicy scent wafting over me.

"Why do you do it?" I found myself asking, fascinated despite myself.

"I don't like to sleep alone," she said simply, as if that made all the sense in the world.

"Have you told Connell that?"

"Oh, is it Connell now? Before you were calling him Mr. Fitzgerald this and Mr. Fitzgerald that," she sneered. "Con and I have an agreement. When it pleases the two of us we share a bed. Otherwise we find our amusements elsewhere. Discreetly, of course." Her violet eyes narrowed. "But he's been less than discreet with you, my dear Mary. And you needn't think I'll give him up to your tender mercies. I intend to stick with this marriage until I tire of Con, not the other way around. I've yet to find someone with enough money to keep me in the style to which I've become accustomed."

"Then why don't you leave Peter alone?" I demanded hotly, knowing full well my protective rage would only fan her determination to destroy him. "He's hardly wealthy enough for you—surely you could find someone in Europe who'd fit your specifications."

"You'd like that, wouldn't you? You'd like me to go off and leave Con and Peter to you. As a matter of fact, I nearly did, and my dear sister-in-law was most helpful in that regard. She'd like nothing better than to be given a free hand with her precious Connell and Daniel." She made a moue of distaste. "But I had misjudged the gentleman's sincerity. So I returned home to the bosom of my loving family. Where everyone so obviously adores me." She shut the secret door with a snap, and I shivered at the thought of my vulnerable state during the months I had been here.

"What I expect of you, Mary," she continued, suddenly brisk, "is to let me in and out through your room at night, without a word to anyone, of course, and to bear me company when I feel like taking a leisurely afternoon visit. Now that Lillian's returning I have to be doubly careful, and you'll provide just the protection I need."

I stared at her, amazed at her self-assurance. "I thought Lillian approved of your flagrant adultery."

She chuckled, a deep throaty noise that was infinitely appealing, and tossed her honey-blond hair back over one white shoulder. "Oh, she does. But she knows that if Con ever found out she'd lied to him he would never forgive her. He might even . . ." She shuddered suddenly. "You're lucky I'm warning you away from him. Con's a very dangerous man."

"I don't believe you," I said flatly.

"You'd like to think I was lying, wouldn't you? You'd rather not believe me when I tell you that I know for certain that he murdered Kathleen, and that he'd murder me if he caught me with a man."

"You're right, I don't believe you."

"Believe what you like. Con knew I was having an affair with Peter, the very man who . . ." she stopped abruptly, shuddering, and despite myself I could recognize her fear as real.

"I think you overestimate his feelings for you," I said matter-of-factly, hoping it was true. "But even if you're right, why do you take chances? Why do you continually give him cause to be jealous if you're convinced he's a cold-blooded killer?"

"But that's half the charm," she replied sweetly. "I know you could never understand that—perhaps you're lucky." She stared off into the shadows for a moment, her angelically beautiful face lost in thought. "Anyway, that's neither here nor there. I'm counting on you to supply a cover for me while I'm off on my various . . . visits. You'll do that, won't you?"

I pulled the quilt around me resolutely. "Absolutely not! You must be mad to think I'd be any party to your filthy habits."

"Oh, I'm not mad, not mad at all. If you don't do what I ask you," she ran her pink tongue over her avid lips, "I will send you away and begin to concentrate all my spare energies on little Daniel. It's amazing to think of the things a person could do to a frightened, overly sensitive nine year old. Perhaps you ought to check on him tonight before you give me a definite answer."

A sudden cold fear clutched my heart. "What have you done with him?" I demanded in a whisper.

"Why don't you go and see?" she smiled seraphically, stretching her lean, sensuous body out on the huge bed.

Throwing off the quilt, I grabbed my nightrobe from the back of my chair, ignoring Maeve's curious stares at my white, nude body. I ran from the room and her mocking eyes on icy, bare feet down the stairs and corridors of the darkened house to Daniel's bedroom door. At first all was silent, and my hand hesitated on the brass doorknob. Until I heard the muffled sobs.

As quietly as possible I opened the door, slipping inside on silent feet. Daniel's bedroom was far removed from all the other members of the family, so that my stealth should have been unnecessary. Some trace of feminine instinct must have prompted it.

He was lying face down in the bed, his thin shoulders shaking with barely suppressed sobs.

"Daniel?" I whispered softly, and was aghast to see him cower away from me in mindless terror.

"Daniel, it's only me, Mary," I said gently, placing a hand on his cringing shoulder.

He let out a muffled shriek of pain at my touch, then subsided into soft whimpers.

"Oh, Daniel, my poor angel," I murmured brokenly. "What did she do to you?" I squeezed his hand reassuringly and slowly, gradually his sobbing lessened and then finally stopped. He raised his tear-drenched face to mine, and managed a semblance of a smile.

"It's all right, Mary. It's not so bad this time, really it's not."

"Your father has to be told," I exclaimed angrily, feeling sick inside.

"No!" he cried. "Please Mary, don't! You don't understand. If . . . if he ever found out he might . . . might hurt her."

"She deserves it," I said shortly, hesitating anyway. "She can't be allowed to do this to you."

He half rose, his pale young face contorting with pain. "I'd rather have her beat me," he said with a pitiful maturity, "than have my father hang for murder. And he'd kill her if he found out, Mary, you know he would."

I sank back down by his bed hopelessly. "I wouldn't blame him," I said fiercely. "I'd like to kill her myself."

There was nothing I could do for his poor thin little back with its flayed and bruised skin. If she had done worse before it was a wonder no one had noticed. But poor Daniel had sworn himself to secrecy, and there was nothing I could say or do to betray him.

I mounted the stairs slowly, holding my murderous rage barely in check. Maeve was waiting for me, a half-smile playing about her pink lips, her lovely eyes bright with amoral humor. I could barely keep myself from flying at her and wiping that small, evil smile from her face.

"What did you use on him, Maeve?" I questioned hoarsely, closing the heavy oak door behind me. "What did you use on the poor, innocent babe to give him such bruises . . ."

She shrugged. "My riding crop, Mary dear. I'm afraid I can't help myself sometimes—I have a wicked temper." The lips drew back over her perfect teeth in a travesty of a smile. "I assume you didn't rush screaming to dear Connell?"

"He's back?" I questioned, torn between my fear for Daniel and the deadly outcome of any disclosures I might make.

"Of course he's back—he can't bear to be parted

from you," she simpered. "But that's to end right now. I have infinite faith in your intelligence. If Con knew I was in the habit of beating his precious blue-eyed son I don't think I'd have long to live. But then, neither would Con."

"How can you do this?" I whispered in horror. "He's your son, Maeve! Your own flesh and blood!"

"I don't give a damn what he is! He means nothing to me, just nine months of discomfort when I thought Con adored me. Little did I know that was all he married me for. Right now he's the only thing his father cares for, and it gives me great satisfaction to do a little damage in that direction. If I can't hurt Con any other way I'll gladly hurt him through his son."

"If you touch him again I'll kill you myself," I said desperately.

"But, Mary, you don't have to," she replied limpidly. "All you have to do is help me slip out of the house every now and then. Just think of all the good you'll be doing, keeping Con's suspicious nature free from doubt, protecting your precious Daniel from his evil mother."

"Won't Con notice that you're absent from your bed at night?" I questioned desperately.

She laughed mirthlessly. "Con hasn't come near me in three months, my dear cousin. Not since he met you."

"What if I refuse?"

She leaned forward, a cold steely glint in her lavender eyes. "Then you'll precipitate a crisis that there's no escaping from. The next time I'll beat him where it will show, and there'll be no stopping Con. How many deaths would you like on your conscience?"

I stared into those beautiful, soulless eyes for a long time, and I was convinced. "Just yours," I snapped. "Just yours, Maeve."

"But you'll do as I say, won't you?"

I nodded. I had seen Con's temper—I couldn't doubt his fury would be murderous.

She leaned back, satisfied. "I thought you would. You're very wise. And I'd advise you not to mention this to anyone, not even to Lillian. Things have a habit of getting around, you know."

"Does Peter know?" I had to ask.

She smiled enigmatically. "Perhaps. You should have learned by now that Peter does what I tell him to. As does everyone else around here. Even Lillian."

"When is she returning?"

"Sometime toward the end of the week, Con said. You should be delighted. Someone to keep you company. You can sit around and talk about how terrible I am." She rose. "We'll try out our new arrangement tomorrow. I'm so glad you've decided to see things my way."

"All right," I agreed numbly, for what choice did I have? "But you swear you'll leave Daniel alone?"

"Absolutely. I won't even glance in his direction. And Mary . . ."

"Yes?"

"Don't forget the other part of our bargain. My husband is to be left strictly alone. You should be glad I'm warning you away from him. All you'd get would be another shanty Irish brat in your belly and Con would be on to new conquests. You should be more grateful . . ."

Something in me snapped. "Get out of here!" I hissed. "I've given you my word. I know honor means nothing to you, but you'll have to accept it this once."

"Oh, I believe you, Mary darling." She started for the door, in an excellent humor now that she had gotten her own way. "You have too much to lose not to obey my instructions to the letter. And don't think you can turn to Peter or anyone else for help. They wouldn't believe you."

"Maeve."

She turned, a beautifully shaped eyebrow lifting in delicate inquiry.

"I hope," I said slowly and carefully, "that someday,

128

someone murders you as they did Kathleen, and that it's slow and painful and very frightening."

She smiled, her pink mouth curving upward smugly. "But then your true love would hang, my dear. Isn't that just what you're trying to avoid? So where would it get you?" And she shut the door softly behind her.

PART TWO

Chapter Thirteen

The next few days were absolutely hellish. True to her word, Maeve appeared at my bed sometime around midnight the next night, a smug, secret smile on her face as she slipped through the door to meet whichever lover enjoyed her favors that night. The thought of Peter's behavior sickened me, and I lay for long hours in that bed, expecting Con to burst through the door and denounce me. It was dawn before she returned, her tawny golden hair tumbling down her back, angry bruises on her slender, delicate arms, a dreamy look on her sated face.

"So you're still awake?" she noted as she shut the panel behind her. "Do you want to hear all about it?"

"Go away, Maeve," I said grimly, "or you'll be sorry you pushed me too far."

"Certainly, my cousin, certainly." She laughed again, and my taut nerves screamed. "I think you're jealous." And with that she left me to three more hours of fitful sleep.

My appearance at breakfast that morning was hardly scintillating—even Connell, who had studiously ignored me since his return to Demonwood, commented on my hag-ridden appearance. "Didn't you sleep last night, Mary? You look exhausted."

"I . . . I had a headache," I lied. "It kept me up most of the night."

Maeve, who to my surprise had made an early appearance at breakfast looking completely rested, smiled triumphantly, and I cursed myself for lying to him. "You poor thing," she murmured solicitously.

"I know what it's like to suffer from headaches. Why I'm an absolute martyr to them, aren't I, darling?"

Con stared at her across the table with a cold dislike, unmoved by her vibrant beauty. "I wouldn't know what ills of the flesh you suffer, Maeve. I'm sure you enjoy a great deal of pain." There was a curiously pointed edge to his voice, and Maeve blushed a deep, unattractive color and subsided for the moment. And remembering the marks and bruises on her arms I was even more nauseated.

"Lillian's returning tomorrow on the afternoon train," Con announced abruptly. "I've decided that Mary should accompany me to meet her."

My heart leapt, then sank as I saw the malevolent expression on Maeve's face. "I fail to see why," she said coldly.

He stared at her for a moment, as if considering an answer to her carping voice. "Mary and Lillian are friends," he replied after a moment. "I thought it would be enjoyable for them both if Mary were to meet the train with me."

Maeve's eyes glittered evilly, and I remembered her son's tortured back with sick alarm. "I don't think I can go," I said hastily. "Daniel and I have fallen behind in his Latin—we should work on it for the next few afternoons."

"I didn't ask your opinion of the matter, Mary," Connell said coldly. "I happen to be your employer—you'll do what I tell you to do." He drained his cup of coffee. "Besides, Daniel's too young for Latin."

"No, I'm not, Father," his son said stoutly. "It's my favorite subject—all those wars and stuff."

"If it's your favorite subject, why have you fallen behind in your studies?" he inquired mildly enough, and both Daniel and I flushed a deep, beet red.

"I thought he needed extra work on his ciphering," I jumped in hastily after a moment. "And I thought his Latin would be all right if we neglected it. He's really very good, you know. He might have the makings of a classics scholar."

134

"And what would you know about such things?" Maeve mocked. "Oh, I had forgotten. You always were a bookworm when you were younger. I should give you a hint or two, Mary dear. You'll never find a husband if you are too clever. Men simply don't find intelligent women attractive. I, for instance, have no pretensions of intellectuality."

"True," I agreed cheerfully. "But then, not all men are like your husband." I rose and signaled for a reluctant Daniel to accompany me.

"We'll leave around two o'clock tomorrow afternoon, Mary," Connell spoke quietly, his voice brooking no disobedience. I hesitated, then nodded coolly before proceeding upstairs.

"You'll have to fall and pretend to sprain your ankle," Maeve informed me that night. "I won't have you going off with him all afternoon, I simply won't have it."

"Then why don't you go in my place?" I asked wearily.

"I suggested it. Con refused flatly. He wants your company, and I know damned well it's not for that bitch Lillian's sake. If you don't say you twisted your ankle I swear I'll shove you downstairs myself," she cried wildly.

"I'm sorry Maeve, I can't. He wouldn't believe me."

"You mean you won't? For all your protestations of innocence you're just dying to go off with him tomorrow, aren't you?" she demanded, her eyes hardening. "We'll see about that, my dear cousin. We'll see." And she stalked from my bedroom.

I dressed carefully for my afternoon excursion. It would be the first time in months that I had been farther afield than church, and my green eyes shone with excitement as I brushed my tangled black curls into a semblance of order. My dress, another castoff from Pauline's mother's mistress, was a soft rose that went beautifully with my pale complexion, and the bonnet I clamped down over my touseled head was

135

the most flattering one I possessed. The thought of spending at least an hour alone with Connell Fitzgerald, without his wife's innuendos and sly amusement was enough to make me feel slightly giddy with excitement, and I ran down the attic steps two at a time, stopping long enough in the hall to take one last admiring glance in the pier glass before descending to the front hall.

As I put my foot out to take the first step, I felt two hands reach up behind me and give me a vicious push. If my responses had been a little less quick I would have tumbled down that long flight, maiming or even killing myself. But instinctively I reached out and clawed at the bannister, just barely managing to save myself. Pulling my trembling body upright with shaking hands I met the triumphant smile of my cousin Maeve.

"Next time you'll miss the bannister," she said, and the blackest, ugliest rage that I had ever known swept down over me. I wanted to take her slender neck and snap it in my two strong hands; I wanted to hurl her soft, seductive body from the landing. I was so furious and frightened that I couldn't trust myself to speak or to move. I just stood staring at her, shaking with rage and fright.

"What's going on?" Connell demanded from the front hall.

"Nothing, darling," Maeve called out. "Mary was a trifle clumsy, that's all." She turned to me, smiling seraphically. "You should be more careful, Mary. You could have been killed."

"There are limits, Maeve," I said in a low voice. "There are very definite limits to what I'll put up with from you. Don't you ever do that again."

"Do what?" she questioned innocently. Bravely I turned my back on her and moved down the stairs.

Connell was curiously silent as he helped me into the closed carriage, tucking the furred lap robe around me with a distant courtesy. We drove down the winding drive, and it wasn't until we were out of sight of the house that he spoke.

"Did Maeve push you?" he asked abruptly, his eyes boring into mine.

"Why do you ask me such a thing?" I evaded.

He leaned back and closed those compelling eyes wearily, his profile stern and yet touching in repose. "Because I know she's capable of it. And I know something strange was going on there at the top of the stairs. Don't lie to me," there was a sudden steely note to his voice. "That's the one thing I can't forgive."

There was a great deal of violence in the man, barely restrained by conventions. I had grown up surrounded by violent, boisterous men, but the violence in Connell Fitzgerald was both more subtle and more frightening. And all the more attractive.

"She pushed me," I said finally. "But I don't think she meant me to fall." This last part was a lie, but I hoped by giving him part of the truth he might believe me. "She just wanted to frighten me, I think. She didn't want me to come with you today."

"No, she made that quite clear, didn't she?" He sighed. "Are you a good Catholic, Mary?"

"I would hope so."

"That doesn't answer my question. Are you a good Catholic?"

I considered it. "I try to be. I fail a lot of the time, as Father McShane can verify."

"And what would you and your good Catholic family think if I divorced Maeve?" The words were cool, measured, the meaning was not.

"You'd be excommunicated! Not to mention ostracized by your friends and acquaintances. No one would be wanting to speak with you." I was deeply distressed, and yet some hidden part of me found it hard to suppress the start of joy I had felt at his words, the hidden meaning I wanted to read into it.

"And would you be wanting to speak with me, Mary Margaret Gallager?" He might have been asking the time of day, so unconcerned was his voice.

"Yes," I said softly after a moment. "I'd be wanting to speak with you." And he nodded, satisfied, and said no more. But there was a curiously tantalizing quality about his silence, as if by our not saying a word we were being far more intimate than if we had chattered brightly all the way to the train. And as we rode along the rutted, snow-packed road, I felt his body next to mine, the heat seeming to burn through our clothes, and despite everything, despite fear and guilt I was happier than I had been in a long time.

I scarcely recognized Lillian as she descended from the train. Of course, it had been months since I had last seen her, but there was more to it than absence dulling a memory. If anything, she was even more badly dressed than she had been in Boston, and her mousy brown hair was arranged in a new style that was both fussy and unflattering. The expression on her round, gentle face as she saw Connell and me waiting for her was surprise, but I don't think it was pleased surprise. But the look of irritation vanished as suddenly as it appeared, and I wondered if I had imagined it. She greeted us both with a vibrant smile, slinging her small, sturdy body upon her brother with an excess of devotion.

I realized then that I had never seen the two of them together. Con disentangled her clinging hands gently, smiling down at her with lukewarm welcome. Her eyes devoured him hungrily, as if they couldn't take in enough, and I rated only a brief, friendly hello before she began deluging her beloved Connell with nonstop, seeming inconsequential chatter. Such sisterly devotion should have been touching, and I wondered why I felt this strange feeling of distaste for her display. And I also wondered what had happened to her distinguished British colonel.

Apparently Connell wondered too, for the moment she stopped for breath he broke in, "You didn't explain in your letter, Lilly. Why are you back so suddenly? I thought we agreed you'd stay on in Florence until summer. And weren't you going to visit Colonel Badham's family in Madeira?"

Her small brown face puckered suddenly, and two large tears filled her brown eyes. "Haven't you noticed I'm in mourning, Con?" She gestured to her frumpy black dress. "He died, Con! Cyril died!" And she dissolved into noisy tears.

Immediate pity sprang up in me. That would account for her nervous excitement, her extreme clinging to her brother. I put my arms around her tiny figure. "Poor Lillian. How awful for you! Let me help you into the carriage and we'll go straight back to Demonwood and a nice warm bed. You must be exhausted after all your traveling." She leaned back against my arm gratefully, giving me a tremulous smile.

"So kind," she murmured damply, mopping her eyes with a handkerchief trimmed with black lace.

"How did he die, Lilly?" Con asked in a curiously harsh tone of voice.

"Oh, Con," she wept afresh.

"How did he die?"

"Don't upset her now," I dared to reprove him. "What does it matter, anyway? The man is dead—can't you see she's too upset to discuss it?"

"No," Lillian recovered bravely. "I don't mind, really. He died quite horribly, Con. He fell from the cliff outside our villa. He must have been watching the sky—you know how he loved birds." She dissolved into tears again, then resolutely blew her nose. "It was very strange, Con. It happened the day you and Maeve left. They think he must have gone over sometime early in the morning, before the household was up. And if we'd only known I could have come back with you, instead of waiting and waiting for a suitable boat. Oh, Con, it was so awful!"

"He died when Maeve and I were still there?" I wondered at his insistence on this point.

Lillian nodded sadly. "Yes, dear. Just think, if

you'd been out walking that morning as you usually did you might have seen him." Her eyes, so different from his shining blue ones, stared up at him with a curious fascination, as if she had just had a most interesting thought. At her artless words a distinctly nasty suspicion came over me, and try as I could I was unable to shut it out of my mind.

In the fuss of seating ourselves in the small carriage the subject was forgotten. Con handed his sister up, then gave me his hand to help me climb in behind her. I don't know quite how it happened, but as the carriage started forward he was sitting beside me, his sister opposite with a discontented expression on her plain, tired face.

The house was deserted when we arrived home—Maeve and Daniel were nowhere to be seen. I forced myself to stifle the onrush of fear I felt at their absence, offering to help the weary Lillian to her room. I was accepted with alacrity. As we made our way slowly up the winding stairs I couldn't shake off a feeling of oppression. I had been looking forward to Lillian's return so eagerly, and yet now that she was here I couldn't rid myself of a feeling of . . . of imminent danger. As if her return had set in motion a chain of events that would prove disastrous for us all.

I had never been inside her bedroom at Demonwood. Indeed, I hadn't been inside more than half the large, ornate rooms in the place. The few that I had seen were alike in their bland, opulent decor, with gilt cupids in the unlikeliest places. But Lillian's room was an exception. She had made it her own, but I couldn't wholeheartedly approve of her style. The walls were covered in a brown watered silk, the windows draped in matching silk curtains that carefully shut out any impertinent sunlight that might want to invade her room. And after five long months, the overpowering scent of violets that she used so lavishly still lingered in the still and stuffy air.

The furniture was dark and heavy, unlike the fragile and impractical French furniture with which

Maeve had filled the rest of the house. The only paintings on the walls were ones of Daniel when he was about five, a pretty, frivolous woman in the style of about twenty-five years ago who I rightly identified as Con's grandmother, the Countess of Carradine, and a portrait of Con that had my full, enraptured attention from the moment I laid eyes on it.

He must have been in his early twenties when it was done. There were no lines in his broad, high forehead, no frown marks around his laughing blue eyes, and his mouth curved in that sweet, disturbing smile I had seen so seldom and loved so much. And standing by his side in the portrait was surely the loveliest creature I had ever seen.

"That's Kathleen," Lillian said unnecessarily, coming to stand beside me while I looked up at the portrait. "She was very beautiful, wasn't she?"

"Very," I agreed with sudden despair. Until that moment I had always thought Maeve the prettiest creature to walk God's earth, but this girl had her beat all hollow. Not in sheer physical beauty, though she had that in abundance, according to the painting. But the sweetness and grace of her character shone through the oils, and I wondered how she could have ever betrayed the man who had loved her so desperately. And how could any man, having loved a woman like that, ever look in my direction?

Reluctantly I pulled my eyes away from the cause of my unhappiness, and turned to my companion. "Would you like some tea, Lillian? I could help you unpack . . ."

"What I'd like most of all, dear, is for you to keep me company for a while and fill me in on everything that's been happening while I've been in Florence. I knew I would get nothing out of Con—typical close-mouthed male, when he knew I was dying for the latest gossip. How is Daniel? Is he happy?"

"Happy enough, I should say," I replied cautiously. "I'm sure he missed you." That was a white lie, perhaps. He had seldom mentioned his doting aunt to me

141

during our long talks, an omission that had disturbed me.

"Did he?" she inquired mistily, stretching her tired body out on the brown silk coverlet of her four-poster bed. "Sometimes I wonder whether he cares for his poor aunt at all. He seems so distant and aloof. Just like his father."

"He's not one given to outward displays of affection," I agreed. "Except, of course, where Con's concerned."

"And what do you think of my brother, now that you've lived with him for a while? Have you fallen in love with him? Most impressionable young girls do." There was a troubled note beneath her gentle prying, and I was glad the dusk hid the violent blush I could feel had mounted to my face.

"I'm not an impressionable young girl, Lillian," I replied tartly. "I don't make a habit of falling in love with married men." No, I thought, I've only done it once. "Your brother is a very attractive man, very polite and well-bred," I continued with a noticeable lack of enthusiasm, "but nothing more than that to me."

I could see her tense shoulders relax, and I wondered why it should matter so much to her. As if she could read my mind, she leaned forward and gestured to the chair beside her bed. "Perhaps I'd better explain something to you, Mary dear. It might make the strange situation around here a little bit more understandable. I love my brother very much. That's obvious, isn't it?"

Seating myself in the uncomfortable straight-backed chair she had offered, I nodded warily.

"I suppose you think I'm too possessive," her voice dropped. "Always clinging to him, never having a life of my own. But, Mary, it's not I who created this intolerable situation. It was Con!"

"Con?" I couldn't keep a slight trace of skepticism from my voice.

"Con is insanely jealous. He always has been, ever

since we were little children. I wasn't allowed to have any other friends, I must always play with my little brother, Con. I thought when we got older, once he married, that it would improve, that I could live a life of my own for once. But no, he didn't trust Kathleen, sweet, gentle Kathleen who adored him. I was to stay with them, so that I could keep watch over her when he was away on business." Her voice was high and taut with remembered strain. "You can't imagine what it's like, Mary, always walking around on tenterhooks, afraid Con will think I'm slighting him. Any beaux I might have had he frightened away—he wanted me all to himself."

"But Lillian," I gasped. "That's . . . that's sick and evil."

Through the twilight of the dusky room I could see her nod. "And then Kathleen died. I was never so frightened in my life. I thought I would be the next one . . ."

"Are you trying to tell me you think Con murdered Kathleen?" I demanded harshly, and I could sense her flinching.

"I . . . I don't know, Mary. After Con found her in her bedroom that night with . . . with another man, he took off into the woods like a man possessed. I'd never seen him in such a rage. When I saw him again Kathleen was dead, and he looked like a man who has seen the depths of hell."

I didn't believe a word of this, I told myself fiercely. It was lies, all lies.

"Why didn't you leave when he married Maeve?"

She sniffed. "That slut? You'll pardon me for saying so, Mary dear, I know she's your cousin. But that was no marriage—it was a breeding contract. Con wanted an heir, so he picked the first likely female he could buy, seduced her, and then when she was safely pregnant he married her. He always made it clear she meant nothing to him."

"Poor Maeve," I couldn't help but murmur.

"Don't waste your pity on that one!" Lillian scoffed,

her dislike hardening her usually gentle voice. "She has what she wanted. An elegant home, a rich and handsome husband who lets her commit whatever excesses she wishes and showers her with money. It's Con that breaks my heart—every year he becomes more irrational."

"Why don't you leave?" I asked reasonably.

"You forget . . . there's Daniel. I couldn't leave him to his father. Con's not . . . not a well man. There's no telling what he might do if I deserted him."

I peered at her through the gathering dusk, trying to read her expression. "Why are you telling me all this?"

She reached out and took my hand in her plump, damp one. "If you're going to stay in this house you'd best be warned what might happen. He doesn't care for Maeve, but she might push him too far. I want you to be fully aware of the dangers inherent in living here. I blame myself for allowing you to come in the first place."

"Are you suggesting that I leave?" My hand felt numb in her nervous, twisting grasp, but there was no way I could politely free myself.

"It might be the best thing," she said eagerly. "I know you've said Con means nothing to you, but he has a way of insinuating himself into one's affections. You're too young and sweet to let that happen to you, Mary. I had to warn you." With that she released my hand and threw herself into a storm of weeping.

I moved over to the bed and drew her frail, shaking body into my arms, comforting her as best I knew how. "There, there, Lillian, you're overwrought. It's been a horrid few months for you, what with your . . . your friend being killed that way, and none of your family around to comfort you. After you've rested a few days from the trip, things will seem a lot better. You'll see, darling."

She raised her tear-streaked face, a pitifully woebegone expression in her damp brown eyes. "You don't believe me, do you, Mary?"

I hesitated. "No, Lillian. I think you're overtired and things are distorted right now. In a few days you'll recognize these worries for the nonsense they are."

And, patting her hand reassuringly, with a confidence I didn't feel, I left her to her misery.

Chapter Fourteen

But the problem was that I did believe her. Oh, my heart told me that it couldn't be—I couldn't be madly, secretly in love with a cold-blooded murderer. And my mind told me it was illogical—a man subject to such crippling jealousies couldn't have lived such a wealthy, successful life without his madness showing through. The respect and affection of his friends and business associates were obvious, surely he couldn't have fooled everyone.

But some nasty, niggling little part of me, perhaps only my overactive Irish imagination, kept saying, "It could be true. It could have happened. Just because you're attracted to the man is no guarantee that he's a white knight in disguise. Other women have been in love with murderers." I didn't sleep well that night, even though Maeve controlled her rapacious appetites for the time being and refrained from creeping through my room.

The next day dawned leaden and cloudy, with the sullen atmosphere thick in the air that augured a bad storm. Tempers were on edge—Lillian and Maeve spent the morning flinging veiled insults back and forth as if it had only been a few days since they'd last seen each other; Daniel whined constantly, and after Connell shouted at us all he disappeared into his study, leaving stern instructions that he wasn't to be disturbed by screaming women and crying children.

I wasn't sure into which category I fitted. It was with an overwhelming sense of relief that I escaped the charged atmosphere of Demonwood and made my way down the pathway to the deserted farmhouse that was my refuge and haven.

I soon had the living room toasty warm by the simple expedience of shutting the doors to the other rooms of the spotlessly kept house, and, curling up in a comfortable overstuffed chair by the fireplace, I made the mistake of falling asleep in the cozy, book-lined room. I felt so warm and drowsy with my deliciously bare feet tucked up underneath me and my cape around me for extra warmth, that I shut my weary eyes for just a moment. And when I opened them several hours later I was looking straight into Connell Fitzgerald's smoky blue eyes.

The room was dark by that time, lit only by the dying embers of the fire I'd built. His face was in the shadows, and I couldn't read his expression. I knew I should jump up, full of apologies and nervous explanations. I didn't move.

"You've been missing for hours," he broke the silence, and his lovely deep voice was harsh in the still air.

"I fell asleep," I replied, as if it was the most natural thing in the world.

Through the shadows I could see a smile flit across his handsome, somber face. "Obviously. Half the men in the area are searching the woods for you. Peter Riordan is checking up by Perry's Ledge. I imagine he's hoping I threw you off."

"Why should you do that?" I asked after a long moment.

He leaned back in the rocker, at ease in the quiet, lonely house. "Surely you've heard by now, Mary? I murdered my first wife. I threw her and our unborn child off Perry's Ledge."

I felt a little frisson of horror run through me at

146

his impassive tone, followed by a swift irritation at my own gullibility. "Really?"

His jaw hardened. "No. Not really. But most people seem to believe it anyway. Why shouldn't you?"

I certainly wasn't about to throw my poor battered heart at his feet, so I merely shook my head. "That still doesn't explain why you'd want to kill me."

He stripped off the elegant leather gloves he was wearing, and I noticed for the first time what beautiful hands he had. They were large and capable-looking, with long, well-shaped fingers. The kind of hands that could control a team of strong horses or throw a woman to her death, perhaps. The kind of hands that could hold a woman . . .

I shivered again, and drew my eyes away from him to stare into the fire, wondering what had brought on this strange and violent mood, after the almost graceful gentleness of yesterday afternoon when we'd picked up Lillian.

"I can't imagine why I'd want to kill you, Mary," he said in a low voice. "Or perhaps I can." He rose abruptly, and in the dying firelight he was very tall. "We'd better get back to the house before someone ends up here. I can imagine the kind of scene Maeve would throw if she knew we'd been here together. I doubt you'd fare too well."

"What made you look here?" I questioned curiously, stretching luxuriantly like a sleepy cat.

He looked down at me, an enigmatic expression on his dark face. "Perhaps I know you better than you think I do," he replied shortly. "Where are your shoes?"

With a gasp of dismay I pulled my bare feet back underneath me. No man outside of my family had ever seen my naked feet, and there was an embarrassing intimacy about it that made me blush furiously. I pointed mutely to the corner where I had deposited my wet and snow-covered footgear, and he fetched them without a word, reluctant amusement in his usually cynical eyes.

"This is not the best climate for going barefoot, Mary," he observed, moving away to stare out the window at the softly falling snow. "Perhaps you'd be happier back in Cambridge."

"Why do you say that?" I kept my voice admirably calm. For not the first time I realized how desperately I wanted to stay in Vermont. With him. "It gets almost as cold there," I continued.

"I wasn't thinking so much of the climate," he replied with his back turned. "It might be better for all of us if you were to leave."

Lacing up my boots, now dry and stiff from being next to the blazing fire, I kept my voice light. "Better for Daniel?"

He paused, and I could feel emotions warring within him. But instead of answering my question he said, "I saw your brothers last time I was in Boston. They're very fond of you."

"Yes."

He turned back, his dark expression lightening for a moment. "You must have been a complete hellion when you were growing up. I can scarcely believe some of the stories Seamus told me."

"You'd be wise not to," I replied. "Seamus is the biggest liar east of the Mississippi."

"And Father Ronan too? He had a few enlightening remarks to make about your character."

"Well . . ." I hesitated, remembering some of the pranks I had pulled on my quiet, introspective brother Ronan before he had entered the priesthood. And the few I had perpetrated since. "I suppose I was rather lively when I was younger . . ."

He laughed, and it was a warm sound in the rapidly chilling air. "I heard about the lovely confession you made three months ago—poor Father McShane nearly had a heart attack."

"He needed something to brighten his day," I defended myself with mock virtue.

He was suddenly very close, so close that I could smell the faint odor of tobacco and wet wool from his

148

greatcoat. And the odd scent of gunpowder from a scorched mark on the arm. "You're very good at doing just that," he said in a husky voice. "Mary . . ." he bent down, and in another minute he would have kissed me. And I would have let him. I even shut my eyes, waiting for his mouth to claim mine once more— it seemed so long since that day on the train platform.

But the moment passed suddenly, and he drew away. "You can open your eyes, Mary," he said in a cold, dry voice. "I have no intention of forgetting myself again, at least not anymore than I have already. As I said before, I'm not in the habit of seducing innocents. Put on your cloak." He tossed it to me, and I caught it with numb hands. He kicked at the dying coals with a sudden cold rage, and started for the door without a backward glance to see if I was following. The room was dark and silent, and some wanton devil in me made me long to fling myself in his arms, and see how unyielding he'd be then.

I pulled the cape around me, tying the ribbons at my throat. Preceding him out the door, I was unprepared for the blast of cold wind and snow that stung my face.

He slammed the door behind us, an inscrutable expression on his face. "It's been snowing all afternoon. If it had been one hour later we wouldn't have made it out of the house tonight."

Wicked creature that I was, the thought warmed me. I would have enjoyed being trapped with him, forcing him to open up to me once more, as he had so seldom. I could have made him come out of that shell of distrust and contempt, made him smile at me as he had before. I knew I could. But fate had denied me the chance. It was just as well; the thought of returning to Maeve's and Lillian's disapproving faces was enough to daunt even my stout heart. I was already seriously frightened of what Maeve was contemplating for her blameless son as punishment for my disobedience.

"It would be better if you didn't come back here,"

he added, as he stepped off the porch into the whirling, drifting snow. "The snows are particularly bad this time of year—you could lose your way and be lost until spring."

"Are you forbidding me?"

"No. I'm merely suggesting. If you find my old house so welcoming, then it's up to you. I'm sure Maeve and Lillian couldn't care less what happens to the old place."

"Why don't you live here?" I questioned, struggling after him through the drifts.

"That should be rather obvious," he answered shortly. "My wives prefer splendor."

I was insatiably curious about Kathleen. I stumbled ahead eagerly. "Did your first wife plan Demonwood?"

"I would have thought that was obvious also," he snapped. "She had a taste for grandeur, just like your cousin."

"I prefer the farmhouse," I said in a low voice.

He stopped, turned, and stared down at me in the dark night, wind whipping around us. "But then, what you prefer doesn't really matter, does it?" he asked coldly, and I felt a twist of pain at the cruelty in his voice. He turned and started onward, and I kept silent, preoccupied with the difficult going and the absurd tears that were welling up in my throat and spilling onto my already icy cheeks.

The faster he walked, the more I struggled, the more I struggled, the faster he walked. And through it all the tears kept pouring down my face. Until finally we reached the edge of the woods, and the fields surrounding the dark and forbidding shape of Demonwood.

"Mind the drifts," he snapped, but I could barely hear him, with the wind taking his voice and spinning it past me. The snow was sharp, stinging needles in my face and eyes and I could see only a few feet in front of me. I tripped and fell, but Connell kept doggedly onward with not so much as a backward glance, so gamely I picked myself up and trudged ahead. The next time I fell down I stayed down, surrounded by the cold, wet, hateful snow, tears of pain and rage and discomfort pouring down my face and into the neck of my dress.

"What are you doing?" I heard Con's angry voice demand.

"Go away, damn you!" I wailed. There was nothing I wanted to do more at that moment than stay in my miserable pile of snow and cry.

Connell, needless to say, was not so obliging. With a less-than-gentle yank he pulled me to my none-too-steady feet and peered down at my tear-streaked face in the snowy darkness.

"What are you crying about?" he questioned crossly.

I tried to pull out of his iron grip, but only succeeded in losing my precarious balance and falling against him. I would have liked to stay right there, weeping copiously, but my rescuer righted me without a word. "Why are you crying?" he repeated.

I had had enough. "Because you're a dirty, rotten bastard," I howled. "You're a mean, nasty, selfish, uncaring brute. You're . . . you're . . ."

Words failed me, and I stood glaring at him, filled with rage and misery and longing in the snow-filled night.

"Is that all?" he asked in an ominously still voice after a moment or two.

I considered whether I had any more epithets to hurl at him. My outburst had relieved some of my immediate misery, and I was slightly shocked at my daring. "Yes," I answered meekly.

"Good." He scooped me up in his strong arms and started forward, ignoring the small yelp of protest I made. "Stop squirming," he said calmly. "Obviously the snow's too deep for you."

"I'm too big to be carried," I protested weakly, feeling very small and fragile indeed.

"Don't be absurd—you're little more than a child," he murmured under his breath.

After my struggles through the ever-deepening drifts I was more than willing to give myself up to Connell

Fitzgerald's strong arms. I was chilled to the bone, angry and miserable, and I told myself I had every right to snuggle against his unyielding shoulder and hide my head from the biting snow. Father McShane would have seen through such excuses, I knew, but I refused to worry about that right then.

We met none of my would-be rescuers on our way in, and Connell strode through the back hallways past the staring Mrs. Carpenter without a word, straight into the cozy library. A warm fire was crackling merrily on the hearth, and the room was filled with a reassuring warmth. With less solicitude than I would have cared for, Con dropped me onto the loveseat by the fire, poured me a good stiff shot of Irish whiskey, and handed it to me with the stern injunction to drink it down fast.

My teeth were chattering so hard I could barely speak, and I held the glass in shaking fingers.

"Mmmmmy . . . father . . . always said . . . to sip the good Irish," I shivered.

"I don't give a damn what your father said, drink it down." He poured himself a glass and tossed it back as if it were water. Throwing off his coat, he went over and poked the already adequate fire into Pompeiian grandeur. He turned back and glowered at me, and hastily I drank the warming stuff, enjoying its fiery path through my frozen body.

He brought the Waterford crystal decanter over and poured me another glass of equal depth, then began untying my snow-packed cape with impatient fingers. It brought his face alarmingly close to mine, and I averted my head stiffly and proudly. He put one strong hand under my chin, forcing me to meet those dark, unfathomable eyes.

"What were you crying about, you silly girl?" he asked softly, the barest trace of a smile on his face, for once devoid of cynicism, and my heart melted. "You should know better than to listen to my bad-tempered ravings."

"Indeed she should," Maeve's light voice floated from the doorway. "I'm so glad Connell found you, Mary. But then, I knew he would. I was sure he'd know just where to look."

Connell had straightened and moved away from me when we had first heard her voice, not with any haste. It was I who was guilty of lustful thoughts, not him. "She was lost in the woods, Maeve. Up in the west pasture . . . I found her wandering around half-frozen."

"Poor little Mary," she clucked, her eyes missing nothing. "And so you had to be such a heroic gentle-man and carry the poor creature through the snow-drifts. You could have put her down when you got to the house, Con." Her voice turned waspish. "You've never bothered to carry me two feet, even in the worst weather."

"You've always been more than able to fend for yourself, my dear," he replied with a cool boredom, totally at variance with his previous gentleness toward me. A gentleness I cherished. Before she could respond with the justified outrage she was feeling, he continued smoothly, "Your cousin was already too tired to make it much farther on her own. If you would have pre-ferred me to let her struggle ahead on her own two feet, we would still be out there."

"I'm sure you did the right thing, Con, darling," she purred. "You always do, don't you? In the mean-time, Mary would be much happier out of those wet clothes. Lillian's waiting for you, Mary. Go and change."

Reluctantly I rose from my exceedingly comfortable seat, letting out a small gasp as the wet, snow-soaked hem of my dress slapped against my legs. I was dizzy from the heat, exertion, and Irish whiskey, no doubt, but I was not a Gallager for nothing. I smiled regally at them, my eyes only slightly glazed, and sedately made my way to the door and through the hallways, barely hearing Maeve's voice hissing, "And you've made her drunk, I can see. It's a shame I came and interrupted your charming little tête-à-tête. In a few more minutes you would have divested her of all those wet, nasty clothes, I'm sure."

And his voice floated back to me. "I'm sure I would. It's too bad you weren't out with your stalwart young groom. But then, he was too busy shooting at me to waste time on the charming widow-to-be. It must have given you a great deal of disappointment to see that he missed."

"I don't know what you're talking about," Maeve's voice came to me, bland and unconvincing.

"There you are," Lillian broke through my eaves-dropping and I jumped nervously. Her brown silk figure bustled up to me and one surprisingly strong arm slid around my waist. "Bed's the place for you, my dear. Come along." And blindly, unthinkingly, I went, my mind still back on the scorched mark on Connell's elegant tweed coat, and the bullet that apparently had caused it.

"Will you come to Mass with me?" Lillian appeared at my bedroom door the next morning, a frumpy black hat clamped firmly down on her bowed head, her muddy brown dress rustling. "We haven't had enough time together since I've been back from Europe. I thought an early service might be nice for us both. I'm sure we're both in need of a little spiritual guidance."

I stopped in the doorway, one hand resting on the gilt doorknob, a small example of Maeve's ornate decor that had made its way all the way up to the attic, while I considered how to refuse her invitation without sounding churlish. Connell would be waiting at the breakfast table, watching for me, I hoped, perhaps with the tenderness he'd shown so briefly last night. Even his not infrequent looks of scorn would be preferable to missing him when he was so seldom here. And I knew deep in my heart that my self-indulgent days in his presence were numbered.

Lillian's nut brown eyes watched me with far more

acuteness than I could have wished. "Con's already eaten and gone, Mary," she said sharply.

I started guiltily, feeling a deep color flood my face. "I don't know what you mean," I said mendaciously, keeping my eyes wide and innocent. "And I'd love to go to Mass with you. Just wait till I get my cloak."

Lillian nodded, not fooled for a moment. "Father LeJeune has been asking for you," she murmured. "I believe it's time you took your immortal soul more seriously." Her mouth pursed in gentle disapproval, and it was all I could to keep from telling her to mind her own damned business. Because, of course, she was right, and motivated mainly by worry for me. I nodded meekly, and went to get my wrap.

The Mass dragged on interminably, and for once the familiar peace that usually filled my tense body eluded me. It seemed that everyone was staring at me, whispering, their eyes cold and dark and disapproving. And I felt they could all read the one thing that preyed on my mind throughout the service—my guilty passion for Connell Fitzgerald, a sin I could not and would not give up.

At the end of the tedious service we moved down the worn aisle, through the whispering voices and accusatory stares, Lillian and I, and she put one of her gloved hands through my arm in an ostentatiously protective fashion, patting my hand reassuringly and whispering in an agonizingly loud voice, "Pay no attention to them, my dear. It's none of their business."

The swell of conversation rose, and I could hear a word or two now and then as I kept my head bent low, color flooding my cheeks. Until I stepped out into the winter sunshine and a ball of icy slush hit me full in the face, as a voice called out a filthy name.

I stood there, stunned, unbidden tears starting in my eyes while a black rage filled my heart, all the blacker for the fact that I knew they were right. I was all the things they called me and more, in my heart if not in my body. And yet surely the desperate longing I felt for Maeve's husband wasn't the evil thing they seemed to think it was.

"Leave her alone!" Lillian called out stridently, her smaller body making an absurdly inadequate shield in front of my somewhat strapping length. "You should be ashamed of yourselves, all of you." And then she broke into rapid, and to me completely unintelligible, French that for some reason did little to soften the looks of scorn and distrust that blanketed the faces around me.

"Lillian." I tugged at her arm urgently. "Let's go, Lillian. It doesn't matter—they'll believe what they want to believe, whether it's true or not."

She broke off, and with a great show of emotion that seemed completely alien to her usual quiet demeanor, she clasped me to her brown silk breast. I could have wished for a little more restraint on her part—by reacting so strongly to the distrust of the townspeople she had only solidified their belief in my sins. But there was nothing I could say to retrieve the damning situation.

Without waiting for her reply I calmly detached her clinging arms and climbed into the carriage. After a moment she followed, slamming the carriage door as another snow ball hurtled toward us. With a jolt the horses started forward, a no-doubt grimly amused Carpenter driving them, and I leaned back in my plush corner and shut my eyes, willing the tears to go away before Lillian recognized my weakness and responded with anymore emotional outbursts. I had had enough for one day.

Chapter Fifteen

The next few days passed at an alarmingly uneven pace, the hours flying by whenever I happened to be in the same room as Connell, the minutes dragging when he was off somewhere away from Demonwood. I made no mention of my harrowing church service that day or during the next few ones, but I had made up my mind to leave. I had no other choice.

I had a hard time keeping Daniel's mind on his studies when he knew his father was around, and my own abstraction didn't help matters. The epic battles of Julius Caesar paled in comparison to Con's company for the both of us, and the seldom appreciated delights of multiplication and long division lost any lingering fascination. Valiantly, I struggled with him for days, and just as valiantly he resisted any effort I made to interest him in his studies. At half-past one on a Friday afternoon I threw up my hands in despair and released him.

"Thanks, Mary!" He smiled a beatific smile, and then, on impulse, threw his wiry little arms around me and gave me a quick hug before running out of the schoolroom, leaving his poor tutor verging between amusement and tears. Leaving him would be almost as painful as turning my back on Connell. More and more the boy was bestowing unexpected hugs and kisses, and more and more I realized how much he meant to me. He suffered Lillian's lavish embraces with a stoic forbearance and shied away from his mother like a wise child, but apparently I was now on a level close to his beloved father.

It was a cheering thought amidst all my gloom, and I found myself smiling as I dressed to go out. The sun had chosen this chilly day to shine for the first time in what seemed like weeks, and I intended to make the most of it. Daniel and Connell would be off somewhere, and I doubted if my services would be required elsewhere. Lillian would have things for me to do, or at least want my company, but I intended to sneak out before she caught me. After the church service and her incriminating defense of me, I was more than a little wary of her company. Besides, I needed some time alone to try and think out my damnable situation, to figure out how I could leave while insuring Daniel's continued safety.

And faith, it was a lovely day outside! The sun shone brightly from the clear blue sky, dazzling my eyes as it bounced off the fresh humps of high-piled snow. I practically skipped through the snow, carefully avoiding the deep drifts as I made my way across the fields. By my own volition I found I was headed for the old farmhouse, and dutifully I turned back. It had been ages since I had been to Perry's Ledge, not since Maeve had returned and bedazzled poor lovesick Peter once more. It was a lovely spot, despite its tragic history, and a good destination on a sunny day like today. Perhaps if I stood on the edge of the cliff and listened very closely to whatever hidden powers my Irish soul had, I would find the answers to the thousands of questions and decisions plaguing me.

By the time I was halfway up the winding, snowy pathway I was regretting a great many things. First, that I had decided to go at all; second, that I didn't have a horse to ride; and third, that I had ever been fool enough to get myself into such an unpleasant situation. Demonwood was dark and dreary, the wind whispering through the pine trees, telling me to go back, go back. No sun penetrated the thick foliage, only wind and snow and ice, and for the first time I could feel an aura of evil and pain emanating from the dark and secret parts of the forest.

Don't be an idiot, I told myself sternly. You've been up here many times, never before have you noticed any atmosphere of evil. But I had never come here alone. I had always had Peter with me, light, sunny, flirting Peter, who only turned solemn once, with his words of guilt and shame.

And suddenly the woods were too oppressive for me to bear. There was evil all around me, and without a moment's hesitation I turned around and started back down the hill to the house, moving as rapidly through the thin crusting of snow as I could in my stout walking boots. And it was with great strength of mind that I kept myself from looking over my shoulder, back into the threatening shadows. And into the eyes that seemed to watch me, waiting for me. Waiting for me to take one misstep, one move in the wrong direction. When I reached the open field I broke into a run.

I had been out far longer than I had thought. By the time I reached the edge of the woods darkness was already descending, my feet were soaked and numb, and the chill of the wind had bitten through my thin wool cape. Not for the first time I wished I could afford a fur-trimmed wrap like Maeve had. A gift from her not-so-doting husband, I supposed, hurrying across the fields, swerving to avoid the waist-high drifts. Perhaps if I had money and furs and jewels I might be beautiful, too. Though not, I had to be honest, as beautiful as Connell's wives.

The thought of a fire was enticing enough to make me throw caution to the winds, and without thinking I dashed into the stable, planning to take a shortcut through rather than around the large mansion.

I had my head bent low against the wind, so that I didn't see him as he approached. A calloused, grimy hand reached out and grabbed my arm, yanking me off to one side.

"Where are you going in such a hurry, little lady?" Robinson demanded, his brown spaniel's eyes staring hotly into mine.

I tugged vainly in his iron grip. "I'm cold. Let go of me, Robinson," I said sharply, trying to control the rush of uneasiness that flooded my chilled body.

"Oh, no," he said softly, his words slightly slurred, and there was the smell of cheap whiskey on his breath. "I've heard that you've taken a fancy to me. I thought I'd give you a little taste of what you're missing." His arms snaked around me, oblivious to my struggles. I tried kicking, but he held me too closely to his large, heavily muscled body. I squirmed and fought, silently, desperately, as his great paws ripped away my cape and tore open the front of my dress. He pressed his mouth on my firmly shut lips, and it felt as if my jaw would break. Pulling one hand free, I raked my nails down one side of his handsome face, and then screamed at the top of my lungs.

A moment later I was flat on my back in the hay, my head reeling from the slap he'd given me. And then his heavy body covered mine, muttering curses and threats and filth as he ripped away at my clothing. I fought like a woman possessed, but I was no match for him. I could feel my strength ebbing, feel myself ceasing to struggle as the nightmare closed in around me . . .

And suddenly the weight was off me. I lay there, winded and stunned in the semidarkness, slowly trying to gather my disordered senses together as I listened to the unmistakable sounds of a fight. I sat upright groggily, pulling my shredded clothing around my shivering body, and as my eyes began to focus I saw two figures rolling around on the floor.

The whole scene was nightmarish—the rolling, tumbling bodies, Robinson's muttered grunts and curses. But the groom, for his burly strength, was no match for his attacker. In another moment Connell Fitzgerald had him pinned to the floor and was slowly, silently, savagely beating him to death.

I opened my mouth to scream, but no sound came out. Instead I was forced to watch in mute, sick horror the animal violence of the man I loved. I couldn't even shut my eyes to block out the sight of Con's merciless face as he bent over his victim.

I had seen fights before, and furious, physical men by the dozen. How could I have avoided it, growing up with red-blooded Irishmen? But I had never seen such a cold, murderous rage as I saw in his face.

Suddenly the stable was full of people. Carpenter was firmly dragging Con away from Robinson's limp body with the stern injunction to "Give over, sir, before you kill the man." He stood upright, wavering slightly, and then his maddened, glazed eyes focused on mine. Focused and recognized the disbelieving horror in my face as I stared at his blood-soaked hands. And then I couldn't bear to look at him a moment longer. I turned and vomited into the straw.

"But this is delightful!" Maeve announced brightly from the door, her filmy pink dress whipping about her in the rising wind. "An absolutely savage battle over a lady's honor. Did you kill him, darling?"

At her cool, cheerful words a fresh spasm of nausea rose in me, and I barely managed to control it. "I don't know," Con replied shortly. "Nor do I care." He started out the door.

"But aren't you going to help your lady fair?" she questioned sweetly. "You shouldn't miss such an opportunity to have her fall into your arms."

He hesitated, then turned back to me for a moment. Just long enough to see my instinctive recoil. An ironic smile twisted his mouth for a moment. "I'm sure your ministrations will be much more welcome, Maeve." And I watched him leave the stable with tears in my eyes, damning myself for a cowardly fool, wishing I could have wiped that look of horror from my eyes before he had seen it.

Maeve looked across the stable at my shivering form, contempt on her pink lips. "What a stupid ninny you are, Mary. Con never lifted a finger to defend *my* honor. If it had been me he was fighting over I

161

would have cheered him on, and when he'd finished he would have taken me right there and then, in the straw like the animals we are. And I would have reveled in it!" And indeed, she looked like a great, magnificent cat, her shoulders flung back defiantly.

Words rose to my mouth, bitter, damning words. I wanted to call her a filthy, mindless slut; a squalid, rutting little beast, but I clamped my teeth firmly down on my battered lips. I knew all too well the words would have been directed at me, not her. And that the sick horror that had filled me as I watched Connell's primal violence had been horror directed at my own insane, debased wantonness. For through the fear and terror that had assailed me I was aware of one strong feeling above all others. When he had beaten Perley Robinson unconscious, I wanted him to come over to me and rip aside my tattered clothes and finish what Perley had started. And I wanted it so badly that even now in retrospect my self-disgust threatened to overwhelm me. I stared at my cousin with hate in my eyes as she stood there, flaunting all the darker things of my soul. It was like looking into a mirror, I thought with horror, despising myself all the more.

I lay awake in my massive bed that evening. Lillian had tucked me in, brought me a steaming mug of coffee laced very liberally with the good Irish, and sat with me for an hour, commiserating over the evilness of Robinson until I wanted to scream at her to be quiet. I wanted nothing more than to go to sleep, to try to forget the horrifying memory of my animalistic reaction in the stable. Given peace and quiet and enough time, I knew I could come to terms with it. But no one wanted to leave me alone.

Even Daniel came up for a bit, speaking cheerfully of his afternoon. I couldn't tell what had been given him as an explanation for my bed-ridden state, for the bruises around my neck and arms. It certainly hadn't been the truth, for after a lull in the conversation he had announced brightly that Perley Robinson had had an accident.

"He's gone away for good, too," he chattered. "Carpenter took him into town to see the doctor, and Mrs. Carpenter says he's not coming back. I'm glad, aren't you, Mary? I never liked him, not one bit. Maybe we'll get someone new to take care of the horses, someone nice and friendly. Maybe he could go hunting with me when Father's gone." This last was a bit wistful, and I gave his thin hand a squeeze.

"If he won't go hunting with you I will," I said grandly, only to meet Daniel's skeptical blue eyes, so like his father's that they practically broke my heart to look into them.

"Girls can't hunt," he announced flatly.

"And who gave you that silly idea?" I demanded, my righteous indignation bringing me bolt upright. "I used to go hunting with my brothers all the time."

"Did you ever get anything?" he inquired with justifiable suspicion.

"Well, not really," I admitted. "But I came close."

Daniel dismissed this, as well he should, and half an hour later made his escape with the cheerful note that, "We won't have lessons tomorrow, will we? Not with you being sick and all."

"Don't count on that, me boy," I replied, and his face fell in ludicrous dismay. "We've missed too many lessons as it is. You'll never be ready for school come next fall."

"But tomorrow's Father's last day!" he wailed. "He's going back to Boston with Aunt Lillian and he won't be back till it's time for me to go to school."

"When did he decide that?" I kept my voice admirably steady.

"Just tonight, I think. We'll be here all alone; even Mother's going. We'll have plenty of time to study then. So, you see, you've got to let me spend tomorrow with him."

And I had agreed, too bemused and distraught to hold out against his pleas. As I lay in my slowly chilling room through the hours that followed, I thought I knew why Con was leaving. The horror and disgust in my face had not left him unmoved, though why he should care about my opinion I had no idea. But I had a strong suspicion that he did care, and that thought kept me wide awake and restless through the long hours of the evening.

Chapter Sixteen

When I awoke the room was pitch black. Not even a tiny glow emanated from the fireplace, and the cold, icy air hung heavy in the room. A small shiver crept over me, and then another, until I lay there beneath my mound of blankets and quilts trembling uncontrollably with the cold. I struggled upright, noticing through the gloom that the secret doorway was open, and a stiff breeze was blowing through the opening. Using words no lady should use, I struggled out of bed and slammed the door shut behind Maeve's path, but by that time the air in my room was scarcely more than a degree or two warmer than the attic. My teeth chattered so loudly that I thought my head would fall off, and without a moment's hesitation I left the room, running lightly in my bare feet, not bothering with the meager protection my thin and worn nightrobe would afford me. Swiftly, silently I moved through the sleeping house, down the chilly flights of stairs and straight into Connell's study. He had obviously been up late, for glorious red coals were glowing in the hearth.

I had to use both hands to pour the whiskey, they were shaking so badly. I swallowed half a glassful of the stuff, gasped, and poured myself another stiff shot. That followed the first, and slowly the heat began to spread through my trembling body. I tipped the bottle into the glass once more.

"You'll be very drunk if you drink all that," Connell spoke from just behind me, and I whirled around, immediately conscious of the thinness of my nightdress, my hair loose down my back like a complete hoyden, my bare feet on the soft, Oriental carpet. "What are you doing down here, anyway?" he asked with complete unconcern.

"I . . . I was cold," I stammered nervously. He was sitting in the wing chair, his long black hair disordered, his linen shirt rumpled, a glass of whiskey in one long, well-shaped hand. I stared at him for a moment, all the longing and despair in my face for him to see. But he wasn't looking at me—his eyes were brooding into the dying embers of the fire.

"I . . . I want to thank you for . . . for helping me this afternoon," I stumbled over the words, feeling shy and incoherent.

He shrugged. "Any time," he offered nonchalantly. At his casual tone a wrenching pain assailed me. Slowly, surreptitiously I tried to edge past his chair to the door, determined to escape before I disgraced myself. His hand whipped out and caught my wrist in a crushing hold, dragging me to my knees beside his chair.

"Don't struggle," he said in a cold, hard voice, "and it won't hurt."

I considered hitting him, biting him, kicking him. Those dark, fathomless eyes had mesmerized me, like a beast of prey hypnotizes its victims into helpless compliance with their cruel fate, and I ceased pulling away. "That's better," he murmured, in no way relaxing his hold on me. My fingers were growing numb in his steely grip. "Surely you wouldn't want to deny me your company? I won't be here much longer."

"Daniel said you were going away," I acknowledged in a low voice. "Why?"

A look of bitter amusement flashed briefly in his

dark face. "I should think that would be rather obvious. Your contempt and disgust were made perfectly plain earlier today."

"I . . . I . . ." I fumbled for the proper words, the right words to reassure him without committing myself. I was far too vulnerable as it was, and I knew with a certainty he would break my heart. "You don't understand," I murmured, looking down. And for the first time I noticed the hand that held my wrist so tightly. It was bruised and swollen, the knuckles raw and throbbing. Forgetting myself completely, I took his hand in my free one, whispering, "Your poor hand!" And I could feel tears well up in my eyes. Quickly I ducked my head, but he was too fast for me. His other maimed hand went gently under my chin, and he forced my face upright to meet the questioning look in his stern eyes.

"I won't apologize for beating Perley," he said, his lovely voice harsh. "I wish I'd killed him. But I'm sorry you had to see it." And that wounded hand, that had a few short hours ago nearly murdered a man, traced my neck and throat with the gentlest of touches, until I was shivering again, but this time not from the cold.

And still the tears kept running down my face. I had always been a great one for crying, tears came often and easily to me and I enjoyed the release. This time, however, I hated them, and the more I tried to control them the more freely they flowed. "Connell," I whispered. "Please. Let me go."

And in answer he pulled me slowly, inexorably into his arms, and his mouth met mine, gently, inquisitively, as if savoring some rare and wondrous delight. I could feel myself opening up and flowering beneath his touch, and my arms went around his neck as I responded, holding nothing back, not even pride or self-respect.

But the cold Vermont winters must have conspired to save my immortal soul. As a blast of cold air

166

touched my bare skin I came to with a start, dragging myself away from his intoxicating caresses, struggling to pull my disordered nightgown back around me. I was halfway to the door before he reached me, drawing me once more into that hypnotic embrace. But this time he didn't kiss me, thank God, or I would have been powerless to resist any longer. He merely held my trembling body against the long, lean length of him, his face dark and unreadable as he looked down into mine. Whatever answer he was seeking from me must have been there in my stunned, defenseless face, for he smiled, that small, loving smile that had shattered me the first time I met him, and his brooding eyes lightened for a moment, so that he looked like the young man in Lillian's portrait.

"You'd better go up now," he said after a long, breathless moment, loosening his hold on me with slow, sensuous reluctance. Without his strong arms supporting me I swayed, feeling faint. "Unless you want to stay?"

If he had touched me, even put out a hand I would have gone to him gladly. But like a gentleman he refused to use undue pressure, and I could not make the move on my own.

"I can't." I started once more for the door, and this time it was his voice, his lovely musical voice with just the trace of the Irish in it, that called me back.

"Are you in love with Peter?" The question came out of the blue, and I turned and stared at him with unfeigned amazement.

"Of course not!"

"You'd never lie to me, would you, Mary? You'd never keep anything from me?" he asked softly, and with a small chill I remembered how many times I had lied to him already to cover his wife's misdeeds.

"No, I wouldn't lie to you," I lied once more, and he seemed satisfied. I was already in the hall when he called me one last time.

"And are you in love with me, Mary Margaret Gallager?" he asked gently. And without answering I turned and ran down the hall, up the stairs to my cold, virgin bed.

I overslept the next morning, and when I awoke the air was warm and leaden, disaster oozing out of the skies. The clouds were dark and threatening outside my many windows, and I dressed quickly, despite the unaccustomed warmth of the air, eager to escape from the depressing climate of my room, eager and yet half-afraid to see Connell once more. I was halfway down the stairs before I realized that some instinct had made me choose my plainest, most somber dress of so dark a blue that it was almost black. It matched my feelings of foreboding, and yet, despite all my misgivings my heart sang beneath my tightly corseted breast.

"You're too late for breakfast," Mrs. Carpenter announced glumly as she left the dining room. "Everyone else in this house has been up and about for hours while you've been enjoying a holiday. If you go out to the kitchen you can have coffee and nothing more. I can't waste my time cooking special meals for other servants."

"Coffee will be fine," I replied cheerfully, my determined goodwill spilling over even to her grim presence. I followed her ramrod stiff figure out to the kitchen. "Where . . . where is Daniel?"

The old witch wasn't fooled for an instant. "You mean where is Mr. Fitzgerald, don't you?" she snapped, all pretense of courtesy gone. "He's out hunting with your charge."

"Oh, yes," I murmured, sipping the scalding, bitter coffee she had grudgingly poured for me. "Daniel said they might go before his father left."

"You should know as well as anyone that Mr. Fitzgerald changed his mind about leaving." Her seamed gray face tightened with disapproval, her apple cheeks trembling with rage. "You ought to be ashamed of yourself, carrying on with your poor cousin's husband beneath her very nose! You're nothing but trash, and the worst kind. You're . . ."

Calmly I walked out of the room, taking my coffee with me, leaving her still spluttering with indignation. She was lucky I hadn't flung the scalding contents all over her stuffed bombazine bosom. When I finally reached a spot where I could no longer hear her spiteful voice I stopped, staring without seeing at the walls in front of me.

So the rumors had spread from the church to Demonwood. That was only to be expected, and who knows, perhaps the rumors came from Demonwood in the first place. And the amusing thing, I thought bitterly, was that there had been no truth to the whole thing other than my own shameful longings. Until last night. Someone must have spread those nasty tales with nothing more than pure evil mischief in mind, and it chilled me to think I had such a wanton enemy.

"Mary, darling," Lillian's soft voice called out to me from a nearby doorway. She had taken possession of the lavender sitting room, and the contrast between her somewhat sallow complexion and the pastel walls was particularly unfortunate. Dismayed at my disloyal thoughts, I forced a warm smile to my lips.

"You shouldn't be up yet," she protested in her gentle voice. "After such a shattering experience yesterday, I would think you'd want to stay in bed for a day or two."

I barely controlled the start of surprise I had felt at her words. For a moment I thought she referred to my accidental (or was it really?) midnight rendezvous with her brother, and then belatedly I realized she meant Robinson's abortive attack. "I'm fine, Lillian," I reassured her. "A good night's sleep took care of everything. I'd almost forgotten it happened."

"How strong you are," she said mistily. "When I think of what might have happened if Con hadn't gotten there in time . . ." she shuddered. "It was sheer

169

luck that he happened to be outside just then, or no one would have heard your screams."

"Well," I said with great practicality, still preoccupied, "Con *was* outside, and he did hear me, so no harm was done."

"I wouldn't say that," Lillian said softly. "They say Perley Robinson won't last another day." I stared at her in disbelieving horror, and she nodded. "Maeve has gone to see him. I hope for his sake she's in time."

"Oh, my God," I whispered, sickened.

"I warned you about Connell, didn't I?" Tears sparkled in her great brown eyes. "He can do . . . can do terrible, terrible things when a rage takes hold of him." She took a few tiny steps toward me, then hesitated. "I'm even afraid he might have had something to do with the Colonel's death."

"Lillian, no!" I protested. "He's not like that."

"You saw him yesterday in the stable. You saw what he did to Perley with just a little provocation."

I was about to point out to her that my being raped and beaten was a bit more than a little provocation, when she continued. "But here I am talking about tragedies when you've had enough troubles in the last few days," she chided herself. "Everyone's gone off for the time being . . . why don't you go see Mrs. Riordan? She's been asking after you quite insistently, you know. The ride will do you good. We're in for a storm tonight or I miss my guess. We might be snowed in for days—this'll be your last chance for some fresh air and freedom for quite a while. Go on, then." She made a little shooing motion, smiling at me like a benevolent mother hen. But the look of worry lingered around her fine eyes. and I was filled with pity for her. She had had too much tragedy in her short life. Given time, surely I could convince her that it wasn't really Connell that was keeping her here, it was her own cowardice. Just as surely as it was my own wickedness that kept me a prisoner, not any words or promises Connell Fitzgerald had even hinted at. He had offered me nothing, not even the possibility of some back-street affair, and I was a fool to stay on in this compromising and volatile situation with my adulterous heart on my sleeve for all to see.

But I knew better than anyone that I wouldn't leave Demonwood until I was forced to. And for the very simple reason that although my upbringing, my moral obligations told me I must leave, my heart stubbornly refused to give him up.

"Perhaps I will go," I agreed suddenly. "It seems like ages since I saw anyone outside of Demonwood. Stonewalls would be just the place." I had more than one reason to visit the Riordans. I needed help badly —I knew in my heart of hearts I had to leave, but I had to make sure Daniel was safe before I left. All I could do was throw myself on Peter's mercy and guilt.

The ride through the damp, silent snow was uneventful, and yet I had a curious sense of unease, as if someone was watching from behind the curtains of pine trees that lined the narrow, snow-packed road. I had felt the same aura of being spied upon yesterday, and determinedly I shook my head to shake the cobwebs and absurd thoughts free from my tangled brain. My pace was slow and steady, as befit my mount. Old Sally was a work horse, a stately dowager who carried my ample weight upon her swayed back with easy dignity. Under normal conditions I would have enjoyed the ride, but hovering around me was a dark, frightening presentiment of evil, and I kneed the old lady forward with sudden fright. If I had been even more of a coward I would have turned back to Demonwood then and there, but grimly I stiffened my backbone and rode onward. I was a Gallager, made of sterner stuff than to run at a shadow.

"Mary!" Peter greeted me with unfeigned delight as I rode up to the unpretentious entrance of his mother's rambling house. "I'm delighted to see you!"

"Are you?" I questioned caustically. "I'm not sure you'll think that for long."

Sudden concern paled his handsome face. "Is something wrong, Mary? Is Maeve . . ."

"Maeve's fine," I replied grimly. "And nothing's happened. Nothing new, that is. I came to talk to you."

"I was on my way to town," he said uneasily, ever one to escape unpleasantness.

"Town can wait. What I've come to say to you can't." I felt for all the world like a stern schoolmistress, bringing a truant to justice, and Peter's guileless, helpless face added to the impression. There seemed to be far more than ten years between our ages, and I was definitely the elder. He hesitated, then reached up and helped me down from Old Sally's back.

"Why are you riding that old thing?" he asked in a light voice. "Surely Con has better horses in his stable than this. What about Moon Maiden?"

"Moon Maiden belongs to your mistress," I stated bluntly, watching him flinch from my frankness. "I wouldn't touch a thing that belonged to her."

"Except her husband and child," Peter shot back, stung, and I could feel a guilty flush mount to my cheeks.

"I suppose you've heard the rumors?" I asked in a flat voice.

"How could I avoid them?" He looked away from me. "They say you're Con's whore, Mary. Is it true?"

My green eyes met his troubled brown ones calmly. "No, it's not. And you should know better than to ask." I moved away from him into the house. "True or not, I've decided there's nothing for me to do but leave Demonwood. But before I go I'll need your promise."

"You can't leave!" he cried, bewildered, following me like a helpless puppy through the warm, seemingly deserted house. I waited until we were alone in the small, firelit study before I replied.

"I've been helping Maeve sneak out to meet you for the last three weeks," I announced bluntly. "You know perfectly well that she creeps in and out through

172

my room at night, forcing me to be an unwilling accomplice to her . . . her trysts."

There was real concern in his face. "Mary, I had no idea she was involving you. I'm sure she didn't realize the position it would put you in. She's young and thoughtless, sometimes, Mary, but not really bad. You should have explained to her. I'm sure she would never . . ."

"Peter, are you blind?" My voice rose in a little shriek of amazement. "She knew perfectly well what it would do to me, to force me to lie to Connell and Lillian, to aid and abet her adultery. She deliberately involved me, and then reveled in my unhappiness." I threw myself down into one of the leather chairs by the fire and stripped off my gloves. "Surely you're not so bewitched that you don't know what kind of woman my cousin is? She's one who enjoys hurting other people, enjoys her power over them. Don't you understand anything about her? Peter," I said desperately, "she beats Daniel. Beats him until the poor babe can scarcely move!"

A variety of emotions played across his face: outrage, pride, defiance, and finally shamed despair. "Oh, God, Mary, I know what she's like. But I swear I never thought she'd go that far!" he cried, turning his back to me to stare into the fire. "I know what a slut, what a monster she can be. But she's . . . she's mesmerized me. When she's around I can't call my soul my own. Don't you think I realize that I'm cheating on my oldest and closest friend, the man that's been like a brother to me? And yet I can't help myself. I tell myself that I won't see her, that I'll refuse to come when she sends me one of her teasing notes. And each time I go, hating myself and hating her. Sometimes I'd like to kill her, like to wrap my hands around her pretty throat and choke the wicked, scheming life out of her . . ." his voice choked up, and I could feel pity well up in me for him. Impulsively, I rose from my chair and moved across the room to his side, placing a gentle hand on his arm.

"I know you can't help yourself, Peter," I said softly. "It's all right, really it is." He had buried his face in his hands, but at my words he slowly lifted his head and stared at me with dawning hope.

"Mary," he breathed after a moment or two, "you wouldn't consider marrying me, would you?"

"What?"

He turned to me then, all eagerness. "Oh, Mary, I could make you happy, I know I could! When we were together this fall I'd forgotten all about Maeve, I'd almost broken free of her spell. If only she'd stayed away longer I would have been free. You were coming to care for me, Mary, I know you were! I could make you love me."

"Peter," I said gently, but he went on like a man possessed, ignoring my quiet interruption.

"We'd go far, far away from here. We could live in Europe, in any city or country your heart desired. I'm a wealthy man. Not as rich as Con, of course, but rich enough. You'd never want for anything." He grabbed my unresisting hand. "Say yes!"

"Peter." I put my other hand on his, restraining him. "You don't love me. You love Maeve."

"I don't love Maeve," he said angrily. "She's a sickness, a disease. You could cure me, if only you would. Tell me at least you'll consider it."

I looked into his shining face, so eager and alive, and my intermittent cowardice assailed me. "I'll think about it," I agreed. And indeed, I would. The picture he painted was a very attractive one, money and an adoring husband at my fingertips. And I had no doubt that he would be adoring, once I had removed him from Maeve's territory. I had always wanted to see Europe, to return to Ireland, the land my grandparents had escaped from. And maybe in time I'd forget the shadow of a tall, black Irishman with the bluest eyes I had ever seen.

"Mary, angel!" He pulled me into his arms, and I turned my face up willingly for his kiss. And it was a nice kiss, warm and loving and full of passion, and it left me entirely unmoved. No tightening in my stomach, no tingling feeling, nothing even close to the storm of emotion Con's touch aroused in me. And I wanted to cry.

"Shall we tell Mother?" Peter asked eagerly.

"Tell her what? I haven't agreed to anything," I said calmly, hiding my intense disappointment. "I won't even consider it until Maeve leaves. She must be made to, Peter! For all our sakes."

"I'll get rid of her," he swore with sudden intensity. "Mary, you won't regret this, I swear you won't. We'll go to Ireland for our honeymoon. You'd like that, wouldn't you?"

"I would indeed," I said coolly. "*If* I agree to marry you, it would be very nice. But right now I think I'd better get home."

"I'll accompany you." He jumped up.

"To see Maeve?"

"I'll leave you at the front door . . ." he swore. A sudden shadow crossed his handsome face. "But, Mary, there's something I have to tell you. Before someone else, someone like that prying bitch, Lillian, fills you full of lies. When you agree to marry me, I want it to be with an open mind, knowing the terrible things I've done and forgiving me anyway. Mary . . . I'm responsible for Kathleen Fitzgerald's death."

Some secret inner part of me had been expecting this, dreading this. "What exactly do you mean?" I demanded slowly.

"I was very young when Con married Kathleen. In my early twenties and very impressionable. And I worshiped Con, always emulated everything he did. So when he fell in love with Kathleen O'Malley, it stood to reason that I would fall in love with her too." He cast a worried look at my stony face, then began pacing back and forth, speaking in a hurried, low voice, as if he wanted to get it out as fast as he could.

"I kept my love for her a secret, Mary. I would rather have died than betray Con then. Until one night when he was out of town she told me she was

175

finally pregnant. She had just heard and wanted to tell someone. It had been a bitter thing between the two of them—her barrenness. I suppose I had always hoped against hope that eventually they'd break apart and she would turn to me. That afternoon when she told me she was pregnant I knew I was lost. I suppose I lost my head then, Mary." He took a deep, shuddering gasp.

"Con was out of town for the week. I went back to Demonwood that night, went to her bedroom, and told her I loved her. I begged her to run away with me. She was very sweet, Mary. She told me she loved me like a brother, but that she was married to Con and loved him more than anything in the world. And that she'd forget I had ever mentioned a thing to her. And she kissed me very gently, like a sister, sending me away, when Con walked into the room."

"Oh, God," I breathed, imagining the scene with real horror.

"He just stared at us. And then he slammed out of the room, out of the house. I tried to follow him, tried to explain, but by the time I got outside he was gone. There was nothing I could do but ride home, Mary, and tell myself I'd explain to him the next day. He had every right to hate me, but I couldn't let him think that Kathleen was anything less than he thought her. He worshiped the ground she walked on, and she deserved it. She was the closest thing to a saint I've ever known."

"What happened then?" I demanded testily, not being terribly . saintlike myself. Kathleen O'Malley Fitzgerald sounded like a shallow, prissy bore to me, but I knew perfectly well why I felt that way. After such a paragon, it was no wonder Con would look at no other woman with any tender feelings.

"I never saw her again." He stopped his pacing and stared at me, reliving the horror of it. "She was found at the bottom of Perry's Ledge the next day."

"And what did Con do to you?"

Peter shook his head dazedly. "Damn near killed

176

me. He showed up at Stonewalls the next morning looking like a crazy man. God knows how I was able to stop him—make him believe me. But I did. He must have known in his heart of hearts that Kathleen would never have betrayed him."

"But you think he killed her?"

He hesitated. "Yes. And only because I saw the look in his eyes that night. It wasn't a rational anger, Mary. It was a madman's rage."

"I wouldn't have thought one would react too terribly rationally if one found one's beloved wife and best friend in a compromising situation," I said drily. "I would have killed you both right there and then." And suddenly a great wave of relief washed over me. That was exactly what Con would have done, if he were to kill anyone. He wouldn't have come sneaking back, he would have done it quickly and brutally right then, in the heat of the moment, before his rage could cool. "He couldn't have killed her," I said with marvelous assurance.

"What other alternative is there?" Peter asked sadly. "I saw his face after they found her—the guilt and horror are hard to forget. The only other possibility was that she killed herself, and that I refuse to accept. Kathleen loved life—she would never have committed suicide. And she would never have killed her own child after waiting so long for it."

"But you think Con would?"

"Mary, he didn't know she was pregnant. I was the first person she told, and only because she was bursting with the news. And Con's capable of fearsome rages. That's why I've wanted you out of the house. There's no telling what might set him off. If he were to find out about Maeve . . ."

I had heard enough for one day. Suddenly I was very tired, and no longer so sure that Con was blameless in the death of Saint Kathleen. I wanted to go home and crawl back into my warm bed in my icy room, shut out the horrible images of Kathleen's body rolling down that hillside. I rose abruptly. "I think I'd better go home now, Peter. You can come with me if you want, but I'm sure I'll be fine."

"Of course, I'll come with you!" he protested. "You don't seem to understand, Mary. I love you!"

Do you? I wanted to say wearily. It seemed as if Peter Riordan had a terribly consistent habit of falling in love with Connell Fitzgerald's females, and with seemingly disastrous results. And I was one of them, forbidden as it was.

Chapter Seventeen

Demonwood was dark and still when we arrived home that afternoon. The heavy threatening dampness seeping into my bones seemed to presage rain rather than snow, and Peter assured me that such was a definite possibility. "There's an old saying about Vermont weather," he announced boyishly. "If you don't like it, stay around for a few minutes and it's bound to change."

He reached down and took the reins from me. "You go on in now. I'll stable this disreputable old nag for you before I head back."

"*Would* you like to come in?" I relented, but Peter smiled in the gathering dusk.

"Now, Mary, I gave you my word. If I'm to win your hand in holy matrimony. I'll have to be a veritable saint. Though I wouldn't mind the chance of proving to you how little Maeve really means to me."

"I don't need to test you," I assured him, scrambling down from Old Sally's broad back. "I've made no promises, Peter."

He looked down at me, his joie de vivre in no way

quenched by my sober warning. "I'll be over early tomorrow," he announced blithely. "We'll talk about it then."

As I watched him lead my sturdy horse away, it amazed me that he had no idea what my troubled emotions were. But then, even I couldn't sort them out. Some blind, unreasoning part of me wanted everyone to go away but Con, knowing as I wished it how impossible it was.

"Did you have a nice visit?" Lillian questioned softly as I shut the massive front door behind me. I jumped a foot in the air, startled.

"Lillian!" I breathed nervously. "I didn't see you."

"The hall is very dark," she said noncommittally, smoothing down her skirts with nervous hands. "Did you have a nice visit with Mrs. Riordan?"

I'm afraid I blushed, and Lillian noticed with a gently raised eyebrow. "I . . . I didn't get a chance to see Mrs. Riordan," I confessed. "Peter and I were . . . were talking."

"Really, dear? How nice. I had no idea that you and Peter had much in common. Apart from Maeve, that is."

The acidity in her tone startled me, and my face must have shown it, for she quickly apologized, drawing her arm through mine. "I'm sorry, dear, I don't know what's gotten into me. It's this weather, I suppose. I hate the winters here. They're so damnably long." She sighed. "We'll be alone for supper tonight; Con's going out."

"And Maeve?"

"You should know by now she never bothers to eat with her female relations. It's men that she cares about solely. We'll have a nice evening together, Mary dear."

The last thing I wanted to do was spend an evening in a tête-à-tête with Lillian, I wailed inwardly, and then wondered at the lack of charity in my thoughts. When I had first met her back in Boston so very long ago it seemed we had so much in common. Now I felt uncomfortable and unhappy with her, so that I longed to escape to the privacy of my bedroom and ponder why Con was obviously avoiding me. Probably regretting his moments of weakness in the library last night.

"That will be nice," I agreed mendaciously. "We haven't seen enough of each other since you returned from Europe." I pulled off my bonnet. "I'll just run upstairs and check on Daniel."

"He's going with Con," she said smoothly before I could move away. "There's nothing for you to do tonight but relax. I'm sure you haven't had a day off in weeks and months—Con's not the most considerate employer, I know."

Words of defense sprang to my lips and hastily I pushed them back. Lillian was far too observant—she recognized and disapproved of my fascination for her brother. "My duties aren't terribly strenuous," I replied noncommittally.

"But you'd welcome an evening off, wouldn't you, dear?" she insisted, and I could do nothing but agree. "Meet me in the library after you've changed and we can have a glass of sherry before dinner," she continued, and I nodded, moving up the long winding stairs with less than my usual enthusiasm.

I spent little time on my dress that night, knowing as I did that Con would be nowhere in sight. The bruises Robinson had inflicted on my milky white skin were less angry-looking than the night before, and I couldn't contain a shudder that passed over me as I thought of the consequences of my shortcut through the stables if Con hadn't rescued me.

I had made my decision to leave—there was no turning back. The knowledge depressed me as I listlessly brushed my hair, but I remained firm. There was no way I could live with myself if I continued to stay in such a situation. The question was, could I live without seeing him?

Demonwood was unusually still as I made my way down the stairs to Con's library. The lamps were lit in the pretty, wood-paneled room that had somehow escaped Maeve's corrupting touch, and Lillian was nowhere in sight. An etched silver tray containing a crystal decanter of sherry and two glasses rested on a little gilt table that must have been spirited in when Con wasn't looking.

"Damn the sherry!" I muttered, and tipped a generous bit of Con's Irish whiskey into my glass.

But the effects of the overheated room after a long chill ride and the spirits were predictably soporific, and in a few moments I was curled up in the cozy armchair that rested back in the shadows, wrapping my black shawl around my green wool shoulders.

I awoke with a start, to see Con and Peter standing by the French doors that led outside to the snow-covered terrace. One small oil lamp had been lit, throwing fitful shadows over the front of the room, leaving me in a concealing blanket of darkness.

I was about to move, to announce my presence, when the controlled rage in Con's voice held me motionless, an unwilling witness.

"This is the fourth time, Peter, that someone has tried to murder me. Twice in Boston, I was set upon by thugs—I have several knife scars as souvenirs of the last encounter. Someone shot at me only a few days ago—at a time when no sane hunter would be out."

"Con, you're a very rich man—you must have a lot of enemies," Peter protested weakly, but Con continued inexorably, almost as if he hadn't heard.

"And then this morning, Peter, when Perley Robinson was far away and completely incapable of anything remotely physical, this morning someone tried to run me down with a wagon."

"You could trace the wagon," suggested Peter.

"I already have. It's Father LeJeune's—stolen this morning and left abandoned on the other side of the Gore." Con's voice was flat.

"B . . . but couldn't you recognize the driver?" he stammered.

"He was all muffled up."

"Con . . . you can't believe that I'd try to kill you! How long have we known each other?"

With a sudden explosion of anger Connell smashed his fist down on the mahogany desk and I winced for him as I thought of his wounded hands. "Damn it, Peter, you can't expect me to trust you! You've allowed yourself to be seduced by both my wives, all the time professing your friendship for me. You've been carrying on with Maeve for over a year now; you needn't bother to deny it. I didn't give a damn what you and she did. But when my dear, faithless wife is obviously trying to murder me what do you expect me to think when there's an accomplice around?"

"You must be mad!" Peter exploded, angry now. "Maeve would never . . ."

"Maeve has admitted it," Con broke in brutally. "Apparently she fancies the idea of herself as a rich widow. She wants both you and my money."

"That's absurd! Mary and I are going to be married."

"What!" If Con had been angry before, now his rage was awesome to behold. "If you've been laying your filthy hands on her . . ."

"What the hell does it matter to you?" he shouted back, lost to all senses of decorum. "You seem to forget that you're a married man."

"I haven't noticed *you* showing much respect for the sanctity of the marriage bonds."

"It's none of your damned business!"

In the blink of an eye Connell had grabbed the shorter man by the shoulders and shoved him up against the wall. Fitful shadows danced around the dark room, adding to the unreal aspect of the scene I was witnessing. "Leave her alone," he grated in a quiet, deadly voice. "Leave her alone or I swear I'll kill you."

Absolute stillness reigned for the next long moments—only the crackling of the apple logs on the blazing fire breaking the grim silence. And then, as sud-

denly as Con's rage had begun, it left, and he released
Peter and strode from the room as if all the hounds
of hell were after him. Peter shook himself, straightened his tweed jacket, and followed him out of the
room.

I found Lillian busy at one of her interminable
pieces of needlework, her squat little body bent over
her work in the gaudy pink-and-gold sitting room that
suited Maeve's lush beauty to perfection. She squinted
up at me out of her soft brown eyes.

"I wondered where you were, dear," she murmured
plaintively. "Con and Peter were having a dreadful
row in the library so I came in here. I do hope you
didn't become involved in their wrangling?"

"No, I didn't hear a thing," I lied, looking innocent.

"Well, they're gone now. Come and sit by me, Mary,
and we'll have a nice relaxing chat." She patted the
orangey-pink brocade seat beside her.

But a less relaxing evening I have seldom spent. The
threatening, uncertain weather must have communicated itself to Lillian, for a strange, inquisitive mood
plagued her; she was restless, probing, almost threatening with her questions and insinuations. I held her
off with vague replies and a look of bland incompre-
hension until, later over dinner, she suddenly demanded, "Are you in love with my brother?"

I stared at her with just the right amount of mild
amazement, hoping my naive demeanor would continue to fool her suddenly suspicious nature. "No, Lillian, I'm not in love with your brother," I soothed
her, still hoping against hope that I wasn't lying to
myself. And her. After all, how could I be in love
with a man I scarcely knew? A married man? It was an
insane infatuation, one that would pass as soon as I
removed myself from Con's vicinity.

"But everyone falls in love with Connell," she replied a little wildly. "You can't imagine what trouble
we've had with the housemaids. One by one they all
succumb to his charm. Who would know better than

183

I how often it happens? He can be so charming, can Con. I don't want your heart broken, Mary."

"My heart isn't about to break," I said firmly. "I'm made of sterner stuff than that. I won't deny Connell's attractive—I'd be lying if I did." I slipped my wool shawl from my shoulders and made a fanning gesture —Lillian always had her rooms damnably hot.

"I've seen you look at him, when you think other people aren't watching," she accused me, jabbing at her rich creamy custard, turning it into an unappetizing jellied mass.

"Have you now?" I could feel a slow flush mounting to my pale cheeks, and I cursed my fair complexion. "You've imagined it then," I said staunchly. "As a matter of fact, Lillian, you've nothing to worry about in that direction. Early this afternoon I received a proposal of marriage from Peter Riordan."

It was her turn to look startled. "Really?" she breathed, some of the strange tension seeming to drain out of her plump little body. "Perhaps I've been mistaken . . ."

"Perhaps you have," I allowed myself a small bit of righteous indignation. Rising with great dignity from the dining room table I tossed my damask napkin down beside the fancy china and started for the door.

"Have you accepted?" she demanded suddenly.

I paused with one shaking hand on the gilt doorknob and met her feverish gaze with cool anger. "Lillian, I have no idea what is wrong with you tonight! It's absolutely no business of yours what answer I give Peter, nor whether I'm in love with Con or not. If I am, that's my problem, not yours."

Hot tears filled her large brown eyes, and she rushed to the door, taking my resisting hand in hers imploringly. "Now I've made you angry! I haven't meant to offend you, Mary dear, it's just that I care about you. I don't want to see your life ruined by my brother's selfish immorality. Don't forget, I've seen the mistresses he's kept during the last ten years, and I've seen how badly he's treated them."

"Your brother has made no immoral or selfish suggestions to me," I replied, concealing the pang I felt at hearing of his other women. At least in this I could be truthful. "I don't think it's something you need worry about. I think you underestimate him, Lillian."

The tears of distress and pity welled over and spilled down her plump cheeks. "Oh, my poor dear, I only wish I did."

There was nothing I could say to this, no reassuring reply I could offer her. She seemed firmly convinced that her brother was an insanely jealous murderer, and who was I to try and tell her otherwise. I shook my head sadly. "If you don't mind, Lillian, I think I'll retire now. I'm still a bit shaky after yesterday." And yet, that desperate struggle in the stables seemed weeks ago. What had Perley muttered? Something about hearing that I admired him. Who could have possibly told him such a nasty, provocative lie? My unknown malicious enemy, I could only suppose. "Have you heard anything more about Perley?" I spoke up.

Lillian simply shook her head, the fuzzy brown strands tumbling from her untidy coiffeur. "Yes, you go up to bed, dear. Perhaps things will have taken care of themselves by tomorrow morning, who knows? I am sorry, my dear."

"Sorry about what?" I demanded, moved by the sudden deep regret in her quiet voice.

"Oh, about everything," she replied vaguely, and turned away.

Alone in my attic bedroom, I tried to shake off the aura of depression and gloom that Lillian's dire predictions had stirred up in me. The damp heaviness in the air, which even a blazing fire couldn't begin to dispel, added to my unhappiness, and I would have given almost anything for a good stiff belt of Irish whiskey to warm my body and soul. But nocturnal wanderings were at an end for me, and in order to purge myself of my lachrymose mood I wrote an eight-page letter to Pauline, full of whining, moon-struck nonsense, which I promptly tore up and threw on the fire, feeling slightly better. I followed that up with a short and direct note telling her I was coming back as soon as I could arrange it and would explain the details later. I put it to one side, suddenly too tired and sad to continue. Undressing slowly in the unusually warm room, I put on a light cotton nightdress as a welcome change from the heavy flannel I'd been huddling in for the past few months and snuggled down wearily into my warm bed.

When I awoke it could have been anywhere from midnight to four in the morning. A crack of thunder sounded from just outside my windows, and I jumped up, startled, to meet the shining, wide eyes of my cousin Maeve.

"Oh, for God's sake," I said with sleepy irritability, "you can't be wanting to go out on a night like this?"

She laughed, her low throaty chuckle that had mesmerized men since she was twelve years old. "But this is exactly the kind of night I do want to go out. I find storms terribly exhilarating."

I was wider awake now, cursing her inwardly. "Who are you meeting?" I found myself asking.

She smiled her cat's smile. "Wouldn't you like to know?" she purred. "Someone very, very exciting." And she drifted out through her hidden door, leaving it open with her usual deliberate carelessness.

I burrowed down in the covers and shut my eyes determinedly. After a few minutes of restless tossing and turning I rose, sighing, and went to shut first the secret doorway and then the one into the hall.

It was almost closed when suddenly I felt it wrenched from my hand and flung open. And standing there, with that murderous hatred I had seen before, was Connell.

I opened my mouth to speak, but nothing came out. He seemed bigger and taller than ever, looming over me with that contemptuous look on his saturnine face.

When he spoke his voice was low, ominously so, with none of the lilt that had so delighted me.

"Where's Maeve?" He didn't bother to sweep those blazing dark eyes over my deserted, firelit bedroom; he knew perfectly well she wasn't there.

I hesitated. "She went out through the passageway behind the paneling," I replied slowly, and his mouth twisted in an ugly sneer.

"What? You couldn't by any chance have decided to tell me the truth for once?" he mocked. "I didn't know you were capable of honesty."

"Connell." I put out a hand beseechingly. "You don't understand."

He moved inside the room, slamming the heavy oak door shut behind him. And suddenly I was very frightened. "Oh, I understand, Mary. I understand only too well. You've lied to me since we first met. I suppose Maeve arranged for you to come and apply for the job, so that you could aid and abet her in her tawdry affairs."

"I didn't know you cared so goddamned much for your precious wife," I shot back angrily.

"Oh, I don't," he murmured, his voice like silk. "It's your damned rotten lies that matter to me. The way you look up at me with those sweet, trusting green eyes of yours, hiding all that deceit underneath. If it was just a case of helping Maeve cheat on me, it wouldn't matter so much. But when you stand by and allow her to torture a poor, helpless child . . ."

"Con, I didn't . . ."

"And I didn't believe her when she told me about you," he continued, ignoring my interruption. "I called her a liar."

"Who?" I asked in a hoarse voice, backing away nervously.

One hand shot out and grabbed a handful of my thick, black curls, yanking me forward. I stayed pressed against him, motionless, hypnotized by his soft, enraged voice. "And are you a slut like your cousin, Mary Gallager? Was it on Maeve's instructions that you came tiptoeing down last night, to see if you could entice the besotted master into your bed? Or did you think of that one all by yourself, to try and tempt me until I was mad for you? Your shy innocence was very touching, my dear. Maybe I should find out how innocent you really are." His strong hand reached under my stubborn chin and forced my face upward to meet his hot, angry mouth. And for a long moment I melted against him, responding helplessly to his passionate, hate-filled kiss. "That's right," he murmured, his dark eyes glittering with hatred. "This is nothing more than you've given Robinson and Peter and probably half the men in Cambridge. Surely you might say I have a right to it after all your lies?" And he ripped my cotton nightdress down the front, pulling it off my shoulders with rough, brutal haste.

It was then I began to fight him, filled with terror and hatred, hatred for him for condemning me without giving me a chance to explain, hating myself for almost giving in to him. I scratched him, hit him, bit him, but he seemed to take no more notice than if I'd been a fly buzzing. Everytime I tried to strike him his hand would be in the way, grabbing my wrist and twisting it until I was faint with pain. I was no match for him—despite my Irish temper he was a foot taller and weighed half again as much. But still I fought him, until he held me away for a moment and clouted me across the face with the back of his hand, so that I fell dazed across the giant bed.

And then his body covered mine, his cruel hurtful hands ripping away at the shreds of my clothing, his handsome face shadowed and brutal in the flickering firelight. And I knew with a sudden cold desperation that there was no way I could stop him, no way my puny strength could ever begin to match his. Slow, hot tears poured down my face, tears of shame and rage, shame that I wanted this more than anything, but under different circumstances, with love, not that mad, murderous hatred shining in his dark blue eyes.

I stopped struggling. "Con," I whispered brokenly. "Con, please. Don't."

He stiffened, staring down at my pleading, tear-streaked face. That killing rage left him, leaving only a cold, bleak expression that somehow hurt me more than anything else. "Oh, damn you, Mary Gallager," he said softly. "God damn your soul to hell." And as suddenly as he had come he went away, silently, shutting the door behind him, leaving me there on the bed, stunned, with my nightgown shredded around me, a hundred emotions warring through my dazed brain: anger, pain, and frustration among them. With a low moan I curled up into a tight ball, holding my weeping head against my knees, completely awash with mindless misery. And stayed that way until the sky, filled with its promised rain, began to lighten.

Chapter Eighteen

I dressed slowly, very slowly the next morning. Dully I noticed the bruises Con's cruel, demanding hands had inflicted on me, and it surprised me not one bit to recognize that they were darker and more vicious than the ones Perley Robinson had given me. And Perley had been beaten half to death for his troubles. I no longer doubted a word of Lillian's horrid accusations—I had seen the killing rage in Connell's eyes last night.

I dressed as warmly as I could, in a dove-gray wool and three flannel petticoats. Lacing up my stoutest boots, I finished packing and started out the door. It was only a few minutes after six in the morning—most everyone would be sound asleep. Certainly Con would be. It would come as a great relief to him when he came downstairs to find the lying governess gone from the cold, empty halls of Demonwood.

It never once entered my mind that Maeve hadn't returned. If it had I suppose I simply would have assumed that she'd gone in the front door like the brazen, hateful hussy that she was. I had her to blame for my present wretched predicament, her to blame for Con's hatred of me. Oh, I deserved it, all right. Deserved it for being fool enough to listen to her. I knew now that Con would have believed me when I told him her threats. I could have trusted him to protect Daniel. But hindsight would do me no good, and it was without looking back that I shut the heavy door behind me and started out through the drenching rain down the long road to town.

I had plenty of time for reflection. I had barely reached the first turn in the road before my clothes were soaked through with the cold, misty rain, and by the time I had gone a mile my body was wracked with uncontrollable shivers. The water on the snow-packed road had turned to ice, and more than once I slipped and fell, scraping my hands through my thin, cotton gloves until they were raw and bleeding, twisting my ankle and splattering my skirts with the patches of mud I always seemed to have the luck to find. The trees around me creaked ponderously in the brisk wind, and vainly I tried to hurry.

When I fell for the third time, I tossed my cumbersome carpet bag to the side of the road, abandoning the few possessions I had hastily thrown together without a moment's hesitation, as I trudged onward. I knew when I arrived at Lyman's Gore I would have at least a few hours to wait for the train, and it would have been far wiser of me to keep a change of clothes along, but I no longer cared. I would have welcomed pneumonia, scarlet fever, and the plague gladly, and as I moved onward I vaguely, self-indulgently considered the increasingly enticing idea of crawling off into the woods and falling into a permanent sleep. Wallowing in self-pity, I struggled forward.

I must have been gone several hours when I first heard the heavy beat of hooves from down the road. The sky was still as dark as ever, and the rain showed no sign at all of letting up, but I knew from the progress I had made along Demonwood's endless roads that I had covered at least five miles. I hesitated, wondering whether I should stand my ground or jump into the underbrush along the side of the road, when the choice was taken out of my hands. I made too swift a move out of the way of the thundering horse and slipped in the snow and mud directly in the path of the approaching animal. I shut my eyes and began a rushed Hail Mary, preparing quite calmly to meet my maker when, with a shrill whinny, the huge animal stopped within inches of my prostrate body.

It *was* peaceful there on the ground. I had a very good idea who had come barreling down the road like a bat out of hell, and I had no great desire to meet his furious face ever again. I kept my eyes firmly shut.

With his usual charm and courtesy he jumped down from the horse, put an iron hand under my limp arm, and yanked me to my feet with one brutal jerk. "You haven't fainted," he mocked, and my eyes flew open.

"No, I haven't," I snapped back. "No thanks to you."

My hostility left him totally unmoved. I had thought I had gone beyond caring, but the cold contempt in his face still had the power to chill me. After a long moment I yanked my arm free from his grip. "And now, if you'll excuse me, I have a train to catch." I started down the road with as much dignity as a new, pronounced limp would allow me. I got no more than a few feet.

"Oh, you'll catch your train all right, Mary. You can count on me to make sure you're out of Vermont as soon as possible. But I'm not going to send you back bruised and bleeding and with a case of pneumonia. For all you've lied and cheated and abused my hospitality, I'm still responsible for you. You'll come back to the house now and Carpenter will take you to the train tomorrow, when you're dried and rested."

"It's you I have to thank for the bruises and bleeding," I spat at him.

He raised an eyebrow. "Now I wasn't thinking it was thanking me you were doing, Mary Gallager," he drawled, and I could feel my face pale. "If you behave yourself I might come back tonight and finish what I started. That's about all you're fit for, isn't it?"

I waited long enough to calm the hot, bubbling rage that flooded my chilled body and made me sick inside. "Don't you dare lay your great nasty hands on me again," I said through clenched teeth. "And if one of my brothers doesn't come up here and kill you," I added with slow, deliberate calm, "then I will."

"But you're forgetting," he mocked, his eyes cold and lifeless as death, "I'm the murderer at Demonwood. Get on the horse."

"Go to hell."

Before I knew what had happened, his strong, sinewy arms had grabbed me once more, and the fear and terror of the night before flooded back, so that I fought against him with a wild, panic-stricken rage, desperate to escape from those cruel, confining hands. But my useless struggles were over in a minute—I was up on the horse, with Con behind me, and we had started back down the long, icy road, back toward Demonwood.

I kept my backbone ramrod stiff, determined not to let any part of me touch his lean, strong body that I could help. My rage still burned red-hot, but the cold, damp rain that had penetrated my clothing and drenched my hair was now reaching into the marrow of my bones, and I began trembling uncontrollably.

"You're soaking wet," Connell observed without expression. "How long had you been walking?"

I refused to answer him, afraid that if I spoke I

would either scream or cry. I kept my eyes downcast. My hands were raw and bleeding through the ripped and torn cotton gloves, and hurriedly I grabbed onto the saddle, hiding them from my captor's all too observant eyes.

"You're a melodramatic fool," he said emotionlessly. "You should have known that I'd make arrangements for your immediate removal from Demonwood."

"I'm not interested in any arrangements you might have made," I snapped back. "I have no intention of accepting favors from you."

"I have no intention of offering any, other than a ride to the station in a warm carriage and your fare back to Cambridge. If you choose to go to Peter Riordan with it than that, my dear, is your business."

"Why should I go to Peter?" I demanded coldly, interested despite myself.

"He informed me that you two were engaged last night. He came courting at eight o'clock this morning, and I discovered you'd run off like a teen-age bride."

I shut my eyes; the rocking of the horse was making me feel both faint and nauseated, and still his cold, cruel voice went on. "You don't, by any chance, happen to know where my erring wife went, do you? I presumed when she slipped off through the attic that she must have gone to Peter, but he would hardly have arrived at Demonwood so bright and early if he'd been having his usual midnight rendezvous."

"You knew about them?" I heard myself ask in dazed surprise.

"Of course I knew about them. I've known about every affair of Maeve's; every affair that I cared to check on, that is. Her comings and goings haven't interested me for years."

"But why . . ."

"Why did you have to lie to me?" he asked harshly. "I wish I knew. Perhaps it's just part of Maeve's idea of fun. Where is she?"

"I have no idea," I said between clenched teeth,

trying to control the chills that were wracking my body. "And I don't give a damn."

The rain was falling steadily now, pouring out of the leaden sky onto the snow-packed landscape as we plodded onward. There was a pause, and suddenly I felt myself pulled back against Con's curiously comforting chest. "You're freezing to death," he said shortly, wrapping his cloak around me with rough concern that he couldn't totally deny, no matter how much he despised me. I made a small attempt to sit upright, and then gave in to his inexorable strength. I rested my drenched head against his hard, unyielding shoulder and shut my eyes, letting my body tremble with the cold and whatever emotions were plaguing it.

The trip back to Demonwood was far shorter than my trip away, and it was with an almost panicked despair that I felt the horse stop. This would be the last time I would touch Connell Fitzgerald, the last moment of tenderness he would ever show me, and I couldn't stand the thought that it had to end. His arm around me tightened for a moment, as if unwilling to let me go, then he lifted me down unceremoniously.

"You'd better go in and change your clothes," he said gruffly. "A hot bath wouldn't be a bad idea either. There'll be time enough for packing later on today."

I looked up at him, at his cold, impassive face. "I'm already packed."

"Mary, darling!" Lillian flew from the house, her small brown face puckered with worry. "Where in the world have you been? The whole house has been in an uproar, what with Maeve and you both missing! What in God's name has happened?"

Suddenly Con's words came back to me from the swirling madness of last night. *She* had told him something. Could it have been Lillian, spreading her vile rumors, sneaking to him, telling him how my every word had been a lie? Or had it been Mrs. Carpenter, who had always hated me. Or, perhaps the most likely, had Maeve herself told him, laughing with those slanted, beautiful eyes as she destroyed me forever in his mind. There was no way I could tell—all I knew was that I could trust no one. I was in a house of enemies.

Before I could bring myself to answer her chirrupy little questions, Daniel appeared at the front door. "Mary!" he cried, and ran headlong down the front steps and into my arms. "I thought you'd left me."

And then the dam of my tears broke once more as I bent down and put my arms around his slender frame.

Lillian grasped his arm in one of her plump, surprisingly strong hands and tried to pull him away. "Leave Mary alone, Daniel. She's had a long, uncomfortable walk. We'll go upstairs while she gets changed. Come along." She tugged at him, her voice sharp. His hold on me tightened.

"No!" he cried stubbornly, trying to shake her off. "I want to stay with Mary! Leave me alone, Aunt Lillian. I don't want to go with you."

Somehow I found the strength to pull myself together. The angry look on Lillian's sulky face augured no good for either Daniel or myself, and Daniel's childish chin was beginning to wobble uncontrollably. I let go of him, reluctantly, and stood up. "Daniel, if I stand around here much longer in these wet clothes I'm going to die of pneumonia, and then where will we be? Why don't you go on up to the schoolroom, and start on your Latin? I'll be with you in a short while after I change into some warm, dry clothes and have a short rest."

"You're not going away then?" he demanded, a ray of hope dawning on his troubled young face, and I felt a pang of sorrow deep within me.

I hesitated for only a moment. "Yes, Daniel, I am. But you can come visit me in Boston if your father will let you . . . you could meet some of your third cousins." And I looked up into Connell's coldly interested eyes as he witnessed this byplay.

This did little to assuage Daniel's fears. He yanked himself away from me, tears welling up in those dark blue eyes so like his father's. "I don't believe you!" he shrieked. "You're lying!" I reached for him once more but he struck my hand away, turning and running off into the cavernous reaches of that cold, ornate house.

Lillian turned to me, her face smooth and untroubled once more. "Pay him no mind, Mary dear. He's overwrought, what with Maeve missing without a word and the realization that you must leave." She tucked a confiding arm in my damp, unwilling one. "Come along with me. I've already had Mrs. Carpenter heat you a nice warm bath, and then a long nap will be just the thing. I'll prepare you one of my own spiced possets and you'll feel much, much better. It might be . . . wiser if you didn't see Daniel again. He's such a sensitive boy, you know. Your leaving will be hard enough for him to bear; I think it might be easier on him if the farewells are brief, don't you?" During this gentle monologue she had drawn me through the drafty halls and up the stairs, her soft voice droning on in a curiously hypnotic way, and I was helpless to resist.

"Let me help you," she murmured insistently when we reached the surprising warmth of my room. The copper and enamel bathtub was steaming in front of me, and the thought of that warm water soothing away my aches and pains made me want to cry with longing. But the last thing I wanted was to undress in front of Lillian's avid eyes, and expose to her my bruised flesh with the marks of Connell's rage still on me.

"I . . . I can manage myself," I said with as much firmness as I could muster. "But if you *would* brew me that posset?"

"I don't think I should leave you alone," she said worriedly, her plump fingers fidgeting with her fussy gown.

"I'll be fine. By the time you're back I'll be warm in bed," I promised, inwardly begging her to leave.

When at last I was alone I sank into the steaming water with tears of gratitude, keeping my weary eyes averted from the dark blue and purple stains on my arms and legs and torso. Using the lavender scented soap which was Mrs. Carpenter's pride, I scrubbed every inch of my body fiercely, including my tangled black curls. They would wave around my face more wildly than ever, I knew, but I had the almost desperate need to feel clean once more. I finally stepped from the tub when the water turned chilly. Drying myself with slow, exhausted thoroughness in front of the blazing fire, I kept an ear out for Lillian's return. Having discovered the extent of my damages, I was even more determined that she shouldn't see what her brother had inflicted upon me. If only he had finished what he had started so brutally I could have hated him. His last-minute mercy left me guilt-ridden and secretly, shamefully filled with frustrated longings I wouldn't even begin to define.

I pulled a fresh, clean flannel nightgown from my trunk, noticing for the first time its tumbled appearance. Surely I hadn't been that overwrought last night, that I had just thrown my clothes in helter-skelter like that? But my mind was too tired to cope with questions that couldn't be answered, so wearily I crawled into my bed, averting my eyes from the gray, wet landscape outside my myriad of windows.

"Drink this." I heard Lillian's voice through a haze of sleep, and found myself swallowing a hot, spicy brew. And a moment later everything drifted into a soft, warm world where I was loved and cared for and protected, and no one would ever hurt me.

I awoke in bits and pieces. Perhaps it was the silence, so strange after the constant drumming of the rain on the roof above my head. Or maybe it was the crackling of the fire, the fresh dry logs burning merrily, spreading heat through the room. I opened one eye and mentally thanked my silent friend who'd cared enough to build up my fire. I listened carefully in the strange afternoon light, and then placed the strange sound. It was the quiet creak, creak of the rocker, and I opened my eyes wider to recognize Maeve's still form, her blond curls trailing down her back, her red dress glowing in the firelight.

"Maeve?" I questioned hesitantly. She didn't move, didn't turn around. "Maeve," I said louder, more insistently. Still she didn't move. Sighing, I rose from my warm, safe bed and padded across the cold floor to her side, reaching one hand to her shoulder to shake her. My hand stopped short as I saw her face. And the red sash wrapped so tightly around her once-lovely throat like a trail of blood, a sash that had cut the life off from her many, many hours before.

I stumbled backward, opening my mouth to scream, but no sound came out. My cousin's corpse just kept rocking, rocking, in a macabre parody of life, and in numbed horror I ran from the room, down the long flights of stairs and straight into Con's study.

He was at his desk, and the expression on his face as he looked up and saw me in my nightclothes would have quelled a braver person. But I was in no state to care.

It took him only a moment to recognize the shock and horror on my face. "What is it?" he asked hoarsely, knocking over his chair as he jumped up. "Is it Maeve?"

Dumbly I nodded. "In my room," I choked out, and he rushed past me without another glance.

I stood there for a moment or two longer, before I realized how very cold this cold, cold house had become. Dazedly I moved over to the fire. Reaching for the cut glass decanter, I unstoppered it and held it to my lips, pouring a good mouthful of whiskey down my throat, then another. It suddenly dawned on me that I had let Connell go up to my room unaccompanied —he could destroy any damning evidence. And I couldn't have cared less. Taking one more stiff drink, I sank down on the sofa in front of the fire and waited.

Chapter Nineteen

The normally empty, cavernous rooms of Demonwood swarmed with people and activity for the next hours. All the servants, inside and outside, seemed intent on hurried and mysterious business, while the constable from Lyman's Gore and his myrmidons strode around looking very grave and officious. Lillian would wring her hands and cast frightened bewildered glances at Connell's stern, impassive face whenever she thought no one was watching, and Daniel stayed huddled next to me on the loveseat, a blanket over the two of us, while we listened in bewilderment to the subtle questions and threats from Constable Hardy, to the guarded, quiet replies of the widower. And never once did he look at me, meet my questioning eyes. Lillian's damp, accusing ones were enough to convince Hardy.

The long, long day passed into an even longer night. The police removed poor Maeve's body with the stern injunction that no one was to leave Lyman's Gore without permission.

"This isn't something that can be covered up this time," Hardy warned pompously, and I watched Con's mouth tighten with barely controlled anger.

Lillian, Daniel, and I made a half-hearted attempt at eating, but Mrs. Carpenter, her rosy cheeks streaked with tears for her beloved Maeve, refused to prepare anything, and none of us possessed the skill or the will to make an appetizing meal.

"Sleep is what we all need," Lillian murmured, pushing away her plate with its half-finished dinner.

"You'll share my room, Mary." There was a sudden assumption of authority, an authority she would never have dared usurp had Maeve still been alive. Controlling a strong wave of distaste, I nevertheless replied with as much forcefulness as I could muster.

"No, I think not, thank you, Lillian. I don't sleep well unless I'm alone." And Con, damn his soul, chose that moment to enter the dining room. One coldly raised eyebrow was enough to flood my fair complexion with blushes, blushes that failed to escape Lillian's avid attention.

"But the police have locked your room. I do admire your nerve, but nevertheless . . ."

"I'll stay in one of the smaller bedrooms on the second floor; that is, if no one has any objections. Near Daniel's room—he's rather off by himself right now." Daniel threw me a look of gratitude from his sleepy, tearless eyes, so different from his aunt's red-rimmed and grieving ones.

"My dear Mary," Con broke in smoothly, "why should we have any objections? Not that I consider you in any way fit to protect Daniel if one can judge by past performances." And with those cold, cruel words uttered in such a gentle voice he turned on his heel and left.

Lillian's mouth was a perfect "O" of wonder, but one look at the stormy, desperate expression on my face was enough to convince her not to pry this time. She shrugged her sturdy shoulders. "As Con said, dear, whatever you wish. I . . . I'm sorry he's in such a nasty temper. I did warn you, didn't I?"

My eyes met her soft brown ones across Daniel's dozing form. "Yes, you did warn me."

I slept fitfully that night, disturbed by the unfamiliar bed, the myriad aches and pains still wracking my tortured body, and the memory of Maeve rocking back and forth in the red-flocked rocking chair. And every sound, every creak, every sigh of wind would make my eyes fly open, certain that Con was outside my door, ready to finish the punishment he had begun.

It was almost daybreak before I slept, and the stillness of the house combined with the cold, dark grayness of the day kept me lost to the world till noon. When I opened my eyes to the dull, gloomy day I wanted to burrow deeper under the covers, do anything rather than face the murderous reality of life at Demonwood.

Grimly I pulled myself out of the comfortable bed, grimly I dressed in a dull black dress that Lillian had unearthed for me from among her mother's stored clothing. Elaine Carradine Fitzgerald, daughter of the famous countess, had been a tall, stately woman with a motherly figure that dwarfed even my well-rounded proportions. The graceful elegance and cut transcended style and modishness, and I was slightly cheered.

The kitchens were deserted when I finally slipped downstairs, and I rummaged in Mrs. Carpenter's usually well-stocked bread box while I heated some of the iron-flavored coffee on the back of the massive cookstove. I dosed it with generous amounts of sugar and fresh cream to try and nullify some of the bitterness and buttered a slice of hardened bread when Mrs. Carpenter appeared, one of Maeve's discarded, frivolous hats clamped incongruously on her iron-gray head. Her tiny eyes were red-rimmed with crying, her prim mouth pursed with hate and disapproval.

I stopped mid-munch, awash with guilt that I hadn't even bothered to mourn my own cousin. I swallowed hastily. "Are you going somewhere, Mrs. Carpenter?"

She sniffed. "I'm leaving, Miss Gallager. And I suggest you do the same. Your precious murdering paramour isn't long for this world—it's time you found yourself another protector."

"What are you talking about?" My guilt and pity vanished before her belligerence.

"Don't you think I don't keep my eyes open? I saw him go to your room two nights ago. I was waiting to tell your poor, deluded cousin, but she, sweet lady, was already dead. Murdered by her own husband." Her cold black eyes were flecked with madness, and I edged nervously away.

"But you needn't think he'll get away with it this time, missy. Perley Robinson is seeing to that. Before that fool of a constable can pull a few strings and let that wife-killer go scot-free he'll be strung up higher than a flag. People in the state of Vermont don't take kindly to having rich murderers in their midst." She smiled then, baring her stained and rotting teeth, and I took my cup of lukewarm coffee and hurled it in her face. And then, being a coward at heart, I ran from the room before she could retaliate with anything worse than screamed imprecations.

"Where's Con?" I found Lillian in the lavender drawing room. She looked up from her needlework with an expression of mild surprise.

"Why, I believe he's taken Daniel over to stay with Mrs. Riordan for a few days. He's anticipating some trouble, although of course I told him he was absurd. No one will ever convict him of murdering Maeve. A man of his wealth and position should be safe from these local people."

"Why do you say it like that, Lillian?" I asked quietly. "Do you think he murdered her?"

Her eyes filled with ready tears. "Oh, Mary," she murmured piteously, but my heart was like ice. "Don't ask me such a thing! He's my baby brother—I have to protect him, no matter what he's done."

I stared at her woebegone face with helpless rage. "Would you tell him I need to see him when he returns?" I asked after a long moment. If he returns, I couldn't help but think. "I'm going for a walk right now. When I come back I'll be in the schoolroom. It's very urgent, Lillian."

"Of course, dear. But what . . .?" I was already out of the room.

But several hours in the strangely warm, damp weather, plowing my way through slushy snow did little to solve my problems, to answer the questions that were plaguing me. When I finally arrived back at the gilt and rose-colored halls of Demonwood, my wet, shivering body matched my sodden spirits. I had nothing to change into—all my clothes were locked up in Maeve's death chamber. The only alternative was to try and squeeze my ample proportions into one of Maeve's gowns, and that I would not do.

Before I could lose what little courage I possessed, I tossed my damp cape onto a nearby chair and strode purposefully up to Con's study door.

He answered my summons politely enough. Swallowing once, I opened the door.

"What do you want?" He made no attempt at courtesy, not even deigning to rise from behind his massive mahogany desk.

"I . . . I came to warn you," I stammered nervously.

"Oh, really?" Sarcasm was heavy in that lovely, lilting voice. "I don't think I'll be needing any help from you, Mary Gallager. Carpenter has deserted the sinking ship, but I'm sure Peter will be glad to escort you to the train tomorrow. Unless you choose to stay on with him." The expression on his dark face was cold and hateful, and some of the dam of pain and anger broke within me.

"Damn you, Connell Fitzgerald, I'm trying to save your worthless life!" I couldn't tell whether it was really horses I could hear coming down the road at a steady pace, or a figment of my terrified imagination. "They're going to hang you. Perley Robinson has got everyone in town worked up . . . he's determined you won't . . ." I let it trail off guiltily, and the look in his blue eyes was ironic.

"He's determined that I won't get away with it again? Well, I can't say that I blame him." He rose, shuffling his papers together in an abstracted attempt at neatness. "I've left instructions with Mrs. Riordan over at Stonewalls. She's promised to take care of Daniel. He'll be happy there—he's always been fond of her."

"But what about Lillian?"

"Lillian can live her own life for once. She's not to have a hand in Daniel's raising," he said coldly. "This is really the best way. It will save everyone a great deal of trouble, don't you think?"

"Don't be daft!" I half shouted at him. "You can't just let them murder you! Daniel needs you!" And I need you, I thought desperately, hating myself for my weakness.

"Daniel will do well enough. He couldn't have done much worse with Maeve as a mother and you as a guardian."

I flinched before his biting contempt. "I didn't dare tell you she'd beaten Daniel. Connell, you would have killed her!" And then I bit my lip, aghast at what I'd said.

"Do you expect me to thank you for that? You'll have a long wait in front of you, Mary Gallager!"

The tears that I'd fought against so long were flowing freely down my cheeks, but still he stared at me with a cold, unmoved countenance. "Won't you even listen to me?" I cried. "Let me try and explain . . ."

"There's nothing to explain. I think you've said everything you ever need to say to me. Now get out."

"They're going to hang you! They're going to storm the jail after you're arrested and drag you out and hang you and no one will be able to stop them," I sobbed helplessly. "And I won't be able to bear it."

In two strides he was across the room, shaking my weeping form until my teeth rattled and the desperate hysteria left me abruptly.

"That's better." There was a momentary softening in his hard, cruel voice. And then his grip tightened as we heard the pounding on the front door, and we stood there, immobilized as we heard the sound of a score or more feet trample into the front hall.

"Warrant for Connell Fitzgerald's arrest on the charge of murder." Constable Hardy's voice was unnaturally loud in the deserted house. We couldn't make out Lillian's reply.

"It seems you were right," Con said with soft grim-ness. And then pulled me into his arms and kissed me as I'd never been kissed before, with a gentle despera-tion and a deep, yearning passion that knew no bounds. And then he flung me away from him and slammed out of the room.

"Good afternoon, Zeke." I heard him greet the con-stable casually. "You boys all here to take me in? I assure you I have no intention of trying to escape."

"I'm awful sorry about all this bother, Mr. Fitz-gerald, sir. I'm sure it'll all be cleared up in no time." Hardy's voice was suddenly nervous and unsure of himself, and I felt a surge of hatred.

"Of course." Was it only me who could hear the gallows humor in Con's voice—the voice I might never hear again?

"I brought along a few boys for your own protec-tion. Seems like Perley Robinson's been stirring up some trouble in town. Nothing to worry about, of course, but it never hurts to be too careful, does it?"

I watched them from the window till they were out of sight, my tears drying on my cheeks.

"You need some rest, Mary dear," Lillian spoke from behind me, and I turned to her wearily. She looked curiously calm for a woman about to lose her beloved brother, and a gentle smile played around her full lips. "I have some tea made. Come sit down and we'll have a nice, soothing cup. And then an early bed. You'll find that things will look a lot better in the morning."

"Will they?" I questioned listlessly, accepting the fragile bone china cup.

"Of course, Mary." She patted my hand. "You drink that down and I'll go get some of Mrs. Carpenter's nice ginger cake. You won't be wanting any dinner tonight, will you?"

"No, Lillian. You needn't bother . . ." But she was gone before I had a chance to stop her.

I sipped at the bitter tea, then made a moue of dis-taste. Without a moment's hesitation I tipped the contents of my cup into the potted ferns and replaced it with whiskey. That would be much more helpful in providing me with sleep and forgetfulness than all the tea in China.

Dutifully I nibbled the stale ginger cake she brought, dutifully I kissed her plump cheek, dutifully I climbed the stairs to my second-floor bedroom. I lay down on the bed, not even bothering to remove my shoes, certain I would never sleep. And before long I was dead to the world, when I thought I would never rest again.

It was the smoke that brought me fully awake, the thick, choking, strangling smoke, blinding my eyes with tears and smothering me as I tried to call out. I struggled to my feet, fighting blindly against the bed-covers, and staggered in the direction of the door.

As I fought my way through the deserted hallways there was no sign of flames, but the ominous crackling of wood being devoured by the conflagration reached my ears, and the heat scorched my skin until I thought my clothes would burst into flames.

"Lillian!" I shrieked into the holocaust, but silence was my only answer. I knew I should try to find her, try to reach her room in the blinding horror, try to save Con's only sister. But all my life I'd had a desperate fear of fire, ever since I saw my best friend's house go up in flames with her parents screaming for help from the third floor windows, help that came too late for them.

"Lillian!" I screamed once more, my voice hoarse from smoke and tears. And then I struggled down into the hall, one hand running along the terrifyingly hot walls, each step fearful that the next would plunge me into fiery nothingness.

I came to the stairs sooner than I thought, and with foolhardy relief I took them two at a time, straight into the heart of the flames.

But luck or God was with me. I knew the house well enough to be fairly sure of my surroundings. As the flames licked my skirts I ran through the hall and out into the cool, still night air to collapse, sobbing, into a snowbank.

I don't know how long I lay there, the damp hissing against my smoldering skirts as Demonwood fell into flames. It could have been minutes, it could have been hours, before I heard Lillian's voice.

"Get up, Mary." I heard her speak, and I leapt up, overjoyed that she'd somehow managed to escape the destruction of Demonwood.

"Lillian, thank God you're all right! I thought . . ." I took a joyful step toward her and then stopped short at the sight of the gun pointed straight at my breast.

"You thought what, dear?" she questioned in her soft, gentle voice. "You thought I was trapped somewhere in that flaming wreck? It's unfortunate for you that I wasn't."

"What do you mean?" I questioned inanely, suddenly, like a blind person given back her sight, able to see all too well what she meant.

"You didn't drink your tea, Mary. That was very naughty of you, after all the trouble I went to to fix it. If you had you'd still be in there right now, and you would never have had to know anything. It would have been a painless death—you would have slept through it." She smiled then, a charming curve of her lips that with a sudden sharp, wrenching pain reminded me of her brother. "Come along now." She gestured toward the woods. "We haven't much time. The fire can be seen for miles around—I expect I'll have visitors before the hour's up. You'll have to be long gone by that time."

"Gone where, Lillian?" I questioned dully.

"Over Perry's Ledge with Con's other whore. You have to be punished. You can't be allowed to live, you know. Not after you tried to seduce my poor innocent brother. He's so susceptible to evil women."

"Seduce him!" I exploded. "Lillian, nothing happened between Con and me."

"You enticed him," she said sadly. "Looking up at

207

him with those innocent green eyes, pretending to be Maeve when you thought you could get away with it. But you didn't know I was here to protect him from scheming hussies like you." She cocked the trigger. "Start walking."

I had no choice but to do as she bid me. I stumbled through the snow, all the time acutely aware of the gun held in the plump, nervous little hands that were more accustomed to the intricacies of needlework than their weapon of death, of the avid, kindly eyes whose expression hadn't changed. "But they're going to hang him, Lillian. Unless you tell them the truth . . ."

"I've thought about that," she admitted, in an entirely rational tone of voice. "And I've decided it's better for him to die a martyr's death than continue to profane his body and soul with evil sluts like you and Maeve. After he's gone I'll raise Daniel and this time there'll be no one to interfere."

"Does Connell have any idea that you . . . that you . . ." I couldn't complete the sentence, so bizarre was the very idea.

"Oh, I'm sure he knows. He's suspected for years, but Maeve's death was the final proof. So he'll go to his death protecting me, a final act of love and devotion."

There was nothing I could say to her madness. It was the night of the full moon, but the angry clouds scudding across the sky blotted it out, so that the light along the dark, tree-lined path was fitful at best. The smell of wood-smoke was strong in my nostrils as we climbed, and I kept my eyes darting into the trees, wondering if I dared to try escaping into the underbrush.

"Besides," she continued suddenly, prodding me in the small of my back with the gun, "other people have begun to suspect." She laughed softly, and my skin crawled. "And then, what with Cyril dying such an untimely death, and then Maeve . . . I need a scapegoat."

"Cyril?" I stopped short, aghast. "The Colonel?"

"Of course," she answered coolly. "Keep moving, my dear. He wanted to marry me. Con was pushing me until there was no way I could escape. So Cyril had to die." We had reached the knoll at that moment, and suddenly, as if on cue, the moon came out, bathing the woods and the breathtaking view in front of us with a silvery light.

"I wish it didn't have to be this way, Mary," she said sadly, with real regret in her voice. "If you'd only taken my warning, kept away from my brother, it would have been all right. I thought you were safe—he'd never shown any interest in inexperienced little girls before. But I was wrong, and in that I'm partly to blame for this." She poked me in the back again with the gun.

"And now, Mary, you must jump. They'll assume you died in the fire and a sad thing it will be. Or if they ever find your body, they will simply think you decided you couldn't live without Con and killed yourself."

"With a bullet in my back, Lillian?" I questioned grimly.

"Oh, no. You'll jump of your own accord—I won't have to shoot you. After all, what do you have to live for, with Con dead?"

I turned to her, desperate for anything to stop the quiet stream of madness issuing from her mouth. "But I'll be with him, Lillian. I'll be with him throughout eternity."

"No, you won't!" she shrieked angrily. "He'll go to heaven and live with the angels like my dear Papa, and you'll go to hell like all sluts. Like Kathleen and Maeve and Mama." Her features were distorted with rage in the ghostly moonlight. "Jump!" she snarled. "Jump, damn you!" And she reached out her little hands and shoved with all her might, and I felt myself falling into blackness.

Flinging out an arm in desperation, by some miracle I was able to grab onto a root growing from the edge of the cliff. I hung there, my feet dangling over the drop, with a now totally-crazed Lillian screaming imprecations to the winds. She leaned over the edge to try and pry loose my desperately clinging hands. She pulled one hand free of its lifehold, and I grabbed at her. My hand caught her ankle and pulled, and she tumbled over my head and down into the endless gully with one long, wordless scream.

I don't know how long I hung there. It seemed like hours and yet later they assured me it was only a matter of seconds before hands were reaching down and pulling me back to solid ground once more. Where my dazed eyes met the blank, unreadable ones of Connell Fitzgerald. And then I finally gave up in a dead faint, rather than face the accusations I knew must be beneath his bleak, distant countenance.

Chapter Twenty

The next few days were nothing more than a blur. By the time we arrived at the small hotel in the little town of Lyman's Gore I was delirious with fever, and it was three days before I took a lucid breath. All the while Constable Hardy and Connell and Peter waited to hear what had taken place at the now charred remains of Demonwood. When I finally regained consciousness, I was allowed a bowl of chicken broth and a bracing cup of coffee (I gagged at the thought of tea) before I was plied with a thousand questions from the officials of northern Vermont, and indeed, by that time their patience had worn thin.

I gave my story in short, succinct terms, as emotionlessly as possible, all the time wondering how Con would react as I betrayed his sister.

"It's all as Mr. Fitzgerald finally told us," Constable Hardy proclaimed importantly as the clerk took down my testimony, and I felt a small measure of relief. "Who would have thought sweet Miss Lillian had so much evil in her?" He took off his hat and scratched his ginger hair. "It's a wonder to me how people act the way they do, it surely is. Why, I would have bet ten dollars that Connell Fitzgerald was the murderer. Just goes to show you never can tell." And he wandered from the small bedroom where I was holding court, shaking his head dubiously.

A sober, official-looking gentleman took my weak hand in his thin, dry one and pressed it sympathetically. "We all thank you for your assistance in this dreadful and tragic matter, Miss Gallager. We'll leave you alone to rest now. In the meantime, there's a gentleman here who's been spending every spare minute by your bed during the last three days. I'm sure you'll want to thank him personally for his concern." And to my surprise he winked.

My heart began to pound wildly. "But I . . . I must look a fright."

"My dear, you look charming," he assured me in a fatherly fashion. "I'll send him in." And suddenly the room was empty of all those large, strange men, and I sat up dizzily, alive with joy and anticipation. Then he must have forgiven me.

But the strain I had been under, combined with my weakened condition, totally undermined my self-control, so that when Peter Riordan walked into the room, smiling, sure of his welcome, I burst into tears.

"I guess it wasn't me you wanted to see," he said wryly, throwing himself into the chair beside my bed, his mouth drooping with just a trace of petulance.

"I'm sorry, Peter," I hiccuped bravely, mopping my streaming eyes with his gallantly offered handkerchief. "I thought . . . I thought . . ."

"You thought it was Con," he said flatly, the light gone from his face and his warm brown eyes turned flat and hopeless. "Perhaps you should know, Mary, that after they brought you in he stayed just long enough to hear you were out of danger. And then he went to Stonewalls to fetch Daniel and we haven't seen or heard from him since. You could have died for all he cared."

By sheer strength of will I stopped the copious tears from flowing. I blew my nose defiantly in Peter's handkerchief. "I'm not surprised," I replied with as much calm as I could manage under the circumstances. "There's no reason why he should care."

"He's a selfish, ungrateful brute," Peter started angrily, but immediately I hushed him.

"What's he got to be grateful for?" I demanded fairly. "I lied to him, helped his wife cheat on him, and believed him capable of murder. I don't find those very admirable things."

"His damned crazy sister nearly murdered you."

"That wasn't his fault," I sighed. "Where do you think they are, Peter?"

"At the old farm," he replied after some hesitation. "Con never wanted to build Demonwood, you know, never wanted to move from the little place. It was all Kathleen's idea."

"Oh, yes, Kathleen."

"I suppose that's another part of his problem, Mary. We had a long talk about her before he took Daniel away. I thought it might bring him some peace, to know for sure that she died pure."

I laughed then, a harsh, bitter sound in the still bedroom under the eaves. "So now she's Saint Kathleen for sure. And she can be enshrined forever in his memory as the one good woman he knew. I wish him joy of her."

"Mary!" Peter protested, shocked. "Kathleen was a wonderful woman."

"I know that full well," I said wearily, leaning back against the soft feather pillows. "And I know that in death she'll be a much more powerful adversary than in life. You'll have to forgive me, Peter. I don't know what I'm saying. It's just that I'm sick with jealousy."

"You love him that much, do you?" There was fresh despair in Peter's face.

I hesitated for only a moment. "Yes, I suppose I do. But don't you dare to tell him, Peter Riordan. It's too late for us anyway—I wouldn't give him the satisfaction of knowing he's broken my heart."

"And you're so sure he doesn't love you?"

"As sure as the day is long, Peter," I said quietly. And suddenly the door was flung open and six brothers streamed into the room, all talking and shouting and demanding answers at the same time.

"What the hell have you been doing to yourself?" Seamus demanded, folding me into a bear hug that left my ribs cracked. "Is it trying to kill yourself you are? When I got Connell's telegram I thought I'd choke. I warned you no good would come of this feather-brained notion. You're supposed to be old enough to take care of yourself. And what does Con think he's doing, letting you fall into the clutches of his crazy sister? I'd like to thrash him within an inch of his life if it weren't for the poor man being a newly made widower once more. And him with a young boy on his hands, too!" He continued in this vein as one by one my brothers embraced me, criticizing me for my lack of self-preservation. "We've come to take you back home, girl," Stephen said finally. "You've had enough of the fancy Fitzgeralds, I would think."

Fresh tears filled my eyes, symptomatic of my weakened condition. "Aye, that I have," I agreed unhappily. "More than enough."

Once the Gallager brothers made up their minds there was no stopping them. The castoff clothing donated by suddenly helpful and sympathetic townspeople was packed in two capacious carpetbags and before twenty-four hours had elapsed I was back in

Cambridge, with Pauline and company bustling around me, cosseting me and letting me cry copious tears on their comforting shoulders. Peter had taken my rejection of his suit quite nobly, promising to visit me soon and swearing at the very least eternal friendship. I could tell my brothers didn't think much of him, and I was doubly relieved that I hadn't succumbed to my momentary cowardice and accepted his proposal. Even Daniel came to see me off on the train, tears in his eyes, promising he would come and stay with me as soon as his father would let him. But of Con there was no trace.

The next two weeks were not the happiest either for me or for the long-suffering Gallagers. As the days passed my despair and depression grew instead of lifting. Connell Fitzgerald showed no tendency to disappear from my dreams, even if I could successfully wipe him from my daytime thoughts.

"What you need is a man," Pauline would suggest stoutly, and as my loneliness grew I decided I had to take some action or I would end up screaming mad like poor, hopeless Lillian.

It was a fresh spring day in late March—one of those warm, windy days that give out false promises of winter's early ending. But I was ever one to be lured on by false promises, and found myself out on the Cambridge streets for the first time since November, on my way to visit Michael Flynn and his constant devotion. It seemed the best option open to me, and I stifled my pangs of conscience. I was due for a well-deserved shock.

"Mary, darlin', how glorious to see you!" he greeted me with an exuberant hug that in no way pleased the watery blonde hovering behind him in a proprietary manner. "I've been meaning to come see you this age, but I've been up to my ears in work. And how did you like hobnobbing with the rich folks up in Vermont?"

"Considering that I almost met my death at the hands of those rich folks I find that question in very bad taste," I snapped with more than my usual acerbity, inwardly wondering why I wasn't crushed at the obvious failure of my evil plans. My eyes met the coldly challenging milky-blue ones of the overdressed lady, and Michael followed their direction with a small troubled expression on his dumb, handsome face.

"Oh, Mary, I want you to meet Lotti Sorensen. You remember my boss, Mr. Sorensen, don't you? This is his daughter," he said unnecessarily, obviously ill at ease.

Miss Sorensen had no such qualms. "We're engaged," she announced abruptly, staking her claim.

A small spurt of mischief ran through me. I could take him away with just a wave of my finger, and then as suddenly as the devilment came it vanished, leaving me with the same ever-present, cold, lonely depression. "I hope you'll be very happy," I said woodenly, and then summoned up my best smile. "And I'm glad for you Michael. Truly."

But I wasn't so glad for myself. It serves you right, I told myself sternly as I walked the long streets back to Seamus's house through the bright sunshine. You would have taken him to try and ease your pain, to provide children for you, and that would have done neither of you any good. You're nothing but a wicked, selfish girl, and you deserve the troubles you've brought on yourself.

A few more blocks in this vein and I was almost in tears. So caught up was I in my extravagant self-pity that I failed to notice the elegant hack standing outside my brother's house in the warm spring sunshine. As I felt the sun pour down upon my head I thought back to the snow-bound fastness of Vermont, where spring wouldn't come for another month yet, and a spurt of anger ran through me. Damn him, I thought, and damn me and damn everybody! And I kicked open the kitchen door.

Well, the Gallagers were all very merry this afternoon, I thought sourly, listening to the sounds of laughter issuing forth from the front parlor. Little do they care that their only sister is dying of a broken heart. At least I had the small consolation that none of them knew the cause of my evil bad temper—except Pauline, of course.

They had all told me, without even knowing the problem, that I would soon get over it. "Time is the fastest healer," Seamus intoned, and was very lucky I didn't hit him. For two weeks now I had alternated between quiet despair and the foulest, blackest mood that had ever been seen this side of the Atlantic, and deep inside the wall of hatred and pain I was truly grateful for their forbearance toward such an unhappy witch of a girl.

"Oh, there you are, Mary." Pauline bustled into the kitchen with a tray full of empty cups and saucers. "Your brothers are having a family conference again, so needless to say it's enough of coffee they've had and on with the whiskey." She shook her pretty head in mock despair. "And God knows when we'll be having dinner." She smiled, and there was a secret smugness about it that immediately alerted me.

"And what are they having a family conference about?" I demanded suspiciously. "It wouldn't by any chance be about me, would it?"

"Whist, now! You'll be thinking you're the center of everyone's attention, and indeed, you're only the center of your own. Though, as a matter of fact, this time you're right." And she let out a little trill of mirth.

"Pauline O'Brien Gallager, how dare you laugh!" I said in hushed fury, having reached the end of my tether. "What are they in there deciding?"

She giggled again, having had more than a drop of the good Irish herself. "Oh, which convent they should pack you off to, I imagine," she chirruped. "A little repentance for your bad temper would do you some good."

"Are you serious?" I demanded, appalled. Not that I didn't love the good sisters, but a lovesick nun was not exactly orthodox. And suddenly a longing to see Con swept over me—a longing so strong I wanted to scream with pain and wanting.

"No, of course not, darling. They're going to marry you off to the first taker. They've been interviewing applicants."

"Over my dead body!" I snapped, and another roar of laughter burst forth from the parlor. I stamped my foot in fury. "Damn them!" I snarled. "How dare they think they can dispose of me that way?"

"I don't think they intend to consult you in the matter," Pauline giggled, then sobered abruptly as she saw the tears of rage and unhappiness starting in my eyes once more. "Oh, now, Mary, don't cry. It's going to be all right, truly it is. Trust me."

"I don't trust anyone," I said with weary bitterness, and at that moment the parlor door opened and Connell Fitzgerald himself walked through.

"I think I'll be making myself scarce," Pauline giggled, and disappeared past his forbidding figure. Neither of us noticed.

"What are you doing here?" I demanded in a rough voice after a moment.

His face was unreadable in the afternoon sunlight. "I came to see how you are," he said stiffly, ill at ease for once.

"As you can see I'm fine," I replied shortly. "You needn't bother your conscience about me."

"It's not my conscience that's been troubling me." He smiled wryly, and my treacherous heart turned over. Firmly, I fought my weakness.

"How's Daniel?" I asked after a moment.

"He's fine. He'd like to see you."

"Would he?" I was furious to find that my voice shook, and I averted my eyes from his dear, distant face. "He's welcome to come visit anytime."

"We . . . we thought you might care to visit us. You always liked the farmhouse," he offered this diffidently, as if my response made no difference to him. As perhaps it didn't. And then he offered the coup de grace.

"I was also wondering if you might consider marrying me."

"Are you mad?" I breathed, numb with rage at the depth of his mockery of me. "What have they been saying to you?" If my secret had slipped out unbeknownst to me I would die of mortification, I surely would.

"What is there that they could have said?" he countered, and I remained mute, staring angrily out the window, anywhere but at his aloof face that would capture me if I let it.

He stared at me then, the man who was so sure and powerful and rich, and he seemed strangely uncertain, endearingly so. "It's not as though I'm a terribly good bargain," he continued, almost as if he hadn't heard me. "I've lost two wives and I didn't treat either one of them terribly well. For what little excuse it offers, I never loved either of them."

"You didn't love Kathleen?" I demanded, a small spurt of hope springing within me.

"It was a family arrangement. We were good friends, but she was very shy and quiet and retiring. I need an amazon like you." He smiled again tentatively, and I could feel myself weakening. "I'm very rich," he added. "You could always marry me for my money."

"Just because you bought one Gallager doesn't mean we're all for sale," I said coldly, moving away from him to stand looking out over the streets of Cambridge. I stared down with unseeing eyes, begging him to convince me.

"Your price is above rubies," he quoted softly. "There's no way I can apologize for what I tried to do to you so I won't even bother. I'm trying to make amends . . ."

That tore it right there. I turned to him with tears of rage in my eyes. "So you decided to come and make an honest woman of me, did you? It's the gentlemanly thing to do, isn't it? But you forget, you stopped in time. I'm still pure—your conscience needn't trouble you."

He swore then, a short expletive that was forbidden even in our man's household. We were so far apart, at different ends of the room, and I could feel any chance I had of happiness slipping away because of my bitter tongue. I knew of no way I could cross the long distance. My pride and my hurt were still too strong.

Perhaps he realized that, perhaps not. "I can see I'm wasting my time," he said shortly. "Forgive me for bothering you." And he turned to go.

"Con!" He turned back, a look of absolute . . . desolation on his face, and an astounding thought came to my wretched mind. "Are you in love with me, Connell Fitzgerald?" I heard myself ask him softly, paraphrasing his words to me. I couldn't even begin to believe in the possibility of it being true.

"I would think it rather obvious," he said wryly.

"But it isn't obvious at all," I replied from the opposite end of the kitchen, holding my breath. "If you care about me . . ."

"Mary Margaret Gallager, you idiotic female, I've been in love with you since shortly after we met! Why the hell do you think I came all this way to listen to your foolish blathering?"

And at such loverlike words I crossed the room to him in two quick leaps.

Dell's Delightful
Candlelight Romances

Dell Bestsellers

Claude - The Roundtree Women

BOOK II
OF THIS SPELLBINDING
4-PART SERIES

by Margaret Lewerth

A RADIANT NOVEL OF YOUNG PASSION!
Swept away by the lure of the stage, Claude was an
exquisite runaway seeking glamour and fame. From a
small New England town to the sophisticated and
ruthless film circles of Paris and Rome, she fled the
safe but imprisoning bonds of childhood and discovered the thrilling, unexpected gift of love.

A Dell Book $2.50   (11255-9)

In this first stirring novel in a 4-part series, you will meet:
Henrietta, the exotic New Orleans beauty who became the
matriarch of the Roundtree clan; Lowell, the fiance of Duncan Phelps, whose spirit runs wild with secret shame about
to explode! And Ariel, Lowell's Paris bred cousin and a restless sophisticate, her destiny calls her back to her ancestral
land—and Duncan Phelps. They are proud. Sensual. Com-
manding. It is in their blood to take what they have to have.

A DELL BOOK $2.50
(17594-1)

Margaret   Lewerth

The Roundtree Women
Book 1

**The Roundtree Women love
only once. Forevermore!**

At your local bookstore or use this handy coupon for ordering:

Come Faith, Come Fire

Vanessa Royall

Proud as her aristocratic upbringing, bold as the
ancient gypsy blood that ran in her veins, the
beautiful golden-haired Maria saw her family burned
at the stake and watched her young love, forced into
the priesthood. Desperate and bound by a forbidden
love, Maria defies the Grand Inquisitor himself and
flees across Spain to a burning love that was destined
to be free!

A Dell Book $2.50   (12173-6)